WITHDRAWN

The Right-Hand Man

The

K. M. Peyton

Right-Hand Man

Illustrated by Victor Ambrus

Oxford   London   Melbourne

OXFORD UNIVERSITY PRESS · 1977

Oxford University Press, Walton Street, Oxford OX2 6DP

OXFORD LONDON GLASGOW NEW YORK
TORONTO MELBOURNE WELLINGTON CAPE TOWN
IBADAN NAIROBI DAR ES SALAAM LUSAKA ADDIS ABABA
KUALA LUMPUR SINGAPORE JAKARTA HONG KONG TOKYO
DELHI BOMBAY CALCUTTA MADRAS KARACHI

British Library Cataloguing in Publication Data

Peyton, K. M.
   The right-hand man
   1. Title
   823´.9´1J   PZ7.P4483
   ISBN 0-19-271391-4

*Filmset in 'Monophoto' Ehrhardt 11 on 12 pt and
printed in Great Britain by
Richard Clay (The Chaucer Press), Ltd,
Bungay, Suffolk*

To Philippa

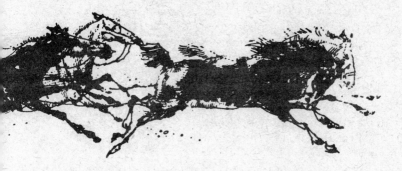

IT WAS quite a long time afterwards, nearly ten months, when he had time to think the whole business over (and in Newgate gaol time hung heavily), that it occurred to Ned that he had met the three creatures he loved best (using the word 'love' in its fullest sense, and the word 'creature' because one of them was a horse) on the same day: the first Wednesday in March, 1818. On the day in question there was no particular impact made by the meetings (perhaps excepting the horse) – merely a passing politeness and forgetfulness thereafter; the day nevertheless altered the course of his life. At the time how could one recognize such a moment? With Ironminster, in fact, first impressions were not auspicious.

Ironminster's first words to him were, 'If you're the driver of this confounded coach, are you aware that it's running twenty-four minutes late?' The voice was cold and contemptuous.

Ned corrected him. 'Twenty-six minutes, sir. It'll take me two more to get a drink inside me.' Frozen with cold, thirty-three miles behind him, not to mention one cast shoe, one doubtful axle-tree, and one confrontation with a very drunk passenger, Ned was not in the humour for appeasement. God rot his imperious passenger, taking the seat beside his own on the box. What did he know of the tribulations of the stagecoach driver?

Quite a lot, as it happened.

'Quick, Mary, a hot brandy, or I'll never make Brentwood alive,' Ned said to the barmaid at the Red Lion. Ned knew he could down a drink in less time than it took to change the horses.

'What's amiss then?'

'There was a man so drunk at Kelvedon I had to knock him down to keep him from getting aboard. He upset the ladies inside – a right tizzy we had. And there's no making up time this weather – holes in the road up to the axle.'

'Well, you've the nobility aboard now. Lord Ironminster and his friend.'

'Not on the box-seat?'

'Little fellow with one arm –'

'I've already met him! *Ironminster*, d'you say! My luck today! God's truth!'

August Ironminster was the best dragsman in the land – or had been, till he lost his arm. His four-in-hand team was second to none. What was he doing boarding a public stagecoach at Ingatestone?

'His own coach is meeting him at Brentwood, I understand. So you've only four miles of him.'

'I finish at Brentwood tonight. John Theobald's taking her into London. I could do without that sort of company, though! He's tried to put me in my place already, and I haven't picked up the reins yet. Pray for me, Mary!'

'Yes, darling, I never stop.'

She took the glass from his icy hand and smiled at his concern: Ned Rowlands – at twenty the youngest, and certainly the most desirable (not to say the cleverest, cheekiest and most conceited) of the coachmen on the Harwich road – needed no one's prayers, not even faced with Lord Ironminster. 'This I must see,' she thought, and followed Ned outside to see the departure, good for a spot of excitement any day of the week, for the Ingatestone horses to the Wellington coach were known as 'the bolters', and required a brave coachman, not to mention passengers. Matched entirely for looks, they were as adverse a foursome as were ever put to.

Late or no, Ned checked the harnessing meticulously, shortened a coupling rein to his liking and paused to examine the beginnings of a collar-sore, and point it out to the horse-master. (No one but he and the horse would suffer for it later: not, unfortunately, the one whose fault it was.) Then, with everyone aboard and the guard blasting the street clear with his horn, and cries of, 'Hold on tightly! Watch yourselves!' for the benefit of the precariously loaded outer passengers, Ned threaded the reins into his hand and climbed up on to the box. He braced his legs and felt his horses' mouths – 'All right, let go!' – watched the ostlers gratefully hustle out of the way, the splendid chestnut backs galvanize beneath him, bars, chains and traces springing – twanging – taut, felt the old coach leap forward under him, fresh clods of mud flying instantly, ladies screaming inside.

'God Almighty! Do you always start like that?' Ironminster, agile beside him, was the only one outside who kept his balance, although his one hand reached out for the rail beside him.

'This isn't the quietest of teams, my lord. But they might make up a little of our lost time.'

They were pulling as if for a wager, and his arms and shoulders were already aching. Useless to let them run themselves out of steam; they had eleven miles to cover and the ground as bad as it could be. He checked them gently, but the near leader, resisting, put in a couple of bucks that threatened to have them all in the ditch. Ned picked up his whip and stung the animal a couple under the bar to remind it of its manners. It only needed a leg over a trace now and there would be another five minutes lost in the untangling: 'Up, up now, you old devil!' By a judicious mixture of authority and coaxing he got the awkward horse going forward, just about in hand. The mud spun up. The ice of the past month had played havoc with the road, and it was a matter of steering the smoothest course, avoiding the worst of the ruts. Ned braced his legs, watching the road. The coach, as always, was overloaded and its balance none too secure. In his hands he held the difference between a safe journey and disaster, not to mention the coach's reputation, upon which their livelihood depended.

'How many miles an hour are you scheduled in this contraption?' Ironminster asked him, quite civilly.

'It averages out at ten, Colchester into London. The last stage – from Witham to the Black Boy – forty-eight minutes: we did it in forty-seven and a half, then into Ingatestone forty-two minutes. A round thirty into Brentwood. We lost fifteen minutes at the start with a cast shoe, and another ten at Kelvedon punching an awkward customer on the nose.'

'Your task or the guard's?'

'Mine, as it happened. The guard's no fisticuffs man.'

'And you are?'

'I've done a fair bit, yes. It's useful in this game.'

'For keeping the clients in order?'

Ned grinned. 'If you like.'

'Are all your teams like this one?'

'Thank God, no. This isn't a team. Each of these horses has a mind of its own.'

'I've noticed.'

'Matched for looks only. Not in stride nor in temperament, which is what matters.'

'I've got the best team in the country and no two are the same colour.'

'Colour doesn't matter. But my guv'nor can't be told.'

'Have you ever driven a first-class team?'

Ned considered. 'Not to match yours, I daresay. And the best I've ever driven have had too much weight to pull. It couldn't match a private drag, like yours. I daresay your weight is no more than a third of the average public coach – and that's for the same number of horses. There's no comparison.'

'No, true. These brutes work hard. I'm only fully loaded when we go to a race-meeting or a fight, or take my mother to Bath for the waters. Going up to town – well, I've done it, Threadgolds to Aldgate, in under the hour and a quarter – I had a wager – but that was before –' He hesitated. 'When I was still driving. I can't now, of course.'

No, by God, Ned thought, with a rare and piercing shaft of imagination – Ironminster had lost more than an arm in his accident, more a way of life. He was no dreamer, no reader of books, music-lover, country-walker, but famous for the hellfire driving of his horses, his riding to hounds, his passion for playing cricket and shooting pheasant: none of which was any use at all to a one-armed man. It was said that he had screamed like the devil himself and had required seven men to hold him down for his amputation, not for fear of the pain, but for a determination not to lose the limb. The story was a rich one, and had lost nothing in the telling. Ned, knowing a good deal of his history, had never set eyes on him before, and was

4

surprised to find he was a small, slender man with delicately moulded features, very pale, finely-drawn – nowhere near as florid as his reputation. He was said to be consumptive; two small spots of colour smudged his cheekbones, either symptoms of the condition or rouge. Ned could not be sure.

'I'm looking for a coachman. Have you ever thought of working privately?'

Ned, at that moment preoccupied with getting his near-side wheeler sharply up to its pole to skirt a large pothole, heard the question put without fully taking it in. The bucking leader was loathe to settle to a trot, and kept breaking his stride, reaching out strongly against the bit, almost pulling Ned off his seat. Ned was wondering whether to lam him again with the whip to show him who was master and to hell with the passengers, or play safe and sit it out. Training prevailed. He must humour the brute, at risk of dislocating his armhole.

'Sir?' Had he heard correctly?

Ironminster repeated his question, exactly as Ned had thought. How was he supposed to answer that and be polite enough to end up with the sort of tip he was expecting?

'I've never thought of it. No, sir. I like this work. If I change, it would be on to the Royal Mail. But they won't have me yet, for my age.'

'Which is – twenty? Twenty-one?'

'Coming up to twenty, sir. My father is on the Mail. Great West Road.'

'George Turner? Harry Rowlands?'

'Harry Rowlands, sir.'

'Ah, I see the family likeness! The red hair, the hands. You'd go a long way to find a better reference than that! Harry Rowlands for a father.'

Ned wasn't looking for a reference, but didn't say so. He knew enough about the life of the private coachees, having rubbed shoulders with them all his life, talked with them, eaten with them, sworn at them, outdriven them . . . They were a sour, haughty lot in their fancy livery, given to taking on the airs of their owners, using their superior cattle to drive their inferiors off the road, given the chance. But their lives were all waiting, nothing for a week and then fifty miles tomorrow, take mother to Bath for the waters, call on Lady

Nincompoop and wait three hours outside in the driving cold when you'd been told no more than fifteen minutes, or put to at four in the morning to pick his Lordship up from White's or Carlton House or wherever. No system. No answering back. No putting the horses to how *you* thought best, only how the master decided, whether he knew a horse from a prize Smithfield joint. Ned didn't fancy it at all. He said nothing, tucking his chin down against the weather. In spite of his heavy boxcoat and beaver and layers of neckcloth, the rain was seeping down to his skin with a familiar clammy embrace; he was cold to the marrow, and aching from his bad horses. At least, with a private drag and only one set of horses, one could get rested and warmed as often as the team – it was the only advantage he could think of and, at that moment, a very fair one.

'I want my team on the road again,' Ironminster said quietly. 'I want a man I can stomach to sit by, without my hand itching to push him off the ribbons. You drive how I would ask. I would give you twice your present wages, and board and lodging into the bargain, a team second to none, and four grooms to work under you.'

'No.' Ned didn't want to be tempted. He had never consciously realized exactly how much his own master he was. He could, in his place now, tell this young Lord Ironminster what to do. He didn't fancy the position reversed, in spite of the blandishments offered. The best team on the road ... he mustn't think of it.

'Think about it,' Ironminster said. 'That's all I ask of you. It wouldn't be an ordinary job.'

No. Ironminster had been no ordinary dragsman himself. Behind them, the sound of the guard's horn warned a scattering of cottages of their passage, clearing geese and donkeys and a carrier's cart out of the way, sending a couple of girls scampering clear of flying mud. Ned eased the horses, partly for the girls, partly to give them a breather for the gradual incline ahead. The guard flung off a couple of parcels outside a door, blasted once more, and dropped the horn to hold on, more potholes staggering them. Inside the coach, a whitefaced lady leaned out to be sick, half-opening the door and getting a deluge of mud over her pallor. Fine driving rain needled the landscape, blurring spires and thatch and rooting pigs, darkening the winter road. Ned screwed up his eyes, feather-edging the miller's cart, tensing himself for the next hole; the smell of sweaty leather and hot animals contrasted sharply with a whiff from Ironminster's lawn handkerchief as he wiped his face – the best cologne. Ned suddenly thought, using his own right hand to check his leaders a fraction, passing the cart: not to *have* a right hand, cologne handkerchiefs and all, to be driving by proxy when all the time you knew you could do it *better* – he was appalled with a sudden wild, rather childlike passion. To have screamed for his arm – how well Ned understood it, feeling his reins and his living horses! He would have screamed himself into oblivion. The sharpest physical pain could not have matched the dreadfulness of the realization. . . .

All the same, the slow hill stretching ahead, and the horses settling together nicely, Ned, glancing sideways at the cold expressionless face, knew that he didn't want to work for Ironminster. For all his pity.

'Brentwood is the end of your ground?'

'Yes, sir.'

'Perhaps you would take a drink with me then, and I'll show you my team? They're meeting me there.'

At that moment, saving Ned the embarrassment of a reply, his whole team, startled by some fool up the road shooting for pheasant, took off at the gallop. Ned let them go, glad of making up for lost time, and too tired to stop them – only, for God's sake, to keep the coach on the road, and prevent it from rolling. If his guv'nor couldn't buy safe horses he was damned if he was going to pull his guts out trying to steady the coach – let them all scream inside! All the same, keeping her upright wasn't easy. Ned held on to his leaders, watching for holes. If he lost control, he might be looking for a job, not turning one down.

Beside him, Ironminster laughed.

'Thank God, I've never had to drive brutes like these!'

Ned wished he could feel as unconcerned. Especially as – God Almighty! – what was happening ahead of them? A horse coming their way at flat gallop, and what looked like a carriage on its side – an accident – somebody standing in the road waving his arms – God's truth! Ned stuck his feet out and heaved, the reins biting into his hands. 'You bloody –!' It was the mad offside leader, ripe for a bullet – the wheelers were

7

responding, resisting their eager fellows, the coach jerking and lurching, bars jangling. The approaching rider was not helping, not slowing down at all and right in their road, but Ned had no responsibility towards him, the poor fool. The road was theirs, and his horses were entitled to it, but he was hoping he would be able to pull up beside the capsized carriage without causing the unfortunates inside to think they were going to be run down as well as overturned.

Ironminster said suddenly, 'There's something wrong here! That shot —'

Ned had got the same idea. The horse coming towards them was bolting; Ned watched it closely. There was no way they could stop it. It was a black thoroughbred, ridden by a slight figure, a boy. It came past them very close, on Ned's side, and Ned got a vivid impression of the rider's face. Not recognizing the horse, he was surprised to find that he recognized the rider, but so evident was it that something was badly wrong, he refrained from admitting it. Poor Kit, by the look of it, had been at the receiving end of something he no doubt deserved — but the horse . . . where had he come by such a magnificent brute as that? Ned had never seen such a beast outside the smart end of London. Even Ironminster remarked on it:

'What a mover! What a beauty!'

Ned, intensely curious, started to pull up. Ironminster was saying, 'Don't tell me this is a hold-up! I never thought to see the day!'

'There's not much wrong here,' Ned judged. 'Not to hear them bellowing. Ridden off the road, I think.'

He held his horses up beside the accident, keeping them still with some difficulty. The carriage was on its side, one horse still floundering in the ditch and the other, its traces freed, standing with a servant at its head. The coachman, covered in mud, was blasphemously setting about getting the other horse to its feet, and two gentlemen were still endeavouring to climb out of the coach.

'What's amiss?' Ironminster called out. 'D'you want some help?'

'We can't stay long, sir,' Ned put in quickly. 'Not if there's no damage. We can send help back.'

'Young rascal rode us into the ditch!' the coachman called

out. 'He meant mischief – Nathan here put a shot into him. Quick thinking, or he'd have done the same for us.'

'Do you know him?' Ironminster asked.

'No. Never set eyes on him. I reckon he knew who we were, though.'

'And who are you?'

The coachman didn't reply and Ironminster said to Ned, 'Armed, and quick enough to shoot. They must have valuables aboard. But no harm done. I daresay the lad knew it.'

Kit knew everything. More than was good for him.

'We'll tell the farm to send down a couple of horses to pull you out of the ditch,' Ned shouted down. 'I'm running late myself.' He didn't want to linger, his passengers on the verge of jumping down to gawp, and all leaning out to one side enough to send them the same way as the carriage. 'Trim the coach! Trim the coach!' He eased his hand and his wild leaders started to prance. 'They've had no more than a fright. I can't waste time.' He got the team moving more smoothly this time; the devils would learn, given enough practice. Under ten minutes now would see them into Brentwood, and himself beside a warm fire drinking brandy – then (he knew himself well enough) curiosity would stir him; it was aflame already. Where on earth did that fool Kit come by such a horse? Ned recalled its raking stride, the glimpse of its fine head and eager eye. Kit was only a wild Irish kitchen boy, more out of work than in. He had never come by the animal honestly!

'Did you see where the young devil disappeared to?' Ironminster was scanning the road behind, but it was empty. 'He must have turned into the woods. Is he local, I wonder?'

'I've never seen him,' Ned lied.

'I'd like to see that horse again. It was a rare mover.'

Ned agreed. He could guess where Kit had gone to ground, and decided to search him out when he was free and find out what he was up to. Meanwhile the wheeler with the sore shoulder was shirking her load and it was up to him to ease her as well as he could and spread the burden tactfully on to the others without losing any more time. The more subtle arts of coach-driving, making the best of poor and difficult horses, attracted Ned, mainly because he had a strong sympathy with the whole genus horse. Fairly callous to human suffering, he

9

did not see why the horse should be subjected to any more cruelty than came its way in the natural course of events; its lot was hard enough as it was, the sole motive powers for all man's needs, however excessive they might be. Ned had defended more horses in fights than he had humans – who could look after themselves. The excitement past, Ironminster settled down watching him again – Ned was very aware of it – and the coach finished its eventful journey into Brentwood, gaining four minutes of its lost time. The new coachman was waiting, and Ned got down gratefully. 'Who left here half an hour ago driving two chestnuts to a carriage? Because they're in the ditch and like as not need a pull.'

'That's the man come down from London – something to do with paying the wages for the diggers on the navigation.'

'Well, he's some digging to do now, if he's to get out. I'll tell Harry – he might earn himself something.'

'You're confounded late. Am I supposed to make it up?'

Ned didn't care any longer, and shrugged. Ironminster and his man were seeing to their luggage and Ned was anxious to avoid the 'talk' his lordship had proposed, and slipped the back way into the kitchen of the White Hart, content to stand with his back to the meat roasting on a spit in the hearth and watch the consternation of the departing coach through the window. Now it was no longer his, he could relax. He hung his hat on a meat-hook above the hearth, his coat and gloves over chairbacks, and started to unwind his neckcloth. Even his shirt was damp, the ruffles drooping sadly above the clammy stripes of his waistcoat.

'Oh, make yourself at home, do!' The cook, almost too old to buckle to his charms, gave him a shove out of the way in order to stoop and baste the meat. The strong smell of her sweat made Ned feel the contrast: the aching cold of his limbs was his inevitable winter penance, and the numb weariness of his arms and shoulders . . . What did a fat cook know of hardship in her steaming, stinking kitchen? Cold drops of rain, slowly corkscrewing down the spiral locks of his red-gold hair, fell with loud sizzles into the cook's fat. She screamed at him again, but he smiled at her with his beguiling brown eyes in his most practised manner and was rewarded – as he intended – with a glass of hot milk topped up with rum.

'That's for you, although I should know better. You're too smooth for your own good, my pretty boy. The girls spoil you and the ones like me, old enough to be your mother, are just as bad. Well, you can earn your keep while you're standing there. Give the spit a turn and spoon the fat over those back legs. I've got the vegetables to do.'

'Where's your kitchen boy then?' Ned, knowing very well, stooped to the task, smelling rum and lamb fat happily in his nostrils, and feeling a whole lot better.

'Hasn't been in for a couple of days. He's a useless lad, too flighty by far. He'll be for it when he shows his face in here again.'

She threw a towel at him and picked up the discarded neck-cloth, shaking it out to dry. 'Your clean linen is on top of the sheets in the cupboard. Annie ironed your shirts last night. You ought to stop and thank her some time – I'm sure I don't know why she bothers. There's a dry waistcoat too if you want it.' She knew perfectly well why Annie bothered and so did Ned, but Ned didn't want to be delayed once he had thawed out. He collected his dry things and made off for his attic room to change. The wind whistled through the ill-fitting window and driven rain had damped the top blanket on his rickety bed. 'I'd be better off over the stables,' he thought, recalling the warm sweetness of the stored hay and the steamy fug from the resting animals below. He was used to sleeping with horses, and enjoyed dozing off to the infinitely soothing noise of munching and chomping – but the room was free. He couldn't complain. Five minutes later, very circumspect, he had borrowed a hack from the stables and ridden out the back way, returning along the road he had just travelled.

Lord Ironminster, warming himself with brandy in the dining-room, waited for his coach without impatience. He had a friend with him, Andrew Field, and his servant, Sam, a man who in looks would have appeared more at home in a betting-shop or rat-pit than in the boudoir.

'I think,' Ironminster said happily, 'I have found my man.'

'A very pretty workman,' his friend agreed. 'I was wondering if you had broached the matter.'

'I did – he's not keen. A pity, but –' Ironminster smiled.

'That won't stop you?'

'Hardly. I shall have him, even if it has to be arranged. He is too good to miss. An artist. And very sharp, not one of your bumpkins. And something of a fighter as well, if his word is to be believed. Almost too good to be true. If I can't talk him into it we'll have to work out a – a method – to persuade him. Eh, Sam?'

'Yes, my lord.'

'Your right-hand man . . .' Field smiled. 'I wish you luck.'

'I need it.'

'You've plenty of friends, August.'

'Yes, well, God knows, I need them now to counter the opposition. Sam, go and find that lad and bring him in here. I want it settled.'

Sam, inquiring for Ned, was told that he had taken a horse and departed for no one knew where, and took the message back to his master.

'Hmm. He knew – never mind. I think we'll probably get our way, if we put our minds to it. Think about it, Sam. Ask around. I'll leave it in your hands.'

'Yes, my lord.' Sam looked cheerful at the prospect, and Ironminster smiled at Field. 'Sam's low cunning is wasted in his present position. He needs a proposition occasionally – a challenge to his baser nature, a spot of skulduggery. Isn't that right, Sam?'

Sam grinned.

'I'll pit you against Ned Rowlands. Have him applying to me for a job a fortnight from now – and it's twenty guineas for you, Sam. How's that?'

'Splendid, my lord.'

'I doubt you'll do it honestly.'

'No matter, my lord.'

'That's settled then. Another brandy with me Andrew? Purely medicinal, need I add. It keeps the cold from my chest.'

He took his handkerchief out and started to cough. His friend's amusement changed to resignation, and he said, 'We'll arrange it for you, August, never fear. I can't see any difficulty.'

Sam went for the drinks.

N ED, riding a tired hack, pursued a line of his own away
from the road, following a track across common land.
It was almost dusk, still raining, and he cursed as he
rode, more at his own stupidity than Kit's. He didn't *have* to
know, God help him; it was his own nature at fault, always
wanting to know more, getting involved. If a hue and cry was
set off after Kit, the last thing he wanted was to be found with
him. He knew this, but he could not stop himself nosing in.
Lucky for Kit that he was the only one who had recognized
him; but lucky indeed if Kit got away with his foolishness and
escaped hanging. The men he had attacked must have had a
good look at him, for it had been light enough, and he hadn't
even covered his face. No doubt they would circulate his description. Ned, aghast at Irish recklessness, knew when he had
come to Kit's cottage – hovel would be more apt a description
– by his own horse's hesitation and inquiring whinny. Another
whinny came back. In the gathering dusk Ned saw the black
horse under the trees, throwing its head up from grazing,
nervous, reins trailing. He halted his own horse, watching,
pursing his lips. Against plum-purple winter woodland and the
golden trampled bracken of the cottage clearing, the horse
stood as if for its portrait, as beautiful an animal as Ned,
connoisseur of good horses, had seen in all his days. The dark
winter coat had the sheen of a crow's wing, muscled beneath; a
large horse but compact, long-tailed, no white anywhere, but a
muzzle the colour of cinnamon. Ned dismounted and approached the horse gently. It was attracted by his own nag, a
mare, and came up quietly, close enough for Ned to catch its
reins.

'Hey, my beauty, my bonny fellow. Come with me then, my
pretty horse.'

The horse was perfectly willing. For a moment Ned was
tempted, realizing that it was the horse more than Kit who had
tempted him on his journey. He wanted to take it and ride

home. Kit wasn't going to use it again in a hurry. But then –
the animal being stolen property – it would be more a liability
than a prize. Ned didn't want to turn horse-stealer and get
strung up for his pains, a sad end to his promising career. He
would have to broach the cottage, and Kit's hellish old mother,
and find out if there was any way of coming by the animal
honestly.

But the cottage was very quiet. Kit's mother was anything
but quiet as a rule, even when her son was behaving himself.
Ned tied the two horses up to the woodshed and went to the
door. He tapped and opened it.

'Anyone at home? Kit?'

The usual stench hit his nostrils. A fire burned low in the
hearth; somebody was crying and moaning in the darkness.
Ned hesitated – he didn't want to *help* at all, nothing had been
further from his mind, only find out and generally nose around
and get the story first-hand from the lunatic kitchen-boy, but
he could hardly not inquire after Kit's health in view of the
circumstances.

'Kit, it's Ned. Where are you?'

His animal curiosity faltered, coldly. There was no excitement here, no jolly panic nor maternal raving, only
agonized breathing, held tightly and let go in shuddering
gasps, half sobbed, and mouselike female whimpering. Ned
wasn't sensitive, but he knew disaster when he smelt it. It was
quite plain. He closed the door behind him and leaned against it,
taking stock.

'Kit?'

His mother wasn't there, only Kit lying on a rumpled bed,
and a little skinny girl Ned had never seen before, who must be
one of Kit's myriad sisters. She was terrified. Ned could see
her eyes glittering like a vixen's caught in the coach lights.

'Get a candle,' he said to her. 'Let's see what's going on.'

She did not move, crouching beside the bed, staring at him.
He crossed over to her, impatient, and put out a hand to pull
her into action. She let out a scream and started to sob wildly.

'For heaven's sake!' Ned was out of his depth instantly. 'I'm
not going to hurt you. A *candle* –' This wasn't his ground at
all, nursing the sick and comforting their womenfolk; he felt
angry, more with himself than anything. What a fool he was!

His eyes becoming accustomed to the dark, he peered at Kit reluctantly, and saw blood everywhere. He wanted to panic then, like the girl, feeling his heart give a squawk inside him like a frightened hen, suffocating. This was anything but a joke. He stood, frozen, wondering whether he could retract, just go, pretend he'd never been. Nobody here was in a fit state to even notice. Nobody would know he'd been near.

And just as certainly he knew that life had caught up with him here, cornered him, repaying him for his inquisitiveness and for having an eye for stolen property and for condoning Kit's irresponsibility. And although he knew he was a bit of a rough animal – compared with the Lord Ironminsters of this world – he wasn't low enough to back out. He only wished he were. He had to make himself look again, force himself to the bedside, and feel himself trembling like a woman.

'Kit? What's up then? What have they done to you?'

Kit was past speaking. Ned swore at him, unnerved by the look in the very blue eyes, which had never looked serious in all their seventeen years until now. Ned knew that Kit was going to die, and wondered how long it would take. The first shock weathered, he now felt very angry. He groped about for candles, and lit a couple from the fire and put them on a chair beside the bed. He had to do something but he didn't know what. Only with horses. He supposed it was the same thing. He had sat with many a horse in its death-throes in his time, sometimes even in the road after a collision, when everyone else had lost interest. Take its harness off, if you could. Kit . . .

'Kit, it's all right.' He had to say something, to appease the look on Kit's face. He wished he hadn't lit the candles. Get some water. Where was the girl?

'Fetch me some water,' he said. The girl just went on crying. For heaven's sake, what had the man Nathan been carrying to defend himself with this sort of shot? This wasn't bird-scarer; this was murder. Ned couldn't see how Kit could have got himself home, the way he was, except by will-power. 'Could you go for a doctor?' He asked the girl. 'Take my horse?'

'No.' The voice was Kit's. His eyes pleaded. Ned could see his point. To be patched up in order to swing wasn't an attractive proposition. He wouldn't have chosen it himself.

'Well, I'm no hand . . . Kit, you are an idiot!' He could not keep the anger out of his voice, manoeuvred as he was, forced into this awful role. He stamped about, throwing more logs on the fire, finding a pan and going outside to fill it from the water-butt. The gorgeous horse whinnied to him. He longed to leave, and feel its lovely stride out on the forest track. The cottage stank of filth and failure.

'It's all right, Kit. I'll see to you.' He couldn't stand the look on Kit's face. It numbed him to the bone-marrow, made his hands shake. He moved the candles farther away, and tried to sort out the mess that Nathan had made of Kit's body, but, beyond pulling away the bloody strips of shirt and riding-coat (and deciding that they were better left to hold him together, for there was little else to do it), Ned could see no constructive course to follow. He pulled a blanket up gently, setting his teeth to stop them chattering. That was a big improvement. He folded an old shawl lying on the floor and put it under Kit's head, and offered him some water to drink, but Kit couldn't manage it. Ned couldn't understand how he had managed to get home, except that Kit's family lived by will-power in the natural course of events, having no work and no money, and to escape from what had gone wrong on the road must have been more important to Kit than anything that had yet happened in his young life. Will-power, having seen him through seventeen years, had seen him to dying in bed, if that was any consolation. Ned, at that moment, thought it very little. What a way to die! Ned put the candles on the floor and sat on the chair and leaned his elbows on his knees, watching Kit's face. The stupid boy looked about twelve years old. I don't even know him, Ned thought carefully; not to get involved – it was useless – yet Ned could feel himself shaking still and the cold sweat of pity, as real as the rain had been earlier, soaking his shirt. Ned, who had begun to feel pretty big and tough since taking his job on the Wellington, was aware that he wasn't far from tears.

Kit only spoke once. He said, 'The horse is – by Whalebone.'

'Where did you get it from?' Ned asked him.

No reply. Kit's eyes were shut. Ned watched him fearfully, afraid of death. Kit's face was like wax, but the nostrils still moved with breath. Beads of sweat stood on his forehead, like the dew on the roses of a master-painter, still and shining. He looked very peaceful. Ned could not reconcile it with what was under the blanket. He sat there tensely, his long, cold fingers twining restlessly, watching, hating the predicament but unable to change anything. Kit's fault – his fault – how *stupid* it all was! Unnecessary. Unnatural. He wanted no part of it, but he was bound by instinct. Fixed to his chair, his eyes fixed to Kit's face, locked by circumstance. Ned felt as paralysed as Kit himself.

Ned sat for a long time, losing track of time. The fire burned low, and the smell of woodsmoke kindly blanketed the evil little room; the soft snapping of fading sparks punctuated Kit's uneven breath. Outside it rained. Rain and rats rustled in the thatch, a familiar sound; rain spat down the chimney into the fire and dripped on to the earth floor. Ned forgot that he wasn't alone with Kit, until – a long time later – the girl got up and put another log on the fire. Ned turned round with a start, and saw her face in the disturbed flare of the embers, thin and white as a witch, haloed by frizzy hair the same colour as his own. She was dressed in drab black, held around the middle with string, her feet bare. She looked about twelve, but Ned guessed that she was older.

'Who are you?' He asked. 'One of Kit's sisters?'

'No.' She offered no more information. She wouldn't come close, but gestured towards Kit with a skinny arm. 'Is he – is he – still –'

'He's still breathing.'

'It's bad? Will he be – all right?'

'No. I don't see how he can be.'

Her eyes were red with crying, and the tears started up again at Ned's opinion and ran silently down her cheeks. Ned felt distaste for her, so dirty and hopeless and useless. But even if he had felt obliged to offer comfort, there wasn't any to offer.

'What was he up to, for heaven's sake? I saw him on the road. He'd ridden a carriage into a ditch. What was he after?'

'They were carrying a lot of money. He said it would be easy. And then he'd come back for me and we'd go away up to Liverpool to his brother, and no one would find us.'

'And the horse? He'd stolen it?'

'Yes. Last night. Ready for today. He'd planned it all very carefully.'

'Not carefully enough.'

'No.'

She sat down in the dirt in front of the fire and laid her head in her arms and rocked herself gently in a primitive sort of despair. Ned decided she was a gipsy of sorts; her voice was strange, not a local voice. Ned supposed that Kit had picked her up out of the hedgerow, just as he'd taken the horse. Probably put more mind to the choosing of the horse than he had to the girl. She was just a slut.

How long was Kit going to take to die? Ned was aware that – should the local vigilantes be hauled out by the constable and a search put in hand – he stood in some danger of being apprehended as an accomplice. To be found with Kit in the circumstances might be thought a little odd. No one would believe that he had come because of a horse – except, possibly, Lord Ironminster. He looked at Kit doubtfully and got up and looked out of the door. It was quiet enough outside. The soft dripping of rain, and the stirring of night birds far away, the barking of a farm dog . . . so uneventful, painfully ordinary – it was hard to believe that Kit was going to – to what? Ned scowled, leaning on the door-post, feeling the night air. What happened? God alone knew. God and, shortly, Kit. Ned, not much of a philosopher, was aware that he was agonizingly grateful at that moment for the ordinary night, the smell of dead leaves and horse-dung, and the promise of its continuance. He wanted to live till he was a hundred. He thought briefly of August Ironminster and how much he sought to extract from his time on earth in spite of dire disabilities; it occurred to him that it was worth taking a good deal of care in this uncertain life not get shot at, maimed or hanged – it had never struck him before; he had never, until today, not taken life for granted. He felt humble and earnest and sad, all conditions very rare to his nature. His eyes, growing accustomed to the dark, saw the wet, miserable outlines of the two horses standing in the rain. He cursed, and went back inside to help Kit to eternity.

It was five-thirty in the morning when Ned got back to the White Hart, riding the hack and leading the black thoroughbred. He felt sick and harrowed, and, in spite of an overwhelming weariness, he took a good deal of time rubbing down the black horse, and the hack, and making them comfortable in the stable. He then slept in his damp clothes until Annie called him for breakfast – and slept on some more – and went down at nine o'clock, pale and bad-tempered.

'Your kitchen boy's dead,' he told the cook. 'I sat with him all night till he decided to go, and someone ought to go down to the cottage and see to his body.'

The news caused a riot, hysterics amongst the women, and some urgent message-running to the acting constable, who came down to the inn to ask Ned some questions. Not having acted on the disturbance the day before – no one, after all, paid him for the job that had been foisted on him and he wasn't one to go looking for trouble – the constable was pleased to have the business cleared up and to take the credit. He would make sure that the irate Mr Crabtree of the Navigation Company would know that the culprit had been apprehended, and that the messy business of taking the boy to court and getting him hanged was unnecessary. The matter of the black horse was slightly more complicated.

'Well, who knows where Kit stole it from?' Ned asked irritably. 'Not from round here, that's for certain. And if no one claims it, it's mine. And if there's a reward put out for it, that's mine too. And meanwhile I'll be responsible for its keep.'

'I'll make inquiries,' the constable said. 'Not too diligently, need I add. You're welcome to the horse as far as I'm concerned.'

Ned reckoned he had earned it, feeling aged by about ten years. He had a conscience, not about the horse, but about the girl, whom he had refused to help. He wanted no gipsy brat hanging on him. To Kit, dying, he had felt obliged (that happened only once in a lifetime) but to the living girl he felt no such loyalty. And in spite of her obvious distress, loneliness, helplessness and youth, he had left her and ridden away, which was no doubt why he felt so bad-tempered. The whole night's business had left him feeling inadequate, which was rare these days. He started to get dressed for his coach, which was due in from London in twenty minutes, winding a swathe of newly-starched neckcloth round his throat. He reckoned he would be half-dead by the time he got to Colchester, worn out before he had started, and with the bolters to cope with, the morning fresh in their nostrils . . . He half-yawned, half-sighed. Annie held out his first coat, in the dark blue livery of his guv'nor's set-up, and then his caped box-coat, the weight of it almost staggering her. Ned, shrugging down into his collar, back to the everyday, didn't feel anything was quite real. Hat, gloves, his whip, a quick brandy and hot water, his respects to the constable, and out to the yard and real life, the bolters drawing to a halt two minutes early and still fresh enough not to stand, one of the wheelers jerking the coach just as an old dame was in the act of alighting, throwing her in the mud . . . confusion, swearing, a spot of professional charm . . . it all came quite naturally. Ned felt himself coming to, checking the pole-chains, the curb-chains, the traces, letting out the leaders' coupling-reins, taking up the reins and threading them between the calloused fingers of his hand and climbing up to his seat. His companion, thank goodness, was an elderly clergyman, already distinctly nervous, not a know-all like Ironminster. For a fleeting moment, contemplating the problem of a smooth start, Ned wished he had accepted Ironminster's offer to drive his beautiful team and have done with the ardours of the public highway – but only for a moment. After all, the bolters were a challenge. Any fool could drive the good ones. Now, to ease them, humour them . . . Ned frowned, concentrating hard, and the coach moved like silk out under the archway, the clergyman smiling and waving to his wife in complete confidence. Ned could feel the clergyman's relief, and the bolters' quivering restraint, at balance in his fingers. Of the wild power he could release merely by relaxing his hand the clergyman had no knowledge, poor fool. Ned, his professional eye on the road ahead, kept his mind strictly on the job, and did not think again of the bloodless body lying in the hovel amongst the trees until he reached Colchester some five hours later, and realized how tired he was.

3

S AM rode on the Wellington from Chelmsford into
London, having made sure that Ned would be driving,
and watched him like a hawk, taking meticulous care not
to be noticed himself. This wasn't difficult, for Ned took little
notice of his passengers unless their behaviour annoyed him –
until the end of the ride when he was pretty ruthless in extract-
ing tips, albeit with great charm. He wasn't an ordinary coachman, being too young for a start, and more reticent than most,
preoccupied with his horses. Also his looks set him apart:
his face not yet florid from too much cold wind and hot
brandy, but pale as Ironminster's own, with a strong nose and
chestnut-brown eyes very lively beneath prominently arched
golden-red eyebrows. Sam, a valet by trade but rather more
than that in practice, considered that the dark-brown
Ironminster livery would set off this colouring to perfection;
the whole turn-out would be much improved in Ned's hands, the
present coachman being habitually shabby and not at all good at
keeping the mettlesome Ironminster horses in hand, irritating his
Lordship beyond endurance. Sam was determined to earn his
twenty guineas, if not Ned's undying gratitude.

Ned for his part did not give Ironminster another thought.
He was hoping, now that he drove into London, to seek out his
father and see what chance there was of getting employed by a
Mail contractor, but he was generally too tired to be bothered
by the time his work was done. The last leg was wearisome
with so much traffic; and one couldn't always be sure if one
was going to get the right of way – a nice advantage the Mails
had over all other road-users. Ned's father knew of a Mail
driver who had divided a marching battalion to exercise his
right. The market carts, hay-carts, coal-carts, post-chaises,
gigs, wandering pigs, and droves of cattle for Smithfield all
made Whitechapel and Aldgate tiresome driving, especially
with the horses either dancing fresh, or near enough home to
be hard to hold. Ned knew the smell of London, recognized

the first sulphurous whiff as far out as Ilford, and knew he was a country lad at heart. By Stratford and Bow he had joined the motley local traffic and the coaches from Abridge and points north, and the passengers grumbled at delays or screamed if he decided to overtake. Mostly Ned was a safe and prudent driver, but he was hard pressed at times, being young and not really very prudent by nature; only his father's stern upbringing reminded him that passengers were not to be frightened. His good tips confirmed that this was wise advice, and so he cursed and swore but proceeded with admirable caution.

That afternoon, taking up the reins of the fresh team at Romford, he was joined on the box by a sharp, well-dressed young man who seemed very anxious about the time of their arrival in Gracechurch Street.

'It's very important to me that we get there on time. In fact, a quarter of an hour before time would suit me very much better.'

A voice from the seat behind added, 'And me too, sir. Three guineas for you, coachman, if you can deliver us into the city by three fifteen.'

'And I'll add two,' said the man beside him.

Ned took a shrewd look at his companions, and decided that they looked as if they could afford it. There were only two ladies aboard, and they hadn't looked a particularly fussy pair, not the sort given to screaming. There was a dandy type inside with rouge and ruffles, and the odd selection of farmers and tradesmen on top. The horses, being the city team and good for advertisement, were the best on the whole ground, and had a stage of only eleven miles, which was well within their compass.

'I'll see what I can do. It depends on the road.' He was cautious, knowing the dangers. Once in a while it didn't matter but as a habit it must lead to trouble; Ned didn't want to be tempted. But five guineas! He picked up his whip, and felt his horses' mouths, easing them out into the street. They were all fit and in good form, and he felt optimistic. What the hell! The guv'nor was safe in Colchester and would never know. He could do with five guineas. He put them into a sharp trot, working out the best place to spring them. Much depended on the traffic through Stratford and beyond and whether or not he got held up behind anything cumbersome. The gentlemen consulted their pocket-watches and Ned could sense their anxiety. He felt the same needle of impatience, skirted a farmer's cart dangerously close and put his team into a canter down a reasonable stretch of ground, biting his lip anxiously at the swaying of the loaded coach. A bit too soon perhaps; the ground improved nearer into London. He didn't want to turn over, five guineas or no. But the traffic would thicken too.

Coming into Stratford and to the junction of the road up to Leyton Stone, he was infuriated by the sight of a private coach coming from Leyton Stone some fifty yards ahead of him. He signalled to his guard to give it a blast of the horn, hoping it would pull in to let him through, but the coach kept its road, travelling at a very sedate trot. Ned got his team on its tail. His horses now, infected with his own impatience, were pulling like blazes, but there was a tilbury coming towards them, and some riders straggling ahead. He swore, forced back into the funereal pace of the private coach, his leaders' noses on its tailboard. As soon as the tilbury had passed, he pulled out and his guard gave an urgent blast again for road, but to his amazement the coach ahead, instead of holding well in to the left, moved over into the middle of the road, far enough to stop his own near-side leader in its tracks. The wheeler, skidding up behind, got kicked for its pains, and in the ensuing mêlée the baulked leader got its leg over the trace, which meant total stoppage for a sort-out. The guard got down to put it right, shouting up to Ned, 'What's he about then? Wanting all the road –'

'Just let him wait!' Ned was incensed by the incident. 'Get that fixed and we'll show him who owns the road! Get your horn ready and blast him to blazes!'

'Yes, with pleasure.'

The trace hooked up again, the guard swung back on board and Ned went off at a canter. The coach ahead had quickened pace and was still taking all the road, but now the road was wider and Ned had room to overtake, although he was aware that the manoeuvre was exceedingly dangerous without the cooperation of the other coach. With the row the guard was making, Ned was gratified to see that all the other road-users ahead were retiring abruptly into ditches and gateways – all but his rival, who started to pull out to the right again.

Ned let forth a stream of bad language, checked his leaders and whipped them suddenly to the left. The excited beasts responded with the alacrity required and went up on the inside at a flat gallop, so close that the front wheel touched the other coach's back wheel and a shower of sparks went up off the metal rims. Ned had a nasty vision of some poor devil on his near-hand up-ended in the ditch, but was too concerned getting himself some room to let it worry him. He was now right alongside his rival who was making no effort to draw in; Ned thought he must be a madman. He got a glimpse of a black beaver, golden whiskers and a white, set face, realized he could expect no mercy from the maniac, and so with a quick and accurate movement of his arm landed his whip a chop on the man's near-side leader, just below the ear, which had the intended result of veering the horse sharply away – so sharply that for a moment Ned thought the coach would go over.

The coachman shouted something furiously, and used his own whip to turn his horses back again. Ned could see by now that they were blood horses with a lot less weight behind them than his own, and unless he held his course very firmly by brute force he wasn't going to finish overtaking much before Whitechapel some few miles ahead. Already the two coaches had travelled side by side for a hundred yards or more and in their swaying had touched topsides more than once with alarming noises, accompanied by much shouting and screaming from his passengers, but Ned was by now far too angry to give way. If once he got his wheel in front he intended to drive the other coach right off the road. Being on the left, he had the enormous advantage in being able to use his whip on the other man's horses, while his rival had no chance of getting at his. It was only this that saved them, for Ned let fly again before the others could draw ahead, and got them to swerve once more, which gave his coach the advantage. He shouted at his own horses and drew them over, so that his own leader started to cross the other. Ned watched the awful, incipient tangle of horseflesh ahead of him, steering implacably, praying hard. There was a farm-cart coming towards them on the other side, much too heavy to move out of the way in a hurry, and to avoid it his rival must surely start to pull up, else he would likely kill his own leader on the approaching shafts. Ned glanced at him, and saw to his astonishment that he was smiling, his face screwed up, very excited, his eyes judging the distance to the farm-cart, but smiling all the while. Ned thought he must be drunk and had a good mind to use his whip on the man's own silly face, but he had no time. To save the farm-cart and its screaming boy, he moved his own leaders over to make room, taking the pressure off his rival who immediately started to pull up, as he was obliged to do to avoid a head-on collision. Ned saw the abused wheelers fling themselves back into the breeching, mud and clods flying everywhere, and then he was through and steadying his own team past the farm-cart, hearing tirades of abuse hurled at him from the top of the load and – for the first time – aware of the cries and exclamations going up from his own passengers. His coach was in pandemonium, the outside passengers sprawled all over the seats, some on their backs, and someone leaning out of the window in hysterics shrieking at him to stop.

'Oh, damn them all!' he shouted to relieve his feelings, and took a look at the man beside him, who was as white as a sheet, although still in command of his wits. 'How are you?' he asked. 'If I stop now to placate this lot we'll have that fellow in front of us again –'

'Carry on is my advice. You're well on the way to your five guineas, I reckon.'

'Well, I won't get any other tips,' Ned muttered. The excitement over, he was a little worried, to put it mildly. It didn't do to lose one's temper on the road, and the insane provocation he had suffered wouldn't really do as an excuse. Coachmen were imprisoned for dangerous driving; a friend of his father's had done a year's hard labour for going over a hump-backed bridge too fast and losing a passenger into the river below.

'No one's hurt?' he queried of his companion, too taken up with the horses to spare a glance. 'If we stop now and listen to all the cackle we'll never make our ordinary time, let alone cut ten minutes.'

'No one fell off. The gentleman below seems a little disturbed.'

'The pretty man? He's got the vapours, I daresay. Give him something to tell his friends.'

All the same, Ned was more careful for the rest of the journey and overtook with meticulous judgement or not at all, arriving a bare eight minutes ahead of time. He didn't expect to receive his five guineas, and was much surprised when it was pressed into his hand the moment he put down his reins.

'Good man!' The two passengers so anxious to be punctual promptly disappeared, and Ned was obliged to climb down and face the cackles of the rest of the crew, who were telling the tale to all their friends and relations. The whole attention of the busy yard had veered round to centre upon the travel-stained Wellington; the stable-boys were examining her splintered panelling and smashed lamp with what Ned considered unnecessary astonishment, and the horse-master was consulting his pocket-watch. 'Eight minutes before time, Mr Rowlands? That's rare going on March roads.'

'Lunatic driving! Lunatic driving!' The pretty man was waiting for him, his already heightened complexion ablaze. 'Who is the contractor of this coach? I insist on seeing him! I shall bring a case against you for risking the lives of your passengers – have you seen the damage inside? Have you considered the suffering caused to the ladies?'

'It would be more to the point to bring a case against the coachman of the drag, sir, if it's lunatic driving you're talking of.'

Ned felt he had to be very careful, and not lose his temper. The best witnesses of what had happened had departed – no doubt not to be seen again – and the passengers inside and most of those outside, with their backs to the horses, or busy talking, probably hadn't noticed the exact circumstances of his overtaking. They would all surely recollect that he had overtaken on the wrong side, but the reasons for it would – if he knew his luck – be quite forgotten, if ever grasped at all.

'Look at this! Look at this!' The man grasped Ned by the arm and propelled him to the open door. The two ladies were still inside, and one of them seemed to be in a faint. The other was dabbing at the swooning face with a blood-stained handkerchief and making a noise like a hen laying an egg. The coach stank of brandy, which seemed to be swilling about the floor from a wicker container, and the window glass was broken, showered about on floor and seats.

'This good lady hit her head such a blow on the side of the window-frame that she has scarcely recovered yet, and when I shouted at you to stop, you took not a blind bit of notice! You are guilty of the most damnable behaviour and I'll make sure you come before the magistrates for it.'

Ned listened to him without saying anything, which took a considerable effort. Such a diatribe was infectious, and several other passengers took the man's part and started exhibiting various bruises and imagined scratches, and calling for strong drink to steady their nerves. Everyone inside the inn emerged to hear the tale, and quite a few people from the street, and Ned began to realize that he could well be in trouble. The coach was visibly damaged, the lady in a faint, and he had cut eight minutes off his normal time. The only man who tried to put a word in for him was his guard, but – not a loud man by nature – he wasn't a match for the elegant complainant.

'I shall take particulars and make sure you pay for this!' The dandy started writing in a notebook, and a party from the inn started to help the half-conscious lady from the coach. The crowd pressed round as if for a hanging, and Ned, bitterly indignant, pushed his way free and sought refuge in the stables. The ostlers were grinning and sympathetic. Ned leaned against the wall and put his hat on a collar-hook, scratching his head angrily.

'To hear them talk –!' The injustice of it stung him, for he knew perfectly well that, having put himself into a situation of great potential danger, he had emerged from it safely by pure skill; a great slice of himself was still exhilarated by his success and his cleverness. He felt that he deserved congratulation, not censure. If Ironminster had been on the box-seat with him – a man like that would have appreciated how nicely he had handled the incident! Just his luck to be carrying a load of old women.

'I reckon you're in trouble, lad,' the old horse-master said gloomily, carrying a load of harness to its hooks. 'When the guv'nor gets wind of this, and sees the damage . . .'

'Damn his job! I'll find another.'

'Depends on the irate gentleman – perhaps when he's had a drink or two he'll think different –'

'He wants to take me to court –'

'Aye, well, he's grounds, hasn't he? I've seen it happen that way a few times –'

'It's the other fellow should be charged – pulling across me like a drunken idiot. It's lucky we didn't have the whole team down.'

He described the incident in detail, using bits of straw for a diagram, and when he had finished the horse-master said, 'Who was this maniac, then? Doesn't sound like anyone I know on this road.'

'No, you're right. I've never struck eyes on the man before. Some yokel down from the country, a Sunday driver.' But a very smart turn-out all the same, for a country yob.

Ned left the stable cautiously, ready for a drink, and found his guv'nor's agent looking for him.

'Bad business. The coach will have to come off the road for repairs. I shall have to go down to Vidler's and see about hiring a replacement until we get it back. And that inside gentleman says he's going to bring an action against us. That means against you, to be more precise, and the guv'nor won't like that. If the gentleman goes through with it, I'm afraid we shall have to finish your employment.'

'Huh! *Very* kind!'

'And even if he doesn't, the same will probably apply. Very damaging to the reputation – it's not the sort of thing we can tolerate at all. I'll send a message through to Colchester on the Mail tonight and see what answer we get back. Meanwhile John Theobald can take the replacement in the morning. You'd better make out a report of what happened in writing, while it's still in your mind. You'll be glad of it if you have to defend yourself against the magistrate.'

The man's quick unsympathetic appraisal of the situation sickened Ned and did nothing to improve his temper.

'You can tell the guv'nor in your message that I've left already! And if that dandy brings an action you can answer for me, for I'm not leaving an address –'

'Not so hasty, Mr Rowlands! You –'

'I've every reason to be hasty! I've held my temper long enough! Nobody asks *me* what happens – no one congratulates me for keeping the coach on its wheels, the horses on their feet – anyone else and you'd have had a proper accident on your hands.'

Ned flung into the coaching-house, stripped himself of his driving coat and gloves, hung up his whip, and went out into the street, walking fast and furiously. It was nearly dusk and the sour smells of the city gutters, the hustling clerks with their letters, old crones and beggars and city merchants in his path all combined to irritate him, reminding him that, without a job, he was just a nobody, less than the mean little men scratching away with their quills behind the grimy windows whom he normally despised. Not much use now applying to a Mail contractor for work, not without a reference, and with the summons likely to be brought against him; not a good time either to go and see his father. Ned did not believe in going home in times of trouble, only when he was riding high and able to impress. He had been independent for too long. But he disliked London save as a coach terminus and decided quickly enough that he was walking the wrong way, into the city instead of out of it. 'But where to?' Blast it, he was bitter and fed-up and he turned into the nearest gin-shop. A drink made him feel better, and another one better still. Cheered, he passed on to a coffee-shop where the proprietor was an ex-coachman, got some food and fell into conversation with a man who knew Jem Belcher and had seen the fight between John Gully and Robert Gregson at Six Mile Bottom.

'Aye, and I saw the Game Chicken beat Gully before that – fifty-nine rounds that one went – you never saw such a sight as they were at the finish! And when it come to Gully and Gregson, my money were on Gregson. Well, that were close-run; thirty-six rounds that one, and they were both beat to pulp by the end, but Gully got up and Gregson didn't, so that were my money gone. But I never saw braver fighters, right to the end, none o'your tricks like the business with Cribb and the Negro . . .'

This talk engaged Ned until, with a few more drinks inside him – and the coffee well-warmed with brandy – he began to feel that the night life of the city of London was weighing heavily. By now the place had filled up with the usual obnoxious young bucks in stays, with padded chests and cossacks as wide as a grandmother's skirts, and old women with their girls in tow, all smelling strongly of sweat and filth over which the scents and snuffs of the gentlemen laid a heady pall. Ned knew of better places to continue drowning his sorrows and got up to go, but as he did so one of the miserable sluts laid a hand on his wrist and clasped him with such desperation that he was unable to shake her off.

'Sir, please!'

She was a skinny little thing with dirty red hair and eyes like cold stones, starved of hope. The face appalled him.

'Let go of me, you little bitch!' He wrenched at her angrily but she was as tenacious as a terrier. He fancied she bared her teeth at him. The other girls were laughing and one of the men drawled, 'Well held, my dear. Don't let him escape!'

But the girl didn't laugh. Ned sensed her utter determination; it was almost a death-hold, the grip of the baited badger.

'You know me,' she said. 'Please.'

The voice was quiet, exhausted, and the appeal quite desperate. Ned, for all his repulsion, hesitated. It was Kit's girl, and there was something in her face that reminded him of Kit on his death-bed, close to giving up the ghost. Ned, as used to seeing starving wretches as anybody, felt angry for his hesitation, but quite unable to steel himself. And for his weakness he felt angrier still.

The old woman was coming at him, her eyes glittering, her palm extended. 'And what will you give me for my lovely girl, my dear?' she whined, gin-bottle clutched to her scraggy breast. Ned would gladly have given her a black eye. The fumes of her breath shrank him where he stood. He took out one of his newly-acquired guineas, flung it at her, and pushed his way out of the shop, dragging the girl with him. In the street outside he shook her off into the gutter, where she stood with her bare feet in the drain-water, gazing at him numbly, like a sheep.

'I don't want you,' he said. 'I only paid to get out of there.'

'Take me back to Brentwood,' she said. 'I won't be any trouble. That's all I want, to get away from here, to go back to the cottage.'

He should have gone, walked on and left her, but he couldn't.

'Why did you come here? You must have known —' There was only one way destitute girls made a living in London.

'The workhouse people came, after the funeral.'

'The workhouse is better than that.' He nodded inside.

She shook her head, mute, beaten. He started to walk away, hunched into the night air, not wanting to be lumbered with her, but she came after him on her silent bare feet like a stray dog. The animal similes kept coming, because she was like an animal. He didn't turn round, but he knew she was still there, a few paces behind. He didn't know what to do. The gin had fuddled him, and he hadn't known what he was going to do even before he had got the girl in tow. Mention of Brentwood reminded him that, if he had a home, it was there – at least his few possessions were still there, in the attic bedroom, and his horse was there, if it hadn't been stolen again. The thought of the horse cheered him slightly. He wasn't completely destitute, not like the poor wretch in the gutter. He walked a bit quicker to see if he could lose her, but she quickened her step too. God, he couldn't take her back to the coaching inn where he had left his coat and whip! They would think he was out of his mind. He turned round.

'You can't come with me!' he said sharply. 'Stop following me!'

She didn't say anything, just stood there, some ten yards away. He knew if he started walking she would come on again. If she had been a dog he would have kicked her. He walked on, choked with indignation. As if his own troubles weren't enough! It was getting late, and the air was beginning to freeze. There was a moon hidden somewhere behind the roofs and the smoke – Ned couldn't get used to London. If he could shake the girl off he would depart, collect his horse and his things and make a fresh start somewhere.

He turned round and berated her again, more in earnest this time, but she wouldn't go. He raised his arm to her and she did not move. He could not bring himself to hit her.

'I've nowhere to go, and nobody to go to,' she muttered. 'I'm not asking you anything, save to take me to Brentwood on your coach. I can't pay. I just ask you, that's all – as a favour to Kit.'

'I've no coach, blast you.'

'I want to get away from London. From *them*.'

Ned could understand. He felt the same, even without her more obvious reasons.

'Wait here then,' he said. They were a street away from the Spread Eagle now. 'I have to go and settle up, collect my coat and things. Don't follow. Just wait here.'

Did she really think he was coming back? He couldn't tell, looking her firmly in the eye, as one would the troublesome animal. He didn't intend to go back. She stood still, watching him, her face expressionless. It was worse, Ned thought, to be a human being for some people, than to be an animal. He turned away and hurried on, disgusted.

The horse-master was going to bed, more drunk than sober.

'What can I take, to ride to Brentwood? Joker? Dolly?'

'And back again?'

'No.'

'You'll have to pay. Why the hurry? You can go on your own coach tomorrow –'

'And watch John Theobald on the ribbons! That's more than I could endure for twenty-six miles. Come on, man, who? You needn't come down with me. I'll saddle up and go.'

'Joker's got a girth gall – he's out for a week. Brandy's shoes won't last out that far – you'd better take the brown mare. She's next to Joker. The new one.'

'Quiet, is she? I don't want to land in a ditch.' Ned's riding was not of the same standard as his driving.

'Yes. A good fast walker. But don't press her – she's worked heavy the last few days. And make sure Jack gets her back here before Saturday.'

'I'll tell him, don't worry. How much?'

'Oh, we'll charge it to your guv'nor, eh? As long as she comes back quick, no one'll know.'

'Good man. Fine.'

'It's a pity – you going. There's a lot worse –'

'Yes, I told them. Here – thanks –'

He gave the amiable old drunkard a coin, and went to seek out the brown mare. She was a workmanlike cob, deep in dreams.

'Poor old sod.'

He fetched his box-coat and whip and saddled the mare and took her out into the yard, nearly getting run down by a departing tilbury overloaded with drunks. He followed it out, and made the mistake of looking to see if the girl was still there. The tilbury having gone the other way, the street was empty save for her, huddled in a doorway. If she had been a dog ... Ned, gritting his teeth, rode ten yards towards Brentwood, halted and went back. She looked up at him, not expecting anything at all, the expression he had seen before, lacking all hope. He got the feeling that she would lie down and die if he left her. The familiar indignation came back but, this time, tempered with a very faint pity. She was so thin the mare wouldn't feel the extra weight, and it would do him no harm. But with two they would be more comfortable without the saddle. He took it off and took it back to the tack-room, came back again to the girl, vaulted on and dragged her up behind him. She weighed nothing at all. She didn't say a word. He was afraid she was going to die.

'Are you all right?' he asked sharply over his shoulder.

'Yes.'

He only hoped he would meet nobody he knew in such company, already feeling somewhat foolish astride the mare in his ankle-length coat and carrying the coaching whip. Thank God for the kindliness of the night, hiding the unwanted. He set the mare's face in the right direction and pressed her on, anxious for the countryside. He could forget the girl was there at all if he was careful, feeling nothing of her clawlike fingers round his waist. The familiar road, unfamiliarly close, shone white with frost, and mists from the marshes stranded the hollows, blurring the few house lights that still flickered. Ned had never had leisure to look about him on the road before, to notice the houses one by one, the smart new ones going up, and the run-down Jacobean cottages, the chained dogs that barked at his passing. It was very peaceful and, in spite of what the day had brought, he felt quite content.

After a few miles he became aware of a strange clittering noise close behind him, and after some cogitation he realized that it was the chattering of the girl's teeth. Quite surprised, he said, 'Are you cold?' He looked down and saw her bare feet rubbing his boots, the toes blue, the ankles purple. She didn't say anything, so he drew rein, and turned round. Her face in the moonlight was colourless like marble, without any sort of animation. She seemed to have no life in her, no spark, no blood. He felt a bit nervous.

'Speak the truth, are you all right?'

He took off one of his gloves and touched her hand. It was like ice. Suppose she died, and went on holding him, and stiffened, and when he got to Brentwood he found he had a corpse embracing him . . . ? She was so strange. He wanted to shake her.

'Look –' He was warm, glowing, in his enormous caped coat, but didn't particularly want to take it off and give it to her. For the first time he noticed that her clothes were only cotton, her shawl as thin and worn as to be almost cobweb. She was shivering all over.

'You'd better come in front, and I can put my coat round you.' He spoke briskly, the idea distasteful to him, but he thought she would die otherwise. She slid off and he pulled her up again in front of him. He unbuttoned his coat, and pulled the skirts round her and the front of it over her shoulders. She was so small that the top of her head only came up to his neckcloth; he was a bit worried about catching lice, but trusted that the cold would be keeping them quiet and at home. It was a few years since he had suffered from such discomforts, his standard of living having risen steadily since he had started work. She was a bit smelly, but not unbearable. The mare started off again, and plodded on under the flooding light of the moon and the frost-fired stars, as bright as Ned ever remembered, the air so still and frozen that sounds carried to his ears from miles away, the owl, the sick cow, the pining dog, the hare in the stiff grass. They passed through Romford, the shuttered market square, past the dead eyes of the cottages, the slumbering White Hart. Ned thought he must have dozed off . . . the mare was walking more slowly, the girl was asleep, slumped in his arms. Two miles to Brentwood – what was he going to do? It was only then, not until he set eyes on the inn and a small cog of memory was jogged in his mind, that he remembered Ironminster and his offer of a job. A private coach, one of the best teams in England, twice the wages, half the work – how slow he was, not to have remembered his lordship! At three o'clock in the morning, the blood running sluggish, the moon growing stale, Ned's ambition fastened gratefully on to the memory. He stirred the mare with his heels, and hurried her the last hundred yards, anxious for a bed and a real sleep to heal the disappointments of the day.

4

'I T WAS very nicely executed, my Lord – better than we might have hoped.'

'You travelled on the coach yourself?'

'No, my Lord. Too risky. But I heard all about it as soon as they got in, and saw the damage for myself. The coach was all scored on the off-side, and the lamp smashed – he overtook on the inside, you understand. They told me it was a very accomplished bit of driving, very daring. They were impressed, and quite a bit scared. In fact, Mr Hargreaves said the next time you wanted a coachman bribed to knock ten minutes off his time –'

'I could do it myself, eh? And ride beside him on the box-seat?'

'Yes, my Lord. That was the gist of it.'

'And the outcome?'

'Entirely satisfactory, my Lord. He was suspended by the agent, Mr Crown, and was angry enough to terminate his own employment. He was last seen riding back to Brentwood with a prostitute on the pillion.'

'*Really?*'

Ironminster laughed and Sam, who was shaving him at the time, deftly withdrew the razor to avoid bloodshed.

'How much did it cost you, Sam?'

'Well, my Lord, five guineas to Mr Hargreaves for the bribe. Fares for five on the coach, and three pounds each to Mr Appleby and the two ladies who rode inside. They played their part very well, and Mr Appleby threatened to sue the company – very vitriolic he was. Mr Crown was upset, naturally.'

'And our Mr Rowlands? What a cruel reward! You're a hard man, Sam. I'll pay your expenses, but no twenty guineas unless the gentleman in question turns up here, you understand?'

'I've got my spies on him still, my Lord.'

'The prostitute?'

'No, my Lord. She was a surprise to me.'

'I'm glad you're still capable of being surprised, Sam.'

'I wouldn't have thought he was in need of a professional lady. He has plenty of admirers along his ground. I found that out very quickly.'

'Yes, he is uncommonly gifted. I confess I want him badly. James is getting intolerably provocative and Rupert – I have to admit – is vastly improved on the ribbons. He can actually round a corner now without taking off the side of the nearest building. And they are out to ditch me, Sam – make no mistake about it.'

'I believe your cousins are ill-intentioned, my Lord.' Sam, like a good servant, waxed vague and conciliatory when the talk was of family. Having served the late Lord Ironminster, August's father, for twenty years, he knew as much of family intentions as August himself, which August very well knew.

'Hot young blood is what we want around here, Sam. You are old and cold for the job, and I am a crock. But I'm not ready yet to retire and think about the Threadgold acres to the exclusion of all else. I want my bit of fun first, Sam. We've been in mourning too long.'

'Two years, my Lord,' Sam agreed. 'Rose-water or Eau de Cologne?'

'Rose-water, I think. Has my mother had breakfast?'

'She is waiting for you, my Lord.'

'But it's ten o'clock! Damnation. Hurry up, Sam. You should have told me.'

Even hurrying, it took nearly fifteen minutes to see August into his morning clothes, the neckcloth to his liking, the black coat brushed and buttoned without a wrinkle, the empty sleeve neatly pinned into the pocket. He weighed scarcely eight stone, and the woollen padding he wore over his chest the whole winter made little difference to the slimness of his frame. 'Like a chicken' according to his cousin James; 'wire and will-power' according to his father. Sam, who slept in the same room, knew that there was more to looking after August than valeting, but immense care was taken that little of this was known outside the family. It was no wonder to Sam that August desired the physical support of a man as vigorous, as positively glowing with health, as Ned Rowlands. His mother, the dowager Lady Ironminster, a lady as strong as Ned himself, desired physical support for August too, but of another sex.

'I think it would be nice if you could arrange to take Amelia to James's ball in April.'

'I don't want to go to any ball of James's, and certainly not with Amelia, if you mean the judge's daughter who never stops talking.'

'You must go to the ball, my dear. It's for Rupert's coming-of-age, strictly family. It would be very offensive if you weren't present.'

'I shall contrive to be ill.'

'Your father would have insisted that you go.'

This silenced August, who had revered his father. It was three days after his own coming-of-age that he had killed him, driving the curricle that had been his present. His mother could talk of it quite rationally, but August could not make conversation on the subject, not to anybody. August had not expected, at twenty-one, to become heir to the Threadgolds estate, with all the responsibilities it entailed. Nobody had expected it. Not even James, in his wildest dreams, whose acres ran adjoining Threadgolds, and who now stood next in line. Until – unless – August got himself an heir. Hence talk of the Amelias of society. 'Get yourself an heir, then you can die,' his mother had said plainly, being a plain-spoken woman, although impeccably aristocratic – this the last time he had attempted to go fox-hunting, three months ago. 'You haven't got a horse in the stables you can stop with one hand.' True. And if he had, it wouldn't be the sort for him.

'James has been civil enough lately –'

'If by civil you mean unsufferably pompous –'

'That's his nature, dear. He can't help it. He has obviously been going to great pains to make his ball very impressive: two ambassadors and a cousin of the Duke of Cumberland's wife are coming, and the architect of his new house in Bloomsbury –'

'Mr Burton? I understand he wants Mole End rebuilt – all stucco and pillars and porticos and what-not. Probably have Mr Burton to the ball and get some free advice. Finish up looking like a London club, instead of a farm.'

'He'll feel at home, in that case. Nevertheless, you will go to the ball, August. I won't mention it again.'

'Very well. But spare me Amelia.'

'As you wish. She will be there, in any case.'

'I shall avoid her.'

Amelia was eligible and healthy and her father had some sort of liaison with Lady Ironminster that August did not like to inquire into too deeply. Amelia had called August 'an exquisite little man' in the hearing of his friends, which had forever damned her in his eyes. She was also thirty, fat, and did not wash her hair.

'I'm hoping I have found a new coachman, Mother.' August decided to change the conversation to a subject nearer his heart. 'We can put Saunders back to gardening.'

'Oh dear.' His mother's face went bleak. 'I like Saunders.'

'Mother, he's impossible! He can't handle them.'

'Now he's cut their feed down, I thought we were doing rather nicely.'

'I only cut their feed down so that he could hold them. It's no way to keep horses, mother – only a temporary solution. As soon as they start losing condition, you'll be the first to complain.'

'My Lord.'

August looked up as Sam presented himself beside his chair. 'What is it?'

'Pardon the interruption, my Lord, but I suggest you look across the park, towards the South gate. I noticed from the window upstairs –'

August got up abruptly and went to the window. 'What are you saying, Sam? Is my twenty guineas at risk?'

'A man on a black horse, my Lord.'

'Go and fetch my telescope.'

'Are you going mad?' inquired her Ladyship.

'No, Mother. It's my new coachman, if we're lucky.'

'You *are* mad. I engaged a new maid yesterday, without the help of a telescope.'

'New maids, Mother, are to be had by the hundred thousand. But a good coachman – that's another matter entirely.'

'To your way of thinking! It's time you grew up, August, and gave your mind to more important things –'

'This is *very* important – nothing more so. Do you want to be in on this, Mother? Shall I see him in here, so that you can quiz him too? Or shall I go out and see him in the stables?'

'Don't be impertinent, August. You may see him in here. Give me the telescope, Sam, and let me have a look at him. . . . Heavens, August, he's only an infant boy! You're not serious? For the coach! For London?'

'Give it me – focus it for me, Sam. Steady it. Yes – ah, Sam, we're in luck! You're right, it's our Wellington man, no mistake – my word, that's quick! And the horse – I've seen that horse before. It's no hireling nag, it's a blood horse. How does he come by an animal like that? What do you know about that, Sam?'

'Nothing, my Lord.'

'We shall see. Put the telescope away, and pour me some more coffee. Show him in here, Sam, when he arrives. And, Mother, not a word about what we've just been saying. We're not sure what his business is, you understand, but I shall deign to see him, the moment being convenient.'

'I don't know what tricks you're up to, I'm sure. But if you ask me, he's far too young.' She went to the window again, stared out and shook her head.

Threadgolds was more modest than Ned had expected. The park was extensive enough, but the house was old without any remodelling: no Corinthian pillars or porticos, but the original red-brick front, very symmetrical and kindly, the drive sweeping up to the door, and then continuing on past the front and the high garden wall and through an archway into the stables, a courtyard of buildings on its own. Ned, having left his horse there with a boy, approached the front door and rang the bell.

He did not feel over-confident, aware of having acted hastily and not at all sure if he wanted to be a servant. He wanted to try the horses, and find out what he was expected to do; if it did not suit, he would travel on. But, having travelled on now some forty miles since his last employment, he was already tired of having no work to do. He was, like a horse, a creature of habit, and he had never done anything but work. Besides this, he had come to think of this part of the country as home, and to get public employment again immediately he would have to travel farther than the grapevine was likely to reach out of both London and Colchester, which would take him almost to the North country, where he had no desire to go. He had turned all this over in his mind on the way to Threadgolds, prepared to turn back when he got to the gates. But, being tired, with only a couple of hours' sleep, and having endured a famous row back at the White Hart for allowing the wretched girl to sleep in the hayloft, he was not in a fit state to take momentous decisions. The man had said double the salary, and there was a team to drive reputed to be one of the best in the country – the prospect had its compensations. On the other side of the village, half an hour ago, a four-in-hand had passed him which he might have said warranted this description; but the coachman, by his dress, looked more like an owner than a hired man; otherwise Ned might have thought that the coach was Ironminster's and the job he had come for was already taken. He still wasn't sure.

A butler answered the door and asked his business.

'It's with Lord Ironminster. He asked me to call. It's about – about horses. Ned Rowlands.' He looked horsy enough, his best pale breeches covered with black hairs from Kit's charger, and specks of lather down the front of his coat. (Riding that horse was a separate adventure altogether, one that reminded Ned that he was far better behind a horse than on top.)

'It's all right, Simmons. His Lordship will see him.' Another servant, whom Ned remembered as having accompanied Ironminster on the coach to Brentwood, appeared beside the butler and invited him inside. Ned removed his hat and stepped into the hall. He now felt nervous, out of his element, especially when he found himself in the morning-room with not only Lord Ironminster and his servant, but a formidable-looking lady about four feet six high with snow-white hair and hostile eyes of a piercing blue-grey. He bowed to her, feeling – faced with his fragile Lordship as well – about ten feet tall and clumsy as a carthorse.

'Well?'

Ironminster was sitting at the breakfast-table, flicking crumbs from his coat with a napkin. The aroma of coffee and warm bread, the gleaming silver and china on the table, the winter sunshine flooding the pale applegreen décor and its exquisite plasterwork, the fire burning cheerfully in the carved marble fireplace, the opulence of the thick Chinese carpet, the perfect, casual elegance of the people he was addressing himself to – the whole setting and the atmosphere was a stunning warning to Ned of the change he was contemplating. Accustomed all his life to the crude rowdiness of the coaching-inn, this monumental calm at the breakfast hour, this lack of urgency, this leisure of precious detail, this smell of genuine opulence – not here today and gone tomorrow opulence but the indefinable, rooted, accepted richness not only of possessions but of a whole way of life – it all came fresh to Ned with force enough to unnerve him momentarily.

'I'm a coachman, if you remember, my Lord.' His voice sounded surly, even to himself. Her Ladyship glared, but August smiled, losing his augustness. He had two faces, Ned had already discovered: an innate arrogance, almost bitterness, suiting his role as heir to a heavy inheritance both in wealth and in health, and a much more attractive carelessness, no doubt his true nature had circumstances allowed it more freedom. For a small man, he had a compelling presence; his delicate frame suggested, curiously, inner resources of great strength. Not physical strength, certainly, but a directness which appealed to Ned, no affectations. His eyes were a clear blue-grey with long black lashes, the eyelids and the hollows beneath the eyes blue-shadowed with strain: the effect effeminately compelling. As if to counteract the unconscious beauty, his dark hair was short and plain, no whiskers, no curls, and his dress severe.

'Yes, I remember. On the Wellington, Colchester to London every morning at nine-thirty sharp.'

'No longer, my Lord.'

'Oh – no? Why not?'

Ned told him the story, to which he listened intently. It was slightly doctored, not mentioning the bribe. When he had finished, her Ladyship said, 'It sounds most unlike a recommendation to me. Overtaking on the inside indeed! Do you do that as a matter of course when your patience runs out?'

'Not as a rule, ma'am.'

'I'm glad to hear it. This job will entail driving me as well, you know, and in my opinion we have a perfectly satisfactory coachman already.'

'I wasn't sure if the post was taken. I saw a four-in-hand in the village, a team of greys –'

'Those are James's, my cousin's – he lives next door.' As there wasn't another house in sight on any side, Ned was slightly surprised by August's 'next door'. 'They are a very good team, but not as good as mine. I think you should see mine. In spite of my mother's remarks, Mr Rowlands, I am looking for a new coachman. We shall go out to the stables, I think, and you can see what you will be working with, if we come to an agreement. Perhaps we might go for a drive.' He got up abruptly, smiling.

'August, Dr Harding is calling at twelve, and Miller wants you to see the accounts this morning –'

'Yes, I shan't be far away. When I've finished –' August was half-way to the door.

'Fetch his coat, Sam!' her Ladyship barked out angrily. Ned took his leave politely, glad to escape her, and followed August across the hall, where Sam was waylaying him with a driving coat.

'I don't want to be interrupted, Sam, whatever my mother says. Come, Mr Rowlands, let me show you –'

They walked briskly down the gravel and under the stone archway into the stable-yard. The actual stables were on the left-hand side, and on the right was the coach-house, whose doors August ordered a stable-boy to open.

'I know I should cut down, the way these things are taxed these days, but –' He shrugged. 'It's no use . . . the coach here, my beauty, is by Adams. Apart from being beautiful to look át, it's perfectly balanced – you shall see – not too light, very stable, but easily drawn – a very fast coach. The carriage – well, it's nice enough, but boring. My mother uses that a good deal. The phaeton – the same. I use this gig – Sam can drive it. And this – well, it's not been driven since –' His voice trailed away and he made a resigned gesture with his arm. 'The fastest thing on two wheels. Have you ever tried one of these?'

The last vehicle was a curricle, fantastically light and high, phenomenally dangerous. Ned looked at it sternly, picturing what his father would have to say about it, but instinctively feeling an odd quirk of desire to mount its spidery frame. *That*, after a stage-coach – it would be like riding a cobweb. With two fast horses –

'Tandem,' August said. 'I always wanted to try –'

'Oh, yes,' Ned said fervently. 'Superb. To drive it tandem –'

'Would you try it? No one else will –'

'Yes. If you get a good free leader – otherwise there's no control.'

'No. You're at the mercy of your leader. But when you get the right one and a smooth road – a bit of good turf, say – oh, you can't beat it! I had one on Newmarket heath once. We did five miles in fifteen minutes – when I was eighteen. I shall never forget it, the nearest thing to flying. They're not much good on the roads we have round here, all right in London, if there's no other traffic about. In the middle of the night is best, but people don't like it. Tandem, that is – they're quite amenable with a pair. And if we had the right horses –' Ironminster was a changed man, standing there in the leather-scented gloom beside his shining vehicles. 'If you are the right man, we could do it all! I have a wager, Mr Rowlands, a long-standing wager, with my friend Andrew Field, to drive this coach from the gates of Threadgolds to Whitechapel Church in under seventy-five minutes. My cousin James is in on it too – he has attempted it twice, and failed each time by three minutes and six and a half. Andrew swears it can't be done, and has put up five thousand pounds. It's stood for three years. I had one crack at it before – well, when I still had two arms – and failed by two minutes, and since then I've never had a man to drive them – the horses would do it, I think, if they were fed and trained hard for a few months. Get the road in summer, hard, and a June night – dawn, say, just light enough to see, but before the traffic's about. James is out to do it – he's no great hand on the ribbons himself, but Rupert – he's the younger brother – he's improving quite a lot. Been taking it seriously. It's probably Rupert you saw with the team of greys – I think he's out to win this money. They count me out now, you see, because Saunders isn't up to this sort of thing. I've had six coachmen in the last two years, and not one of them have I been able to stomach for more than a few weeks.'

Ned, confident of his own talent, was undaunted. In fact,

definitely attracted. This wasn't what he had been expecting. This sounded like serious work, a challenge after his own heart. To take risks, to have no passengers' complaints to consider: it was a prospect almost too good to be true. He tried not to feel excited, remembering his first doubts. To work at this, *and* get paid for it . . .

'And the horses,' Ironminster was saying. 'If I thought the whole business was a possibility, I'd look for a new leader. The rest are good – come, I'll show you – but we have tendon trouble with Apollo. He wouldn't last out, not on hard ground. And a bit more blood, I think. My off-side leader – she's pure-bred. She raced as a filly. She is very free, difficult. Saunders can't cope with her at all, but I found her perfectly manageable, using quite a lot of tact, that is. I used to ride her, but she's too strong now I've only . . . you can imagine. I can only ride nags now, and there's no interest in that.'

Ironminster, talking about horses, was a different man from the cool, autocratic figure at the breakfast table. He seemed much younger in the space of a few minutes, much more animated, the colour rising in his cheeks. He crossed the yard to the stables, and three grooms lined up to do his bidding. The same grooms eyed Ned with undisguised curiosity and he guessed that they knew his business.

'Fetch Nightingale out,' Ironminster ordered. 'We'll see her in the open.' He turned back to Ned. 'That horse you rode here on – I saw you across the park – was it my imagination, or was it that horse we met that day I rode with you? The trouble-maker's horse?'

'Yes, sir.'

'I knew I'd seen it before. I'd like to have a good look at it. Can we have it out? Who does it belong to?'

'It belongs to me, my Lord.'

'Does it, by God! And how did that come about?'

Ned explained, leaving out his knowledge of Kit.

'That's luck, if you like!' Ironminster exclaimed. 'To come by it for nothing!'

'Unless the rightful owner sees it, and can prove his right – but it's mine at the moment. The constable knows the circumstances.'

'You wait – here's Nightingale. They are very alike, do you

agree? Strip off her cloth, John. Let's have the two of them together.'

The grooms brought the two horses out and stood them sideways on, one in front of the other. The mare Nightingale was dark brown, very fine, very interested in her new companion, whom she kept backing up to, turning her head with its keen, troublesome eye. Ned could see that she would be a handful, restless and temperamental. His own horse by comparison was kindly, exactly the same height, but with more substance. He reached out for the mare and she squealed, wheeling round. Ironminster laughed.

'They're a good match, look at them! Does he go in harness, I wonder? He could be my new leader.'

The two animals, showing themselves off to each other with ears pricked and nostrils distended, the cold March light polishing their dark coats, underlining the veins and hard muscle, were remarkably alike. The two men watched them keenly, both struck by the possibilities, both equally stirred by professional interest. Ned had never thought of his beast in harness, but now wondered why not, when the thoroughbred was being used more and more. From racing to coaching, like Nightingale, was no uncommon move now that the roads were getting faster.

'He's by Whalebone,' Ned said.

'And she is by Waxy, out of a Hambletonian mare! There's fate for you.'

Ned, groping to relate, said, 'Waxy is the sire of Whalebone? And Waxy is a grandson of Eclipse, Whalebone a great-grandson – that should win us your wager.' He grinned, exicted by the coincidence.

Ironminster said, 'If I can use your services as well as those of your horse – what do you say? They've taken to each other, and what a match! Come, let me show you the wheelers, and Apollo. Esmeralda – she's the nearside wheeler, a mare of remarkable stamina, and willing – she will give you her life before she stops. . . .'

It occurred to Ned later that he had decided to take the job the moment he stepped under the archway into the stable-yard. From the examination of the horses in the stable, it was perfectly natural to progress to putting the horses to the coach and going for a drive. And the moment Ned picked up the reins and felt the coach move beneath him, he knew that there could be no going back, whatever the disadvantages of becoming a servant (and besides, what had he been on the Wellington but a public servant, as opposed to a private one?). Never had he felt such response at his finger-tips, such a feeling of power contained, power unexploited – ('They're half-starved at the moment, to keep them from bolting with Saunders. This is only a fraction of their proper energy') – the sense of responsibility it gave him was awe-inspiring. Not responsibility to old bags inside the coach to keep their nerves from being jangled, but responsibility to the animals themselves, not to fail their rare spirit. It wasn't that he hadn't come across horses like Ironminster's before, but he had never driven four so perfectly matched in class, nor ever felt his own skill so stretched to match. It demanded a much purer skill, not the all-round routine of checking for inadequacies and overcoming them by a form of guile that had become second nature – there were no inadequacies here; the requirement here was all hands. Ned had forgotten that mouths could be so sensitive, directions conveyed by such a fine moving of a finger. Did Ironminster's sharp gaze notice his lack of finesse? But after a turn round the park Ned knew that he had already adjusted; he could feel them working for him, sense already the extra tact required for the mare Nightingale, the solidity of Esmeralda on his nearside, the very slight hesitation of Apollo's stride on the hard gravel. The coach, unencumbered, was light as a cloud, yet kept to the ground without swaying in an unusually roadworthy manner.

When they got back to the stables and put the coach away, it was by a common instinct that they then decided to try Ned's gelding as a pair with Nightingale. The grooms brought out an old breaking-cart from the barn and stood round helpfully while Ned gentled the horse into a breast collar and pad and brought him up to the pole.

'Ah, he's in love with the mare, and we're half-way to it already,' August murmured, tense with longing, at Nightingale's head. The gelding stood quivering, suspicious. Ned stroked his neck, and looked at Ironminster. Once do up the traces, and they were committed . . . the two animals were

46

like dynamite, ready for the match. It was crazy to work so fast, yet Ned loved the challenge, and could feel Ironminster's commitment.

'Yes, hook them up,' Ironminster nodded.

The grooms, one on each side, drew out the traces, moving very quietly, and fastened them. Ned already had the reins in his hands, standing out of kicking range.

'Go to their heads,' Ironminster said to the grooms, 'And then we can get up.'

He knew no caution, Ned decided, recognizing daring when he met it. Other men might have called it stupidity, but Ned was with him, close in spirit. This was what he had been brought up to deplore by his father, but what his heart had too many times hankered for, the recklessness to grasp an opportunity. Ironminster obviously did not hesitate over such matters.

'The mare will do it for us,' he said gently, hopefully. 'Get up. The boys will hold them.'

He could quite easily have ordered Ned up and stayed behind himself. Ned felt strongly that, in essence, Ironminster's fingers were on the reins too. Working for this master was going to be strange partnership; Ned was aware of it already, aware of being, in a sense, enslaved, yet willingly. because Ironminster's intentions were Ned's own. Ironminster wanted a pair of hands, another arm, not really a coachman at all. Ned saw it very clearly, and was glad that the situation was so plain.

It was as if his gelding too was under a similar influence, obedient to the mare. At a word from Ironminster the grooms let go. They were out through the archway with the park before them, the two horses quivering before them, charged with all manner of incipient emotions which Ned was bound to control. The grooms were still watching, talking among themselves, waiting – no doubt – to pick up the pieces. Ned willed the mare to walk on, to take her trembling partner with her; Ned could feel the gelding's fear literally harnessed to the unusual sweetness of the mare. He could only make it work through the mare's coquetry, her kindness to the new partner, desiring him. If he lost out, the gelding could well kick them all to bits. He kept talking to the horse gently, trying to keep the mare walking out against the gelding's fits and starts, his swinging away from the pole. The grating of the wheels on the gravel was frightening him. Ned turned them on to the grass, but the mare felt the turf and tried to lengthen her stride. The gelding held her. She started to plunge. Ironminster was laughing.

'It's safer to let her go!'

Safer than what, Ned thought? They were insane to be doing this, but he eased the mare and felt the gelding take the bit, thrusting up into his breast-collar strongly. The cart bucketed forward, and Nightingale started to stride out. The black tails streamed ahead of them. Ned took a stronger hold, and avoiding action for the group of spreading elms ahead. The gelding was wild, but the mare was in hand, although moving fast enough. He had to keep to the best turf, afraid of turning over, and strive to keep the gelding straight. He was now bearing away from the mare, and taking them down towards a small lake.

'Where's the safest ground?'

'To the right of the water. It's boggy on the left. You'll have to get him up to the pole.'

Or drown. If he couldn't handle the gelding . . . the thought of drowning his Lordship on his first day . . . Ned, taut with fear, used his whip to turn the gelding and checked the mare strongly. He thought the rackety little cart would fly apart and the pole break, or the jerking traces snap: the vision of the ensuing tangle was best not contemplated. The whip had frightened the gelding, but the mare was steadying; Ned's hold on her was stronger than she had known before and she did not like it. Now he had to ease her, humour her before she started to fight him – but the lake was out of their path and the ground started to slope gradually uphill, a considerable help. If only the gelding would keep up to the pole – Ned's fingers felt as if they had been disjointed . . .

'They're coming, they're coming,' Ironminster said happily. 'See if you can get them trotting. The hill should help. The mare covers a lot of ground, you've noticed – but I doubt if the other will relax enough to show his stride properly.'

His Lordship was unperturbed, his whole attention on the two animals.

'If you can survive the shock of this method – it's a good

one,' he said. 'A certain amount of risk, but an intelligent horse soon takes its cue from its partner.'

The lesson continued without incident, although it took all Ned's ability to achieve – at last – a level trot on the drive. For about twenty paces the two horses strode out shoulder to shoulder, fast and level, the reward of two hours of effort.

'Beautiful!' said his Lordship. 'A most rewarding morning, Mr Rowlands.' He consulted a gold watch from his pocket and added, slightly subdued, 'Afternoon, perhaps I should say. I suppose we must put them away.'

Sam was waiting in the stable-yard with a message that his Lordship was wanted in the house.

'People to see you, my Lord,' he said apologetically. 'They have appointments.'

'Yes, no doubt.' Ironminster's expression changed abruptly. The grooms came up to take the horses and Ned climbed down, handing over his reins.

'You're to come up to the house with me,' Ironminster said to him. 'None of those appointments is as important as the arrangement to be made with you first.'

'Yes, my Lord.'

He wanted the job, and it was settled in a business-like fashion in Ironminster's study. 'Sam will show you your living-quarters. There is a room over the harness-room. I take it you're not married? I suppose you will want to go and fetch your belongings? If you wish, you can take the Stanhope – it will be the best for carrying your luggage in. Your horse can remain here. Would that suit you? Can you be back tomorrow? Or have you affairs to see to?'

'No, my Lord. I can be back tomorrow.'

Ironminster stood up, smiling. 'Don't change your mind. Although I suppose, in all fairness, I shouldn't misrepresent the post. You will be driving in London a good deal when we go up to our place there and her Ladyship, my mother, will have to be conveyed about town at a decorous pace – you understand? And there's the business of livery and turn-out to Park standards – you won't be used to that side of it, although no doubt you know what is involved. Sam can tell you what is expected.'

At this moment her Ladyship swept in and said with some

heat. 'Harding has been waiting two and half hours, August! I've sent Miller away, but there's a man here about making the new gates, and the Rector is calling at four about the Easter service —'

'Yes, Mother, I'm coming. Perhaps you would like to have a word with Mr Rowlands here? He is our new coachman.'

'Really?' She gave Ned a daggers look. 'You're punctilious enough when it's a coachman, I see. We've wanted a new butler for two weeks, and now a kitchen-maid, since Polly has lost her virtue. If *I* took nearly five hours giving interviews to new staff I would get as little done as you, August.'

'I only want you to be perfectly safe when you're on the road, Mother,' August said sweetly. 'Mr Rowlands will ensure that, I'm sure. Sam, will you tell Saunders to let Mr Rowlands take the Stanhope and one of the spare horses?'

'Yes, my Lord.'

'How old is he, August? Have you asked him?'

'No. How old are you, Mr Rowlands?'

'Twenty-two, my Lord,' Ned lied.

'And we expect our servants to take baths, Mr Rowlands, once a fortnight. Did he tell you that? All over, not just the feet. The pump is very handy to your quartèrs, so there's no excuse.'

Ned was glad to make his escape, leaving Ironminster to his chores. He felt confused about the job, anxious for it to work out, but slightly anxious too about driving her Ladyship 'decorously' in London with the same team that was being fed and trained to win Mr Field's wager. His fine Lordship hadn't intimated how this was to be achieved. He also realized, after he had fallen asleep twice at the reins on his way back to Brentwood, that he was very tired and very hungry.

At the White Hart, having stabled the Ironminster horse and washed down the Stanhope, he spent a rather hectic evening arguing with various people about his intentions, gathering together his clothes and few possessions, drinking to his new job, and trying to shake off his responsibility in landing the inn with a prostitute who refused to leave the premises.

'And it's no good saying it's nothing to do with you, because you brought her here — you admit it. We gave her some breakfast out of pity, and George was to take her down to the workhouse, but when he went for her she bit him.'

'She *what?*'

'Bit him. Drew blood, she did. George was right shaken.'

'Where is she now?'

'She's still in the hayloft. You'd better see to her. Get her out. You brought her here.'

'She's Kit's girl, that's why she hung on me. I don't want her.'

'Get rid of her, that's all I ask.'

'Can't you give her a job? I don't think she's stupid, apart from what happened to her. She's got a bit of spirit if she bit George for wanting her in the workhouse.'

'I took on two girls last week. And one of them was more out of pity than want. I've no more room.'

'But if you turn her out, and she refuses the workhouse, what will become of her? She'll be taken as a vagrant and whipped in the street . . .' He didn't wish that fate on her. Then suddenly, with a stroke of genius, he remembered that Lady Ironminster wanted a new maid.

'She can apply there, as long as she makes no sign that she knows me. If you clean her up, she will probably do.'

'Are you daft? A slut like that, no references –'

'Write her some then. You want to get rid of her, don't you? Tell them she's your niece or something. Annie can find her some clothes, and I'll give her a lift in the morning. Drop her off outside and she can make her own way.'

The landlady was outraged and called down a hail of invective on his head. But when he went to harness his horse the following morning the girl was waiting for him, shining clean, in Annie's cast-off shoes and cloak, a letter of recommendation in her hand. She said nothing. Handing her up into the gig, Ned was merely grateful that she didn't bite him.

5

NED was measured by the Ironminster tailor for his livery. 'As soon as it comes we will take the team to London, Ned,' said Ironminster. 'They haven't been in traffic for over a year. Saunders would only risk the carriage and pair. And we'll get that curricle going too, as soon as the new leader is ready.'

'Yes, my Lord.'

'Never thought we'd see the day,' said Pegram, the groom who was old enough to be Ned's father, when he heard the news. 'That curricle's never moved out since the day it came back after the accident. Only been driven three times ever.'

'I'd better start practising,' Ned said.

'You've never driven one before?'

'Not one like that.'

'Well, it's only for idiots, isn't it? Or suicides. You'd think, with what happened, he'd leave well alone. Not that he's ever thought of anything else but the driving since he was just a lad, and he's got the courage all right. Not much else any longer, but he's never lacked that.'

'What went wrong, when the accident happened?'

'Well, it doesn't take much with one of those, does it? A coster cart crossed them, running away, and his Lordship had to swerve to avoid it, pretty quick sharp. The wheel hit a pavement bollard and the whole thing went over. That's their trouble, no stability. His old Lordship was thrown clean over a set of railings into an area basement and smashed his skull on a window-sill, and his young Lordship got himself impaled on the same railings. Nasty business. By the time they got him off, his arm was all but severed, and they took him in the house and a passing doctor finished the job off for 'im. Well, you can imagine – it made a big stir at the time –'

'I remember,' Ned said, not feeling much heartened.

'He was very quiet for a long time after. Because of having killed his father, on his conscience you understand – not that

52

his father was much different, mind you. He was a splendid whip in his day. It was he that taught his young Lordship. He was a lovely whip too before he lost his arm; he could make a horse do anything, not by force – he's never been a strong lad. The weakness is the family failing, isn't it? He had two sisters that died as children – the same thing. Nobody mentions it, of course. Well, he gets ill – you'll see – they tell you it's just a fever. Some say it's not a bad thing he lost his arm, you know, because now he can't do the things that exhaust him – the four-in-hand, and riding to hounds. Could be a lot of truth in that. I don't know. He has been better this last year, and that's a fact. He's no heir, which makes it worse, and his mother's trying to get him married, so's the title won't go to the cousin up at Mole End, James Saville. Saville's not a popular man in the neighbourhood, although he acts the part. Likes to make a show. Everybody knows he can't wait for young August to come to his end . . .'

Ned, having listened to this recital, felt almost incredulous when he next saw August, who was laughing at the time, almost into convulsions, at some story of his friend, Andrew's. With such a heavy history behind him, and all its consequences on the immediate horizon, Ned was astonished that August still had this genuine capacity for delight and enjoyment. In a short time Ned had had plenty of evidence of it, probably more so than most of his Lordship's acquaintances, for it was in Ned's company that August found his greatest joy, behind the horses. And for all the obvious physical limitations, he had more of what Ned could only think of as energy of spirit than most people in robust health. That he completely ignored his frailty Ned could not at first grasp; with his own natural vigour Ned had been inclined to an instinctively protective role towards his employer, but within a very short time he had adjusted his attitude, not through any reprimand, but through recognizing the formidable will-power; when August was doing what he wanted to do, it completely transcended any weakness. When he was enduring (and this is how Ned sensed it was with him) his arduous role of master of the very large estate, it was not so apparent. He could then be as short-tempered as the most querulous of invalids.

Ned, obeying a summons to the morning-room some three

weeks after his arrival, was greeted by August – after his amusement had subsided – with, 'Ned, your livery's arrived – you'd better try it on. This is my friend Mr Field, whose wager we are going to win, God willing, when you've got those horses fit.'

'And I'd far rather, if it's to be won at all, which I doubt, that it fell to you, August, than to any of the other contenders. Your cousin James, for instance.'

'Ah, yes, my cousin James. It's on no account to fall to my cousin James. But Rupert's not whip enough yet. We shall have our horses fit before Rupert learns to handle the ribbons sufficiently.'

'Rupert is learning all the arts, I understand – not only on the ribbons, but fighting, too, at Mr Jackson's academy.'

Andrew Field was a tall, fair, rather unassuming man, of gentle good nature and complete affability towards servants. He shoved the breakfast things out of the way for the tailor's boxes and smiled at Ned.

'I hear that you're the man on whom it depends,' he said. 'Lord Ironminster's right-hand man.'

'And his horse,' August put in. 'Not only has he a beautiful pair of hands, but a horse to match. By Whalebone. You must see it afterwards. A perfect match with my Nightingale, an identical stride. And great courage. Just what we want. I think we shall have the edge on James, come the time the roads are dried up. We shall have to draw him out on the matter at the ball, Andrew, and see what his intentions are.'

At this point Sam opened the door and announced, 'Lord Railton, my Lord.'

'Good. Come in, Alex. And you too, Sam. You can help Ned with his new clothes, and let's see how he looks. Alex, this is the coachman I've been fortunate enough to obtain – the one who is going to win us Andrew's wager.'

Ned knew of Railton by hearsay – a reckless, hard-driving, hard-spending young heir to a large estate in Suffolk; he was unexpectedly charming, slight in build and fastidious in his dress, but careless and friendly in his manner, without arrogance. He was said to have very good horses, and spent a great deal of money on them.

'Mr Rowlands? I've heard all about you. If you please

August, you must be a whip indeed. Congratulations.' He shook Ned's hand. His fingers were fine and white, but strong as steel. He did all his own driving, which was said to be hard and spectacular.

'I came to see who you are taking to this ball of your cousins', August? The confounded Amelia, I take it?'

'My mother insists, yes.'

'I understand Miss Redbridge has been invited.'

'Yes, Alex, and if you are a good friend, you might relieve me of Amelia for part of the evening and give me a chance to talk to her. I get precious little opportunity the way things are. My mother doesn't approve.'

'Rupert approves – of Miss Redbridge, I mean. It is said he intends to marry her.'

'She's far too good for him. I'll tell her so. She cannot waste herself on a Saville.'

Only half listening to the ensuing conversation, Ned was watching Sam undoing the boxes on the table and disappearing amongst clouds of tissue-paper. There seemed to be a great deal of the paraphernalia, including three hat-boxes, a pile of striped waistcoats . . . Ned's eyebrows went up. There was a waisted brown coat with fringed epaulettes and a whole armoury of gold frogging down the front, and one of the hat-boxes, opened, revealed a tricorne hat. 'God's truth!' Ned muttered to Sam, appalled, knowing that tricorne hats went with white wigs and silk stockings, 'This isn't for *me*? I'm not a confounded footman!' 'Only the very rare occasion, in London,' Sam said soothingly. 'For her Ladyship, to a Royal garden-party perhaps. This is the everyday livery, quite plain by the standards of the nobility.' He lifted out an impeccably severe dark brown coat with gold buttons, and a waistcoat striped in pale grey and gold. Ned tried them on, not at all reluctantly. In the mirrors on either side of the fireplace he looked imposing, even to his own eyes. Sam tied him a neckcloth, high and severe, and he tried on the pearl-grey beaver and liked the effect very much. And afterwards he took the coach out for Ironminster and his friends, to see how well the black horse – which they had christened Starling – went as leader with Nightingale – a somewhat hair-raising performance, for he had not been put with the team before. The outcome was encouraging.

His new livery – although he changed out of it after he had put the coach away – had not gone unnoticed by the servants' hall.

'Ironminster will have to look to it if he's to sit beside you on the box, and that's for sure!' said the cook. 'Trust the horses to get the prettiest master in this establishment – you should have kept it on, Mr Rowlands, and let us all have a look at you.'

'I don't want gravy down it the first day.'

'I can't answer for your eating habits – that's another matter.' She put a large plateful of mutton before him, its gravy floating a small armada of suet dumplings, and shouted to one of the maids, 'Matty, bring Mr Rowlands his ale! And a new loaf.'

All the other outdoor workers had already eaten. The cook was used to Ned's irregular hours, and kept the best back for him, and let him eat at the indoor servants' table, which was near the fire and laid with more refinement than the other. Ned was used to being a favourite with the stout vigorous women who made up the cooks and landladies of the nation, and took his favours amiably. He had none of the ingrained stiffness of the indoor male servants, whom he considered a pompous lot – even Sam spent a lot of his time on his dignity – and was only just getting used to the etiquette of private service, a good deal more formal than he was used to in the coaching-inns. Not unduly so, though – 'We're pretty well off here,' the housekeeper told him. 'Her Ladyship doesn't interfere. As long as everything runs well upstairs, she doesn't go on about trifles, like some of them.'

'She's got too much to think about, finding a wife for his Lordship,' said the parlour-maid, and they all laughed.

'Well, he doesn't do much for himself, not that I've noticed,' said the cook. 'Even his old Lordship had more women about the place than young August. Plenty of gentlemen friends, and horse-dealers, mind you.'

'There's only one lady round here that he takes notice of and that's Miss Redbridge,' said the parlour-maid.

'Miss Redbridge, the doctor's daughter! But she's no match. Her Ladyship would never hear of it!'

'Of course not. I'm only saying he *speaks* to her, of his own accord, without her Ladyship prompting him. After church, every Sunday. You notice.'

'I would if I had the chance,' said the cook, who wasn't one of the morning church party. Ned, who took the coach, and sat in the back pew while the boys looked after the horses, resolved to notice Miss Redbridge next Sunday. His mind was then taken off the subject by noticing the maid who brought him his ale. She smiled at him. She looked familiar, yet his mind did not connect her with Threadgolds. He smiled back, prompted by the conversation into realizing that it was a few weeks since he had thought about girls, a record in his lifetime. She was small, with a round white face and golden-red hair, very curly. Quietly, so that the cook wouldn't hear, he said, 'Where have I seen you before?'

'With Kit, sir.'

'Kit!' He was so surprised that he spilt half the glass of ale in his hand with the start. The little prostitute, like a stray dog! It was incredible what a scrubbing-brush could achieve, and a clean dress. Her child's body had filled out with a few weeks' good feeding; and the dreadful, dead look of despair in her eyes had gone. He had only ever seen her with the haunted expression, the touch of death. It had set her apart in Ned's mind; he had never imagined that she could possibly look like an ordinary desirable girl. But she did.

'What's your name?'

'Mathilda, sir. Matty.'

'What do you do here?'

'Kitchen-maid, sir. Thanks to you, sir.'

'No thanks to me! I did little enough!' Little enough to have had a bad conscience whenever he had recalled her, which had been seldom.

'Oh, yes, sir. I owe everything to you.'

Well, he might make use of those sentiments one day, Ned thought, grinning. Afterwards, back at work, he kept seeing her face in his mind in a most disturbing fashion, and he realized that he had succumbed to the charm of this unexpected infant – for surely she was? – and the knowledge annoyed him, for he could see no way to getting satisfaction for his feelings. She was much too young and delicate a flower to woo – not to say highly unsuitable – Ned was used to chasing cheeky, brazen girls, their quick tongues a match for his own (and their ardour too); it was a game to him, and all for fun. He did not expect his emotions to be engaged. It was all he knew of loving, and he didn't wish for another pattern.

Prompted by the gossip in the kitchen and, possibly, by sympathy for Ironminster in his own particular problem regarding the female sex, he made a point of looking out for Miss Redbridge the following Sunday. As it happened, even without his fore-knowledge, he would have had to be deaf and blind not to notice the lady, for she came with August all the way to the coach, and they stood talking for some time beside it. Ned guessed that this breach of decorum was caused by the absence of her Ladyship, in bed with a chill; and perhaps their obvious desire to stay with one another was caused by the day being exceptionally mild and springlike. Even Ned could smell it, stirring the blood and the senses: this peculiarly British burgeoning of spring after the iron grey mornings of March, tart and wet and scolding. It had made the sermon seem interminably long, teasing the senses with its flavour, the sun winking in through medieval glass, the thrushes and blackbirds pouring out their songs in far more effective hymns to the glory of the universe than the mangled noise they contrived to raise within. It made Ned feel magnificently optimistic and cheerful and restless, like the horses he held with difficulty for his Lordship. A fine to-do if they played him up amongst the gravestones, in front of the gentry . . . for Harry, the youngest groom who doubled as footman when needed, had left their heads and was waiting to open the door. In fact the spring, along with the powerful feeding and copious training exercise, threatened to make the church-and-shopping runs distinctly hazardous, more so every day. The turn-out looked immensely impressive; everyone stopped to admire it on the way out of church, standing well back and ready to run, and the rest of the motley collection of carriages and gigs wisely gave them plenty of room. Ironminster brought Miss Redbridge to inspect the horses but she, seeing Ned's difficulty, said to him, 'Perhaps you shouldn't linger, my Lord. They seem very impatient. Like my father,' she added, nodding in the direction of a formidable-looking gentleman waiting by the gate. August laughed, and bowed an amiable farewell, and the lady moved away. Ned, from the quick look he was able to take, approved his Lordship's fancy, for Miss Redbridge was gravely handsome, dressed without affectation, and gave the impression of being a lively capable person – not above handling a pair of horses herself. August told Harry he would ride on the box, and climbed up.

'And I'm not stopping to offer Dr Redbridge a lift home and be snubbed for my pains, Ned. I think the gentleman disapproves. Come, give them their heads. Let them go. Her Ladyship is not here to be considered.'

The church stood close to the North gate into Threadgolds, and the way home was merely a mile through their own park, which the horses took at a flat gallop all the way. August laughed and shouted to them, in mighty spirits, but paid for it by an attack of coughing when they got into the stable-yard, which had him breathless for a few minutes. He stayed on the box, leaning forward with his elbow on his knee, hand dangling, and Ned sent Harry for a glass of water.

At the same time they both heard the sound of approaching hooves, hard-driven, and Ironminster straightened up painfully.

'You haven't met my cousins yet, Ned? I feel the pleasure is about to be granted.'

Ned glanced at him, half-amused by the situation, but worried by the effort it required of Ironminster to appear in a fit state to face his cousins. The coughing had left him sweating and weak, but when the Saville drag pulled up beside them he appeared perfectly composed, watching Rupert's efforts to make a smooth halt with an expression of tolerant pity nicely calculated to annoy.

Ned looked across at the two brothers side by side on the box, and was sobered by an impression of overwhelming physical strength. They were both heavily-built and very alike; James, fifteen years older than Rupert, was running to fat and tightly-laced by the look of him, his thick neck jowled with fat around the jaw. Rupert, no doubt to go the same way, was as yet a fine physical specimen, tall and dark, with the same black, formidable eyebrows as his brother and sharp, dark eyes. His bare hands on the reins were enormous, brutal, black hair running down to the knuckles from beneath the spotless white cuffs. Ned watched their effect on the horses, and realized that the Savilles thought that everything could be achieved by brute strength: arrogance and self-importance stamped the very way they sat, legs straddled, chins raised. He understood, seeing them, why Ironminster had desired the moral support of his own mere youth and physical stature; yet he also saw, as a stranger to the trio, that beneath the Savilles' sharp greeting to Ironminster, there was a wary hint of respect. For all that Ironminster was as thistledown to these apparent oaks, Ned sensed that where the real strength lay was undecided. The antagonism was undisguised.

'When you manage to stop, Rupert, the boys will see to your horses. I take it you are calling on my mother?'

'That's right. We would hardly be according you the honour, August.'

'I will go and warn her of your visit. Drive me up to the house, Ned. Rupert can watch how to turn horses in a confined space – he lacks your experience.'

'He lacks your experience too in meddling with other people's affections,' James angrily. 'As we hope not to meet you again, August, perhaps you will tell us what your intentions are as regards Miss Redbridge?'

'I have no intentions, my dear James. Discuss it with my mother. She is the one with intentions. She will be only too pleased to air them with you. Drive on, Ned.'

Ned obeyed, aware that Ironminster's brief exchange had tired him. Out beyond the archway he groaned and said briefly, 'I'm told Rupert wishes to announce a betrothal to Miss Redbridge at his coming-of-age ball. That's more luck than he deserves, Ned.'

This confidence was unexpected, and Ned could only be non-committal: 'Yes, my Lord.'

He did not envy Ironminster his cousins and the power they held over him, to inherit. He could see their desire, their greed: their eyes reflective on Ironminster's slender frame, on the flush of fever on his cheekbones. To claim Threadgolds on August's death would be fortune indeed, its well-farmed acres marching side by side with their own.

That afternoon they took the coach to Romford and back, and averaged thirteen miles an hour, which was very gratifying. Ned was very much aware of the improved strength and stamina of the team, and was distinctly nervous of taking it into London, which was to be his lot the week after the Mole End ball. August said life in London would be insufferable without the horses to keep one amused; Ned gathered that her Ladyship insisted on going up every three months or so 'to keep in touch' but August only liked it for the journey and the excursions out of town which it entailed, and the opportunity for showing off his team. Not that this wasn't fair compensation: August spoke happily of 'springing them' across Epsom downs on race day, and 'carving up' his haughtier acquaintances in Hyde Park. Ned decided not to get rattled. There was time enough. Close at hand, something more prosaic arose to nettle him.

'When you take the drag to Mole End tomorrow night,' Sam informed him stiffly, 'there will be a full party – her Ladyship with Miss Amherst and her father, as well as his Lordship and his friends. There will be two footmen to wait on, and her Ladyship gave orders that you are to wear full livery.'

Ned scowled at Sam. 'You said only in London, for royalty!'

'It's not my doing. I don't give the orders. You'd better get dressed upstairs here – I'll see to you after I've got his Lordship ready.'

This was the side of private service that Ned disliked. Having spent all day getting up a party shine on the four horses, the coach and the harness, he had then to submit to the same treatment himself. Sam led him up the backstairs to Ironminster's appartments, where Field and Railton were sprawled in the two window-seats in their evening finery, and August was sitting hunched in front of a large fire dressed in white silk stockings and satin breeches and woollen dressing-gown, obviously short of breath and strength but looking perfectly cheerful. Ned, pausing in the doorway, saw the lavish branches of candles burning in the sconces and through the long windows the sun going down in equal glory over the tangled woods, red and wild through black tracery, red-splashed in the curved arm of the Threadgolds lake beyond the lawns. It was a brief, sudden picture of the Ironminster irony, that all these riches, inside and out, lay on the shoulders stooped so painfully over the fire.

Sam took Ned into the dressing-room where the livery was laid out and Ned undressed gloomily.

'We never ordered a wig,' Sam said. 'I was going to get one from the wigmaker when we went to London. You'll have to wear your own hair powdered.' He proceded to lard Ned's head with pomatum. 'I spent half my time at this job when I was a boy.'

'Waste of time,' Ned said. 'I wonder they suffered it.'

'A gentleman couldn't go out unpowdered. It wouldn't have been countenanced.'

Ned, although he wouldn't say so, was quite impressed by his new silvery image, and the cravat Sam tied him, and the ornate, full-skirted coat with its heavy embroidery.

August smiled when he saw him and said, 'You carry it a lot better than old Saunders, Ned – a credit to the house. Almost as smart as your horses.'

'Thank you, my Lord.' Ned was never familiar with Ironminster in company, although easy enough when they were alone. August, now ready to leave, looked very frail in his pearl-grey evening coat with its high collar framing his face, the candlelight deepening the feverish colour already there. His demeanour was plainly that of a man steeled to see through a programme that his physique was not wanting to contemplate. His friends seemed aware of this, and treated him with a careless sort of concern that Ned was to become familiar with in time: it treated the condition as a joke, but with a sympathy obviously born of deep affection. Ned found it surprising, and rather moving.

'Are the ladies ready, Sam? You'd better see. Then Ned can bring the coach to the door.'

There was no turn-out to touch the Ironminster team in the Mole End courtyard that night, Ned was gratified to remark, and the satisfaction of being responsible for it eased the boring prospect of waiting around into the small hours. He managed to get a good look at Miss Amherst when she alighted, and saw a small, slightly plump lady, much lacquered and painted, rather imperious, and with a great deal to say. He felt sorry for Ironminster, and much in accord with his confidence regarding Miss Redbridge, for as he was turning the coach after dropping his party, the Redbridge phaeton came up to the doorway and Miss Redbridge, alighting, sent him a smile of recognition. There was a touch of conspiracy about the smile, her father being occupied with giving instructions to a groom about the horses, and Ned got a strong impression that the favour was bestowed because he was Ironminster's coachman, not for any other reason. It was instinctively given and instinctively appreciated. Ned very much doubted, from that moment on, that there would be any announcement of a betrothal to Rupert Saville that night – or any other.

He took his horses to the stable-yard and prepared to sit out the long hours until he should be needed. The Savilles were too mean to provide anything for the servants; a good many of the carriages went off home again, to return later, but he had been given orders to stay, in case the ladies wished to retire early. He was watching a boy putting rugs over the horses' backs when a very smart curricle came into the yard, driven by its owner with a footman behind. Ned looked up, curious, and in the light of a groom's torch saw a dandified young man throw down the reins and jump down. Ned knew immediately that he had seen the man before: the face gave him a shock, a feeling of disturbance, which he couldn't account for. He watched the man give orders to his groom and walk away in the direction of the house, and could not account for the familiarity. The frustration of not being able to place him, nor recognize the strange feelings his face had provoked, eventually compelled him to approach the groom and ask.

'His name's Marney, Anthony Marney, of Brentwood,' the groom replied.

The name meant nothing to Ned.

'Why do you ask?' the groom asked.

'I know the face, and can't place it.'

'Who do you work for?'

'Lord Ironminster.'

'Ironminster!' The groom gave Ned a startled look. 'You're not the man off the Wellington – what's his name – Rowlands?'

'Yes.'

'God's truth, the man they tricked! No wonder the face is familiar. He's the man who lost you your job. Too good for a stage, they said you were – did you never find out?'

'Find out what? What do you mean?'

'Marney, my guv'nor, is the man you overtook in the Wellington. He's a friend of Ironminster's. It was all planned – for him to baulk you. They wanted you to get the sack, and they worked it all out, even to the passengers who bribed you to make a good time, and the man inside who threatened to sue. Ask that valet of Ironminster's – Sam Arnold – he planned it all. Ironminster paid him to get you into his employment.'

Ned felt himself gaping. Of course, the blond-whiskered maniac who had laughed when he overtook – a *friend* of Ironminster's! And Sam – *Sam* had engineered it . . .! He felt coldly angry. The groom was grinning all over his face.

Ned shrugged. 'It was change for the better, the way it turned out. They needn't have gone to such lengths.'

He wasn't going to reveal his feelings to the idiot; but the indignation and the anger were so strong that he had to turn away and go and occupy himself with his own horses, making an excuse. He was literally trembling with rage. He could feel himself burning with humiliation. To be deceived, to have his mind read like a child's, to be taken advantage of, to be *used* . . . The shock of it was unnerving, drenching his pride. And Ironminster, of all people, whom in this short time he had come to respect and – dammit! – *like* . . . he truly until now had never admired anyone more . . . he laid his hands on Starling's back and bent his head down on the glossy back, too shaken to face the world until he had recovered his composure. What a fool, never to have guessed! He did not know what on earth he was going to do about it.

It was cold, and the time dragged, and after a while he went and sat on a fence behind the stables to keep out of everyone's way. He knew, for his pride, he would have to have it out with Ironminster: he could not go on working for him; it was more than one could stomach. If that groom knew, God knows but every lackey in all the stable-yards between Threadgolds and London must know about it. He must be a laughing-stock at every dinner-table where dragsmen recounted their adventures. What a good story it was, if one was on the right side of the encounter! Even now, coldly, he saw how cleverly the trick had worked. He had a good mind to climb back on his box-seat now and drive home, and leave them all to stew, and go.

Someone was calling him.

He came off his fence and went back to his horses, not hurrying.

'The lady wants you,' someone said.

It was Miss Redbridge. He suspected more trickery, touching his hat warily. It was very strange, to see her standing there, obviously upset and – once more – conspiratorial.

'Mr Rowlands – Ned, they want you to take the coach round the drive to the library windows. They're waiting for you. Lord Ironminster has to go home – he's been taken ill. I'll show you where.'

Ned, puzzled, called a groom to help him tighten girths and bearing-reins. He flung the rugs into the boot.

'Why the library?'

The drive round the side of the house was narrow, between banks of laurel and rhododendron, and only the lawn to turn round on. Ned cleared the rose-beds and negotiated the bend in the drive without a wheel going off. And all the time he wondered why he was doing it, to help Ironminster. Damn Ironminster. Let him cough his damned lungs out.

'They don't want anybody to know. Not the Savilles, at least. They so delight in August's bad health. Mr Field and Lord Railton say we can go this way without disturbing anyone.'

Ned pulled up outside the windows indicated and Miss Redbridge jumped down. In the darkness she was a quick, strong presence, very sure of her actions. The windows opened and Railton and Field, half-supporting, half-carrying Ironminster, manhandled him into the coach. Ned, occupied with holding four restive horses, could not see much of what was going on, but presently Railton climbed up beside him and said, 'Carry on. Let's get him home.'

Ned didn't see how, surrounded by herbaceous borders. A wide flight of steps led down from the library windows on to an expanse of lawn and Railton said, 'How about down there?' and Ned, in his state of bitterness, picked up the whip and forced the surprised team down the steps on to the lawn without question. They skirted an ornamental lake and went down a yew walk at a canter, crammed their way through a planting of young hazel saplings and came out on to the drive again. Ned, in silence, put the team into their long, level trot, smooth and fast, and concentrated on holding them steady, only too aware of their inclination to gallop after their long cold wait, smelling home. He felt dour and angry still, and without sympathy for the situation.

Railton said, 'He shouldn't have gone, dammit! We don't like James to see him in one of his states. It gives him ideas above his station.'

Ned, in spite of himself, said, 'What's wrong with him?'

'Consumption, of course.'

In spite of himself again, Ned said, 'I found out how – somebody told me – how I was tricked into this job.'

He felt Railton looking at him, dubious, not knowing how to accept his statement.

'You're angry?'

'Yes.'

He shortened his reins a fraction on the leaders, feeling the wheelers beginning to fret, and cleared the gates of Mole End, two inches on either side, without slackening speed. Railton let out his breath with a hiss, and said, sounding slightly uncomfortable, 'You'll not stay angry?'

'No. I shan't stay at all.'

'*Ned!* You mustn't take it like that! Confound it, don't you see – you wouldn't come of your own accord – they worked it out because there's no other whip to touch you! No one else would do. It's a compliment, for God's sake. Nobody else was worth all that trouble, believe me!'

He sounded desperate, which made Ned even more angry.

'I don't like being *used* – deceived! It wasn't the way to do it, destroying my reputation –'

'Destroying it! What you did merely established it, you fool! Don't leave Ironminster, Ned, not now. He's got precious little else to make him happy, you must see that. Don't act hastily.'

Ned didn't know how to reply, the anger and the indignation subsiding into a cold and unworthy fit of sulks. He didn't know where he stood now, torn by indecision, and remnants of his liking for Ironminster. He tried not to let this make any difference when he brought the coach to a halt and was obliged to get down and give a hand, the grooms coming out to take the horses. He thought Ironminster was going to die. They got him on to the doorstep where he leaned over the enormous brass door-handle and vomited blood all over the scrubbed stones. Sam came out and took him in his bruiser's arms, calm and practised. 'Help me with him, Ned.' Up the stairs, sweating and staggering. 'Go and get Mrs Burns and that girl Matty. They're supposed to be waiting up.' Sam had worked the whole plan out, Ned remembered, and been paid for it. 'Tell Matty to bring me some hot water.' Ned did as he was told, then slumped down in the window-seat, not dismissed, but not eager to have to do with this miserable business, watched the shadows flare and swoop over the curtained bed, watched Matty fetching and carrying, helping, standing at Sam's shoulder, remembering her the night Kit . . . God, life was short and hard for some. If he had been as clever as Sam he might have done more for poor Kit. What had he got to be complaining of . . .? Matty, now, with food and a roof over her head, was far removed from the waif Kit had picked up. Where had she come from, Ned wondered? She did not have the look of a yokel, a village slut. She kept darting him glances while she waited on Sam, because of his smart livery and powdered hair. The gold clock over the mantelpiece chimed two, and he realized that he must go to bed and get up again by six. His clothes were in August's dressing-room. He got up to fetch them, taking one of the candles. Sam was very tidy; he could not see them immediately, and held the candle up, illuminating the rows of immaculate coats and boots, shelves and drawers full of snowy linen, piles of hat-boxes, cabinets full of lotions and powders . . . and on the wall, hanging in pride of place, a driving whip with a chased silver stock. Underneath was a boxful of driving gloves, faded and unused. Ned held up the candle and saw engraved on the whip a name and date: August William Montagu Ironminster. 21st March 1815. One of the accessories, presumably, after the famous accident, which took place so shortly afterwards. Ned, chilled by the evidence of August's ill-fortune, collected his clothes and crept out. Matty was going down the stairs carrying the empty water-jugs, and stood back for him to pass. Ned hesitated, wanting to say something to her but not knowing what, drawn to her, and yet for some reason bereft of his usual glib girl talk. The jugs in her hand gave him the excuse. 'Can you draw some hot water for me?' He was never going to get his powdered head clean under the stable-yard pump, and there would be no time in the morning.

'Yes – in the kitchen.'

'Is anyone else up?'

'Only Mrs Burns, waiting for her Ladyship, and seeing to the gentlemen. She won't come in the kitchen.'

'I'll come down with you.'

They crossed the hall and Ned followed the girl down the dark flagged passage into the kitchen and servants' quarters. A few candles were burning, and the embers still glowed in the big cooking grate. Matty went to the water cauldron that hung in the corner of the chimney and started to fill one of the jugs with a ladle. Ned watched her, sitting on the table, feeling soothed by her presence. He could not be bothered with his anger and his indignation any more. He would take it up again in the morning, not now.

'What's happened to his Lordship? He's terribly ill.'

'Oh –' Ned could scarcely bring himself to explain. The hints and hearsay of August's condition had been proved only too forcibly, and everything else beside that seemed meaningless.

'He's like to die?' Matty said, awed. She set the jug on the table beside Ned.

'He's consumptive, they say. I don't know.'

Sitting on the table, Ned saw Matty's face on a level with his own, the eyes regarding him, round with respect. He looked back into them steadily, aware of being out of control of the procedings of the evening, and without the will to alter the situation. Matty's eyes wavered, dropped, and came back again. The light was dim, and Ned could not divine their message, but he felt it in his bones with a deep and unerring certainty. To be more exact, in his nerve-ends and his male instincts. His bones were tired. He could have slept on the table without any trouble. He lifted his hand to the jug.

'I'll use the scullery to clean my head. The fire will be out by now in the harness room and the water cold.'

He couldn't find the ends of his cravat to untie them, and Matty found them and unwound all Sam's yards of linen and

Ned felt as if his head was going to drop off without it. Matty helped him off with his coat and undid the hooks on his shirt. Ned started to smile.

'I'll have you for my valet,' he said.

He had never known home comforts in all his life before. It made her very desirable, not because of the roundness of her breasts and the softness of her skin, but because she knew where the basins and the soap were, and a towel, and he groping round wearily in the darkness avoiding the black-beetles and cockroaches out of the damp bricks and not able to see what he was doing . . .

'Let me,' she said. 'It needs more soap.'

She was very capable and gentle. How lovely to be a gentle-man! Like August having Sam to tend him – but a girl was better. August ought to know that, being a man of the world. August needed all the tending he could get. Ned yawned hugely.

'I'm glad I'm not a footman,' he said.

'Oh, they never wash,' Matty said. 'Just put more on top. It's full of fleas. William's is anyway. I crack them for him.'

'Lucky William.'

'You're ginger, like me,' she said.

'Not *ginger*.' Ned didn't like being called ginger.

'Well, no. More golden.' That was better. She wrapped the towel round his head. 'Sit by the fire. I'll rub it for you.'

'It doesn't matter.'

'Please.'

Ned was too tired to argue; indeed, only a fool would have resisted laying his head back on Matty's bosom and letting her have her way. When he opened his eyes he could see her face in shadow, giving nothing away. Her hair was pinned back into her maid's cap, little corkscrews escaping over her ears; he wished it were loose, making a cave round his head. He would put his hands up and clasp them behind her head and hold her captive. But he didn't. She bent down and kissed his forehead. Strange, he thought, that although he had found her living with Kit, and afterwards as a prostitute, there was a chasteness in her character completely at odds with her history. Even in her kiss . . . 'I love you for what you done for me,' she said. 'For bringing me here.'

Ned, remembering only his callousness, the offhand, joking way he had offered to relieve the landlady of the White Hart of her unwanted lodger, was discomfited by her gratitude. All he had done, unwillingly, had been at no cost to himself. He felt his colour rising, and twisted round out of her grasp, nervously. He did not want to be loved, a tiresome burden in his experience; only to be cheeked and cuddled and amused – again, at no cost to the emotions. She was altogether a serious child, with a strange tenacity of purpose, not a girl to sport with.

Sliding away, practised, a fish from her fingers, he said lightly, 'I hope your luck holds out. Our master's future seems a little uncertain. He has my sympathy for his state of health, but not much for his methods of recruiting staff.'

'What do you mean? That he shouldn't –'

'Take servants who want his job – yes, but not trick a man the way he did me. I had a perfectly good job which I liked, and when I refused to change and work for him, he got me the sack by a trick. That was the night I took you back to Brentwood. I didn't know – until just now –'

He told her the story, and in the telling took a fresh hold on his indignation. Matty, from being a digression from his night's revelation, now fuelled his righteous anger with her sympathy. It was a good story, and with Matty's eyes in the candlelight all awe and admiration, Ned vowed to have it out with his Lordship. 'In the morning, I shall see him. I shall tell him –'

'But he's so ill.'

'I don't see that it makes any difference. He's not too ill to remember, I'll wager. I can't pretend I don't know, not now. Besides –' Ned did not believe that Ironminster wouldn't quickly recover from his night's illness. He had seen him at the point of exhaustion before, and never known him give in to it. Ned could not take the treachery lightly, not from *Ironminster*; it kept swamping him with amazement, rage, humiliation . . . It was gratifying to have Matty's loving concern, balm to his wounds. He went to sleep in a state of fuddled, warm self-righteousness and woke at six with a raging headache and the prospect of extra horses – Railton's and Field's – to do before breakfast, cold, angry, and vicious. The boys leapt to their chores, recognizing the mood, and the stables resounded to diligent sweeping and shovelling and washing-down; the horses were brushed and fed in nervous silence, the coaches cleaned and polished, the harness started on. Ned drew his hot water from the harness-room fire, shaved and cleaned himself up, dressed in his proper clothes and went up to the house for breakfast. Sam was just starting his, as irritable as Ned.

'I'm seeing Ironminster after breakfast,' Ned informed him. 'I've something I want to have out with him.'

'Yes, yes, I've heard. Railton told me. You'll do better to have it out with me – I was responsible for the most of it, and his Lordship is in no state to see you. Your views on the matter can be aired without any inconvenience upstairs.'

'It's more than inconvenience, believe me. You'll not stop me seeing him, say what you like.'

'Much joy may it give you then.' Sam shrugged, too tired to argue. They ate in silence and when Ned flung back his chair and made for the back stairs, Sam came after him, swearing. Afterwards Ned, wondering what he had been expecting, realized that he had been visualizing August sitting up, pale and weak, but taking coffee, perhaps, talking to his friends. Quite ready to defend himself – possibly, even, with an entirely convincing argument; Ned was not so incensed as to discount Ironminster's infinite skill in handling people. He knocked at the door and there was no answer. Sam came up behind him and flung it open. 'Go to it,' he muttered. 'Don't say I didn't warn you.'

The room was very warm, a large fire burning in the grate. Railton and Field were standing by the hearth, looking jaded and grave, in dressing-gowns, and Matty was sitting by the side of the bed. Ned gave a sharp bow to the gentlemen, and crossed over to Matty's side. He was aware of Matty half-rising, a pink flush coming up into her cheeks, and of a sudden silence from the men. He hesitated, glanced at Ironminster, dropped his eyes.

'Go to,' Sam said bitterly behind him. 'He'll hear you.'

Perhaps, Ned thought – if the sound of his breathing allowed it. So much for disregarding his weakness: Ironminster, propped high on pillows, his head thrown back, was in no state to comprehend anything save the agony of trying to draw breath. Ned, not much versed in sickness, could recognize that much. He opened his mouth, saw August's eyes come to his own, acknowledge him. No more. His Lordship was past speaking. The eyes, deeply shadowed, were desperate.

Sam came up beside Ned and bent over the bed.

'Mr Rowlands wants to speak with you, my Lord – an important matter. You'll hear him? Just for a minute –'

August moved his head to face Ned, questioning. Several swollen leeches were fastened to his throat, which Sam commenced to remove by burning them with a lighted taper, replacing them with fresh ones out of a jar. August lifted his hand in protest but Sam held it down. Ned glanced at Sam, and back to August, feeling his determination crumbling. Sam had engineered it; he was smiling. Ned could feel the silence; he could not speak. Without turning round he knew that the two men behind him, and Matty too, were all hanging on his hesitation. But his anger was completely routed. God knew, he had a grudge against Ironminster, but even in the height of his passion he had never wished *this* on him. He felt completely thrown, his purpose overturned. He put out a hand and touched Ironminster's, now resigned on the sheet.

'It's nothing, my Lord. I didn't know you were – bad . . . I came to say, I'm sorry, I'm terribly sorry –'

August stared back at him. The perspiration trickled down the sides of his nose like tears. 'Ned, don't –' The two words were gasped out.

'No!' Ned said desperately. 'No, it's all right –'

Sam said gently, like an uncle, 'He's fine, my Lord. Don't fuss yourself. We're all right now.'

Ned retreated, shaken to his marrow-bones. Sam came with him firmly, opened the door and came out with him into the cool corridor.

'Go for Dr Harding then. He'll need to do some blood-letting. It's a better idea than the other one you had.'

'It's awful –'

'We're used to it here. You don't know the half of it, Ned, over the years. His lungs are rotting away. He knows it, we all know it, but there's nothing to be done. He will fight to the end. You go for Dr Harding, and forget what you found out last night. Stay with Ironminster while he needs you. It won't be much out of your life, but it means everything to him.'

Ned needed little urging; a good fast ride out in the clear morning was exactly what he needed. He felt the air rushing into his great leather lungs, pure and deep, feasting on it, his nostrils dilating to it like Starling's own. His only emotion now was gratitude for his lot. It had not needed Sam to say his piece. Ned was Ironminster's till death.

6

IRONMINSTER'S recovery was not rapid, but that it took place at all was something of a miracle. Having prayed devoutly for him in church for two Sundays, Ned was rewarded the following Tuesday by being summoned to take him for his first outing. He harnessed Esmeralda and Sunbeam to the barouche and presented himself at the front door, but was immediately sent back to the yard to exchange the turn-out for Starling and Nightingale to the phaeton, in spite of fierce protests from her Ladyship, which August countered quietly by saying, 'I shall go how I choose, or not at all.'

Ned was amused, watching as the boys brought out the two leaders and put them to; his Lordship was running true to form. In the barouche he could have sat in the back with his mother like a gentleman, but in the phaeton the passenger seat was up with the whip, and there was no room for his mother, unless she wanted to play groom. She didn't.

'It's ridiculous, August! You will undo all the good –'

But nobody listened to her. Sam lifted his Lordship bodily up beside Ned and tucked the rugs round him. Ned said nothing until they were away, alone, then: 'It's good to –' and found that August was saying the same thing at the same time. They both laughed, and August said, 'Come, Ned, spring them. We're out of sight and the drive is smooth enough to the gate.' It was crazy, but the need was so fervent in both of them, like a flinging of hats out of school, a peel of celebration bells, that he eased the reins and the horses' strides lengthened before them, gradually, easily, as perfectly in accord as their passengers. The two men watched their action, the impressive strength of the muscles bunching and extending and the smooth coats flowing; Ned could pit himself against the strain and feel it pulling right through his body so that he was joined to the action; he was so used to it now, using the same horses all the time, that he could judge their mood and their state of health to a degree. He could not let his concentration wander for a minute – especially now, the phaeton being so light, and the two horses fresh from their stalls – not like Esmeralda and Sunbeam who had done a morning's shopping for her Ladyship. They stormed down the drive, and he had a devil of a job to pull them up for the gates. August was still laughing, but the shaking had provoked the familiar cough. Ned cursed himself for a fool, shortening his reins and steadying the horses with his voice.

'I wish I were a fraction as fit!' August said, speaking steadily with obvious effort. 'They are bursting, Ned –'

'Yes, too fit, my Lord. Her Ladyship doesn't like it. I'm hard put not to frighten her at times.'

'She told me. But that's how *we* like them, Ned. Give us another month and I reckon we can try for that wager. Don't run them down, whatever she says.'

'How about in London?'

'Oh, the others will have to get out of our way! You're not on the bottom cheek? That'll help – and the bearing-reins up a little.'

'Not enough to worry them. I don't like holding them that way – makes 'em fret. You see too much of it.'

'You'll just have to work it out of them – two hours before breakfast. Keep them going like this whatever happens. This sick spell of mine – badly timed – damnation –' A fit of coughing shook him. Ned, terrified it was his fault, brought the horses back to a walk and sat by waiting for it to subside. August leaned back, wiping his face with a handkerchief, spent. His eyes were full of tears.

'Do you want to go back?' Ned asked softly.

'No, by God. This – this is what I – *need* –'

They had passed out of the park gates and the horses were treading delicately, necks arched, mouthing their bits, down the lane outside. Tall elms and high hedges, just in leaf, made a tunnel; the ground had dried out and the ruts had been harrowed and rolled after the winter; the phaeton moved smoothly, the horses' hooves making no sound. It was warm, the sun flooding the gaps, dappling the horses before them, sparking off the metalwork on the harness. They were quite alone, very close. Ned, holding the horses to their work, was conscious of August's distress; he had never seen him not perfectly in control before, yet under these circumstances it seemed the only human reaction possible, entirely sane, not to be deprecated, not even to be covered up.

'It's all right,' he said.

Useless words, but only to show that he was with him in spirit. Not to mind giving in. Too much civilization clotted the natural cry of pain. Ned did not believe in it.

The horses walked on, and after a while August said, in a choked voice, 'I don't know why, sometimes . . . whether it's worth the fight – no one, thank God, depends on me –'

Ned was silent. Only August could be a judge of that. What the fight cost him, Ned could only imagine.

'But in the night, sometimes, when you think –' August paused, readjusted – 'When there's a lot of time, on your own, to work it out – well, it's things like this –' he gestured with his hand – 'that come to mind. Always. Not the estate and the title and the – the things that ought to matter, but always the horses going well, and the ground firm, the smell of – what is it? What does it smell of, Ned? You know – I'm no poet. My sentiments aren't noble at all. I'm not proud of them. But if you come very close to giving the whole silly business up, and know, in any case, that you will pretty soon, you know in your mind what you will miss most. I'm ashamed to say this – wouldn't dare, to anyone else. I'll miss you sooner than my mother, Ned.'

August smiled when he said this, and straightened up in his seat, and stretched his arm out along the folded hood. Ned appreciated that the moment of weakness was short indeed; he might well never see another. But, strangely, it strengthened his respect for August, rather than diminished it.

'Don't let's admit to anybody what a coward I am, Ned. Only Sam knows the truth of it, and he'll not say a word. I suppose we must recognize our limitations and proceed at a seemly, convalescent pace – if you can, of course. You'll be more tired than me when we're through.'

'We'll go round the back of the village, the quiet way – not meet anyone,' Ned said. 'The road's smooth enough. It's not bad practice for them, besides, to learn a bit of decorum, before we hit Piccadilly.'

'Will you sell me Starling, Ned?'

'Why, my Lord?' Ned was startled.

'They are a perfect pair. You must never leave me, Ned – unless you sell me Starling –'

Ned glanced at him, and saw that he was smiling again.

'No, I won't leave you while you want me. And I won't sell you Starling either. You may *have* him, that's different.'

'A gift for life?'

'Yes.'

'That's excellent. And afterwards, Ned, you can have them both. They shouldn't be parted, do you agree? I will see that it is put in writing. Have you got him leading tandem yet?'

Ned grinned. 'When it pleases him. We've had some right tangles. But I think we shall get the measure of it.'

'Have you seen my cousins' team out on the road? We must keep our spies on them, in case they try for the wager before us. When they hear we're ready, they'll try and beat us to it.'

'What I've seen of the young Mr Saville, he's not much of a whip. But that won't put him off, I daresay. I've seen him a few times, yes.'

'Well, he's better than James – so you can see why I haven't been much worried until now. But he's taking lessons, so he's serious. And with Mr Jackson too! That's something I envy him. When we're in London, Ned, we'll call at Mr Jackson's and see what we can pick up about Rupert's prowess in this direction. You'd be interested?'

'Yes, I would. We might see Tom Spring or Ned Painter – even old Tom Cribb –'

'You could try a few rounds yourself, if you've a mind. Railton goes there, and Mr Jackson knows me –'

'Oh, but I'm rough! My fighting has just been fairground stuff. Hit and hope for the best, to make a bit of money.'

'I wonder? You must have more strength in your arms and shoulders than anyone you're likely to meet at Jackson's. If you land square you could hammer 'em.'

'Yes, I've got by that way. I've won a bit.' Ned didn't want to denigrate his talent, but 'Gentleman' Jackson's was the top school of the land where the sporting aristocracy – who loved a fight – paid large sums to spar with aspiring champions.

'What's your style?'

'I'm not particular. Hitting or wrestling, whatever seems most likely to work out – I've not fought many men who were above foul play, so I'm not above taking advantage myself.'

'All the champions started that way.'

Ned had never aspired to be a champion, only to defend himself in a hard world. Serious fist-fighting as practised by champions was a hard and brutal way of gaining fame, for the rules required a fight to continue until one contender was no longer able to stand up, which resulted in fights between good men going to as many as fifty or sixty rounds, with dreadful damage inflicted. Ned had always been careful to accept challenges that he felt confident of winning fairly quickly; it hadn't always worked out, but he had only been beaten once out of nine fights.

'It's a pity,' August remarked, 'that I seem to get most of my enjoyment out of sports not at all fitted to my physical capacity. God knows, if I'd been a poet or a botanist by nature, I'd have been satisfied with my lot.'

August, in spite of the bitterness of the remark, seemed to have regained his usual graceful acceptance of his lot and did not mention his condition again. He was very weak, but the phaeton was well-sprung, and Ned chose his road carefully. More cleverly than he knew, in fact, for skirting the village by a bye-lane and passing a large, newish house standing on its own amidst well-tended gardens and orchard, he recognized the figure of Miss Redbridge. She was close to the road and could not fail to look up at their approach. She straightened up, smiling, and Ned scarcely needed Ironminster's summons to halt. He brought up immediately beside her and kept his eyes to the front like a good servant.

'I see your bantams are laying apace.' Ironminster removed his hat, smiling.

'Yes, my Lord – if only I can find their nests. How are you?' Her abrupt question was filled with concern. Standing there amongst the flowering hawthorn, bare-armed, her skin exactly the same colour as the little tawny eggs in her basket, softly-freckled, her hair untidily caught back and shining in the sun, she looked to Ned more desirable than any other girl he had set eyes on. The setting and the circumstance were undeniably picturesque, but Ned had seen similar pictures many times before without being quite so struck as he was on this occasion. His good servant veneer was hard to maintain, his eyes drawn despite his good intentions.

'I am better, thank you. Recovering fast – and much better for meeting you. What a pity I can't ask you to accompany us. I sent the barouche back to the stable, but if I'd known . . . Do you collect the eggs every day about this time?'

She laughed. 'I might do.'

'If a barouche were to come by with a spare seat . . . who knows, you might fancy a little spin? Especially behind such splendid horses. I think it would speed my convalescence enormously, to have such a pleasure to look forward to.'

Very good, Ned thought enviously, prettily put. There was no doubt that August had the edge on him when it came to a wooing with pretty words.

'It would please me more than anything to speed your convalescence, my Lord. We have all been very worried about you.' From the look in her eyes, she meant it. Ned was familiar with the expression, but this time the glance was not for him.

'Would it please your father?' August asked pertinently.

'As far as riding with you, it would please him as much as it would please your mother. That is different.'

'I don't reckon to please my mother,' August said.

'I haven't the same power over my father as you have over your mother. The world is that way round. The ladies are the losers.'

'Oh, not so serious! If I am just passing, there can be no harm –'

Miss Redbridge smiled dryly. 'Not much, my Lord, if we are seen in this village! But I don't much care about gossips. If you come by, and it can be managed, it will make me very happy.'

'And me too, Miss Redbridge. More than I can say.'

Ned looked in front of him, and waited for the order to move on. He felt as speared now with envy for August as, half an hour before, he had been moved by pity. The warm feeling of loyalty and affection that had been evoked earlier was flattened. He had been paying far too much attention to his work lately, and not enough to sporting with kitchen girls as in the old days. He felt a great cold gap of want, such as he hadn't experienced for a long time. He remembered little Matty in the kitchen, and how she had moved him when he had first recognized her; he knew she looked for him now and sought out excuses to speak to him. He did not want for opportunity. But Matty now could only be a shade of Miss Redbridge, a sub-Sarah, a shadow girl.

They drove on in deep silence. The sun was so warm that the fields had the drowsy fullness on them of high summer, thick with larks and thrushes and pipits trilling and warbling at the beck of foolish nature, spilling prodigality after the long hard grasp of her unkind winter. Deep inside the woods some boys and dogs were digging out a badger, to hound and bait it through the village; a fox starved in a snare. The two horses, settled now to their curious pace, took the phaeton smoothly down a grass ride through the far Threadgolds covert, crushing foxgloves under the wheels. August lay back against the cushions, holding his hat in his lap, silent. Ned glanced at him once or twice, but his expression was so grave and sad and far-away that there was no question of disturbing him; his thoughts were beyond Ned's power to alleviate.

Future rides out were not uneventful. August, with rapidly returning strength, was not – having made up his mind – a patient suitor. Ned took the barouche to the front door the next afternoon and August came out with Sam and his mother. Ned observed the famous will-power in action as he walked firmly down the steps and climbed in. Sam shut the door.

'You should take a footman, August. You have no sense of what is proper.'

'No, Mother. We are doing a tour of Threadgolds, not Hyde Park. Drive on, Ned.'

The driving seat on the barouche was high, formal and exposed, the passenger riding behind in the open, low-slung carriage; there was no familiarity, not even – given August's lack of lung-power – any conversation. Ned knew that it was no carriage for August in his ordinary frame of mind, but for August as suitor it was eminently convenient. Ned drove decorously, feeling rather sour. He knew that August was eager to reach the doctor's house, but he was unsure of the barouche's springing and did not want to distress him: Starling and Nightingale had the joys of spring in their feet, and were not above throwing an occasional buck. Yesterday's confidences were immeasurably far away; Ned felt he was back to his conventional place, thrown over for Miss Redbridge. He half-hoped she wouldn't be there, but when they reached her home she was waiting in the orchard, sitting on a bench hidden from the house, dressed in going-out clothes – although her bonnet was a mere excuse for a hat and she had no gloves. (Lady Ironminster would have been appalled.) Ned pulled up and she came quickly to the gate.

'Don't get up, my Lord. I can manage!' But August got down and did the footman's job, although it stopped him talking for the first few minutes. Ned received a darting smile, and that was his lot for the afternoon, save the tantalizing softness of her voice in conversation with August, and an occasional laugh. He could not overhear what was said for the sound of the horses and could not possibly turn round to see if they were touching hands. August told him to go through the woods, and once more the two horses turned into the tunnel of shade down the cleared rides. The sun came through in shafts like the light through stained glass, trembling and moving with the wind in the leaves, and the horses were pricked and agog, their hooves dancing on the peat, the sweat of excitement coming up in foamy lines down neck and flank like the remains of a tide on a beach. Ned had to gentle them, talk to them, sweating in his smart livery with anxiety and envy and downright pain at the turn of events. Whether August intended any more than to alleviate the boredom of his convalescence Ned never knew, but, whatever the intentions, the afternoon rides through quiet woods and along the cart-tracks of fields newly sown and thrusting with corn, through somnolent lanes heavy with the blossom of faded hawthorn, became a far more serious diversion than mere flirting. Ned was not above interpreting the deep silences that preoccupied August when they were alone, and his increasing irritation at any frustration of his plans; he also knew, with a deep and acute sympathy he had not known himself capable of, what was going on behind his properly impassive back, minutely tuned as he became to nuances of murmured conversation, the meaning of a laugh, the length and poignancy of mere silence. There were times when the silences were so deep, so charged with emotion – or was it all in his mind? Ned wondered – that it seemed the very horses, the woods themselves were a part of the conspiracy; the horses curiously tranquil, rubbing each other's crests when they were halted, as if imbued with the lovers' spirit, and the woods so quiet, cathedral-dim, quivering-cool, protective – a shell of privacy for this strange, hopeless, yet completely happy court-ship. Ned could not deny the last part.

'Stay here, Ned, until we come back,' August said, and Ned waited, still as the trees themselves, pretending to himself that he had no feelings on the matter, that he was not concerned, interested or involved, just waiting like any coachman, the inevitable lot, doing as he was told, not to think, to wonder, to complain, to show impatience, but to be resigned to whatever he was put to. Far, far away, out in the sunshine, a cuckoo called. Ned had a strange feeling that he no longer existed, save as hands on the reins, a machine, a perfect servant. It was better that way, in fact, particularly when they came back, walking towards him up the ride hand in hand, Sarah trailing her bonnet, looking at the ground, smiling, and August delicate beside her, as shadow to the sun, his expression distant, inscrutable. Sarah looked up at Ned and smiled again, the pink rising up in her cheeks and the happiness bursting out so that she flung her bonnet up over his shoulder into the carriage and threw out her arms and said, 'Oh, it is so lovely here – I wish it could last for ever!' She spun round in a shaft of sunlight and stood waist-deep in foxgloves, laughing at August, pink and white and gold, glowing, vibrating with such *life* as Ned had never seen in the well-brought-up female species; it was almost incontainable in her, a perfect, pure spring of brimming happiness. Ned recognized such joy when he saw it, and was affected with a corresponding spasm of intense sympathy – for her, for himself, for August: for every-thing that was promised, and could not happen. He met August's eyes, and had to look away, withdraw, put up his servant's shutters. Their feelings were all too plain, shouting out; it was improper. As if Sarah felt it too, she came to the carriage, looked up at Ned and did not smile this time, but shook her head slightly, and August opened the door for her. Ned drove on at August's command, and knew, without look-ing, that August lay with his head on Sarah's breast, with her tawny arms round him, but what was in his mind he had no way of knowing, whether such love made him happy or not. Sam, obliquely questioned when they were alone over tea in the servants' hall, was sound enough in his knowledge of what was permissible and what wasn't.

'A doctor's daughter for his Lordship! It would be scandalous – her Ladyship would throw a thousand fits.'

Ned smiled. 'Does he always do as he's told?'

'No, And as for scandal, he doesn't trouble about that either – or didn't, I should say, before his accident calmed him down. The biggest impediment there, won't be with his mother, but with her father.'

'With Dr Redbridge?'

'Yes.'

'Why?'

'Because he's a *doctor*, of course. He's a very dour man, austere, not at all a snob. He is hardly likely to want his only daughter to make a liaison with anyone as precarious in health as his Lordship, and especially to produce an heir for a hereditary consumptive. Not a man of his outlook and upbringing.'

'Hereditary?'

'Yes. His father would have died of it if August hadn't done for him first. The family is riddled with it. Dr Redbridge knows the history well enough without being told.'

Strangely, Ned hadn't considered this side of it. It seemed perfectly feasible as stated coldly by Sam.

Sam said; 'He and Miss Redbridge are coming to tea tomorrow. You will receive orders to call for them at four o'clock. I understand that his Lordship wants to introduce Miss Redbridge formally to his mother before they go to London – where he's going to see a great deal of Miss Amelia Amherst and family whether he likes it or not.'

'I reckon his Lordship has a better eye for a woman than her Ladyship.'

'Perhaps, but I'm afraid her Ladyship is very much of a realist. Miss Amherst's father is a High Court judge and knows the family intimately. Think how useful such a man would be to her as a member of the family, if things run their course. It's the father she wants to bind by marriage as well as the daughter.'

'Dr Redbridge could well be more useful in that respect,' Ned said sharply, not liking the picture Sam drew.

Sam shrugged. 'Unfortunately there's a limit to a doctor's powers.'

Ned felt depressed. When he took the barouche with a footman to the Redbridge home the following afternoon, Sarah was very demure in her father's company, and had only a formal nod for him. They were silent on the drive to Threadgolds. Ned delivered them to the house, and wished he were Sam, to eavesdrop, to see Lady Ironminster's reception of the lovely, unsuitable Sarah. The only glimpse he did see of the proceedings was when he was changing out of his livery into working clothes until he should be called again: over the garden wall he could see August and Sarah walking on the terrace alone. After a few turns in earnest conversation, they moved down the steps to the shelter of a convenient yew tree and embraced passionately. Ned, not intending to spy on such intimacy, nevertheless remained watching, feeling immeasurably sad and, curiously, not jealous at all. August, even for the simple act of embracing, was handicapped by having only one arm; Ned, watching, could almost feel the lack himself, knowing August's desire. But Sarah held him; she was tender and tactful and passionate, surely leaving August with no sense of inadequacy when they parted. He was laughing, not at all touched with Ned's own sadness.

When Ned drove the visitors home afterwards – without a footman, for the doctor had said it wasn't necessary – he overheard the conversation that passed behind him. It was brief and bleak.

'There is no future in the relationship, Sarah, and you know it, however serious his intentions.'

'I love him.'

'I could never condone your bearing a child by Ironminster. For her Ladyship to wish for an heir as she does, for purely worldly and financial reasons, is selfish and wicked. To give him his due, Lord Ironminster has more sense than his mother. He has a healthy disrespect for posterity which, considering the circumstances, is the proper attitude.'

'I love him.'

'Yes, he has some excellent qualities. I can appreciate

your feelings. But there is no question of this being anything other than a friendship. If necessary I shall make it plain to him.'

'I love him,' Sarah said for the third time.

'It will pass,' said her father.

Ned drove home alone, the sun in his eyes, trying not to think about what did not concern him. He was only paid to drive the horses. But, changing out of his livery and supervising the evening stables, he was unaccountably lacking in spirits, quiet and sharp with the boys so that they exchanged looks with one another, rolling their eyes. Over mutton and peas in the servants' hall he questioned Sam again. Sam gave him a shrewd look over his forkful of food.

'Seems to me you're mightily interested in young Ironminster's lady yourself. I'd look nearer home if you want someone to warm your bed.'

'What do you mean by that?' Ned asked sharply, not liking the accusation.

'That little girl Matty – she'd die for you if you gave her half a chance. They're all the same – even the cook gives you the best cuts, and she old enough to be your mother. I'm only mentioning it . . . the way your mind's running . . . I wouldn't like to see you pining for want of a lady, when there are so many others near at hand.'

'When I want your advice I'll ask for it,' Ned said coldly.

Sam laughed.

'Well, Ironminster will have to cool his heels – we're going to London on Saturday, and it's Miss Amelia for him, the next couple of weeks. You'll have your work cut out, my lad, all the gallivanting that goes on up there, and the shine that's expected. Her Ladyship has hired you a valet for your own use, did you know? She thinks it will be too much for me, keeping you up to the standard as well as his Lordship. Quite right, of course. His Lordship's been a lot of work lately, and I'm not getting any younger . . .'

Ned finished his supper and pushed his plate back. As he got up to go, Matty came to get the dirty dishes. Sam glanced up and laughed, and Ned felt himself firing up with embarrassment. He ducked his head and hurried out. 'God's truth! I'm losing my grip,' he thought. 'Ironminster's infecting me.' And not with consumption. He spent the next three days working fiercely, overhauling and cleaning the coach and curricle, greasing the wheels and minutely inspecting all the working parts, taking down all four sets of harness, cleaning them meticulously and examining every strap and buckle for wear, every chain and trace and length of stitching, getting the horses reshod, washing their manes and tails, giving them all an extra half-hour's strapping a day. The night before they left he took a bath in the yard trough and cleaned it out thoroughly after him. London could expect no more.

7

IRONMINSTER was laughing.

'We might not live to win this wager,' Ned said bitterly, cautiously inching out his leaders' reins in the earnest hope that Starling had finished his exhibition of rearing in the middle of Pall Mall.

'Avoid St Albans Street and the Haymarket – go on down. We don't want any of these houses falling on us. We've enough to cope with without that.' Clouds of dust marked the demolition workers' trail; an overloaded brick-wagon, minus one wheel, in the middle of the road had been the reason for Starling's dismay. Ned overtook a cart full of sand and a closed carriage and turned very neatly northward for Piccadilly. His choice of words had not been very fortunate, he realized, but he had more to think about than mere tact. He had worn out two pairs of the white gloves favoured by her Ladyship in four days, and could feel raw palms again, and the reins slippery with sweat. It was oppressively warm, which did not help – not for him nor the horses. The work was every bit as exacting as he had expected, both the arduous waiting around for her Ladyship in the carriage and the very fast and impatient passages through crowded streets with the team which was Ironminster's idea of fun. Ned felt that he was, in essence, Ironminster's right arm; doing what the man himself willed, in the way that he willed it. Ironminster required him to take risks which he would have preferred not to; Ned was beginning to appreciate just what sort of dare-devilry had given him his youthful reputation. Confidence in his new coachman was reviving it.

'Look! Rupert – just turning out of Jermyn Street! Now, Ned, if he turns west into Piccadilly, you must overtake him before the turnpike gate. Come, he hasn't seen us. He'll be going down to their farm in Kensington, I daresay, if he's driving out of town. Yes. Very good. It's up to you, Ned.'

Carving up Rupert was Ironminster's particular joy. They

had done it once, spectacularly, on the road over Clapham Common on the way to the Epsom races; to do it in Piccadilly was going to be difficult. With luck, Rupert would draw over for him before he realized who it was. Round a dray-horse and neatly through the usual clutter of smart carriages up St James . . . let them stride out up the hill . . . Nightingale breaking her stride with excitement, check her, hold up the leaders at the junction just in case – a fraction . . . Esmeralda and Sunbeam still into their collars, and they were away with scarcely a pause, clearing the bollard by an exact two inches.

'There, very nice. A sitting duck,' August said.

Let them go, a sight for all the smart ladies and their escorts on the hot pavements: the finest coach in London moving fast down the outside, all eyes drawn to the gleaming horses and then, in curiosity, to the tense, fragile figure up on the box, smiling in anticipation, to the equally tense coachman, frowning, the two footmen behind nervously holding on and trying to retain the nonchalent hauteur of their trade in face of great provocation; inside, the least of all the glory, were Miss Amelia Amherst and her mother, returning to their home in Park Lane. August started to laugh again, with excitement, and even Ned started to grin as Starling and Nightingale went up alongside the unsuspecting Rupert. He half-turned his head, checked his own horses to draw over, then recognized Starling's eagerly curling nostril and cinnamon muzzle. Ned flicked his whip over the leaders' backs to forge ahead, heard Rupert shout angrily and saw him pick up his own whip.

'Now, Ned – quick – before he –' But Ned didn't need telling. He had to be quick, or risk collision with a carriage coming towards him. His coach sprung away, the horses galloping for some twenty yards, the wheelers twitching it neatly across Rupert's path a bare few inches clear of his leaders and some infinitesimal number of inches more clear of the oncoming carriage.

'God Almighty!' The action successfully concluded, Ned felt the tension breaking out in sweat, larding his choking cravat and trickling down from under his beaver. Amelia's mother was hammering on the window behind them. Ironminster bent down and shouted back, 'Nothing to worry about, my dear Mrs Amherst! We'll be at your door in a moment!'

Starling and Nightingale, with the precedent set, were pulling like maniacs. The dust settled over the lather of their excitement in a grey pall. God, the cleaning and washing and settling-down the evening promised – should Ironminster not visit some damned club and be requiring them again at two in the morning! Ned was not enamoured of London life. Neatly to the Amherst door and stand the horses four-square, heads up, perfectly still – not lurch silly old Mrs Amherst into the gutter at her moment of touch-down. The footmen, glad to get down, went to the horses heads. August made charming farewells. Amelia was sallow and greasy in the evening sunlight, her large bosom breathless with the heat. Ned felt a pang for the cool woods and the airy Sarah laughing among the flowers; thoughts of her disturbed him when he least expected it, and he would turn his mind to the available Matty, trying to transmute his desire to where it would be appreciated. When he got home he would . . .

'Tomorrow I'll take you to Mr Jackson's,' August said suddenly. 'I promised you. I said I'd see Railton there.'

'Yes.'

August's thoughts evidently did not linger after Amelia. He was always more than pleased to deliver her back to Park Lane.

'I'll see if we can arrange a few rounds for you. If you're good – well, it's easy enough to fix up a meeting between friends. The magistrates need never know.'

August was as good as his word. They drove to Bond Street in the curricle, carving a hair-raising passage through the chaos that Mr Nash was currently stirring with his grandiose plans for the new road north across Piccadilly.

'The man's a maniac,' August declaimed. 'Tearing everything apart – Swallow Street – half the stabling in London's been pulled down – and all these squares, you can't tell one from another. My mother says she never knows where she is these days, everywhere looks exactly the same. I know what she means.'

'There's a lot of money in it, in property. You can't go wrong with a bit of land round here.'

'No, and even farther out. An acre of cow pasture in Marybone now is fetching a fortune.'

Ned approached Gentleman Jackson's gymnasium with mixed feelings. This was a place where the sportsmen, the 'fancy', the inveterate gamblers came together on common ground: one might meet anyone from Lord Byron himself to some Irish paddy seeking his pugilistic fortune, lucky enough to have been seen by someone who mattered. Enormous amounts of money were made and lost in this sport. Ned had noticed that Ironminster, away from the home cloister, laid heavy bets on any sporting event he attended, and numbered some florid betting personalities amongst his friends – Captain Barclay, Squire Osbaldestone, Lord Castlereagh. Yet Ned knew that, if he were even able to hold his own with his fists, he would be perfectly accepted, even admired. And Ned had never lacked confidence in his own powers. His everyday job was one greatly respected amongst the sporting peerage – some of whom were not above dressing themselves as coachmen and aping their mannerisms; he was already a part of this scene. Even so, the names, made flesh, were impressive.

'Mr Jackson, my coachman Ned Rowlands . . . Mr Belcher . . . Captain Barclay . . .'

Jackson, a charming giant, shook his hand. Ned, unusually, was awed into speechlessness, managing only a gasping smile. Captain Barclay had trained Tom Cribb for his great fight with the Negro, Molineaux, and was said to be able to lift a man of eighteen stone with one hand. Tom Belcher, the younger brother of the legendary Jem, familiar Railton, laughing, the blonde Marney, Lord Yarmouth . . . the faces passed before him.

'Well, if we're to see what he can do, perhaps he would like to spar a round or two with Tom?'

Ned guessed that this opportunity had been laid on by Ironminster; it came too easily to be pure coincidence. When he had stripped and Railton was tying the 'mufflers' on to his hands he saw August regarding him in what he could only interpret as a speculative manner. He was saying something to Jackson, whose enormous but graceful body was bending down politely to listen; Ned got the impression that this induction was more than just a bit of fun. 'I can't fight with these things,' he complained to Railton anxiously.

'No, well, it's the law in here. Save your knuckles for the real thing. You'll soon get used to the feel of 'em.'

Perhaps if it was Tom Belcher he was going to fight, Jackson's 'law' was a good way of keeping whole . . . Belcher, although only a middleweight, stripped like a Smithfield bull, donned his mufflers and came up with a smile.

'You coachmen are all the same – shoulders like fighters before you even begin – gives you a head start –'

Belcher was out of condition. Ned, on his mettle against so renowned an adversary, did not wait to be hit but went in to the attack at once, landing several blows with some force before he found himself neatly sidestepped and his head clamped fast under Belcher's left arm. The right arm landed him a warning crash to the ribs; the next second he was on his back, neatly thrown and acknowledging, even as he lay, Belcher's superior science.

'Up, my young fire-eater!' Ned did not need the invitation.

'He's a natural,' Jackson said to Ironminster.

'Very keen to mix it. No caution,' August agreed.

'Just needs the science, to spare himself.'

'Perhaps you could give him a little?'

'Certainly, my Lord. A pleasure.'

Ironminster was all smiles, excited. Ned's nose was bleeding.

'Begad, August, what's your mother going to say? Her smart coachman –' Railton was highly amused.

'We could come early, Mr Jackson, if you could fit it in. Before my mother's likely to need the carriage. Before ten o'clock. You'd like that, Ned, wouldn't you?'

Ned's eyes regarded him cautiously over the top of a wet towel held to his face. August smiled, and didn't wait for an answer. 'Say eight o'clock, Mr Jackson. That will do us splendidly. Get dressed, Ned. I've got an appointment in the City in twenty minutes, and my mother wants to drive out to Kew for lunch.'

Ned departed and Railton said to August, 'What are you planning, my dear boy? Or am I being unduly suspicious? Your bold Ned has aspirations to the fighting fraternity . . .? I hadn't noticed. Or is it something to do with Mr Saville taking lessons?'

August smiled again.

'A very good point. How is my cousin progressing, Mr Jackson? I understand he comes here fairly often?'

'Quite right, my Lord. Twice a week. He takes a very keen interest.'

'Is he good?'

'Yes, my Lord.'

'But Ned must have more potential –'

'Your coachman doesn't mind being hurt. He's had a hard upbringing, no doubt, and fighting comes naturally. It's the best school, the best background by far. I would rate his chances very highly.'

'Good. We shall come every day while we are in London, Mr Jackson. Do your best by him.'

Ned drove Starling and Nightingale to Ludgate Hill aware of a rapidly-swelling nose and a chronic ache in the ribs. Ironminster was in a very good humour.

'Jackson says you're a natural. He puts it down to a hard upbringing.'

'Huh.'

'Was your upbringing hard?'

'My father was hard. I fought my brothers and my friends quite often. The worst I ever got myself was a flogging from the magistrates for stealing a bucket – hardly fighting. I never got hurt much fighting.' Ned, his eyes strictly ahead, thought privately that he was more likely to get hurt driving Ironminster's curricle than in Mr Jackson's gymnasium. The angle of the reins to the hand was all wrong, and it was a hell of a long way to fall. He had nervously noticed the imminence of iron railings below, remembering Ironminster spitted, but Ironminster seemed to have put his experience behind him.

'I'm going to look at a barouche, Ned. It's by Chapman and only one owner. First set of wheels. We could use it at home and bring the best one up here.'

'Yes. We could use a barouche this weather.'

'We'll take the coach to Kew, and the new chariot to the Theatre Royal tonight. Andrew and Railton want to see Miss O'Neill, so I got tickets. The Amhersts are coming but using their own transport. Afterwards we can drop my mother at home and go on to White's.'

Three hours sleep, Ned estimated, and another hammering at Jackson's in the morning. It was supposed to be sparring but Ned found it hard not to make it the real thing, and Tom Belcher treated him more roughly than he did the more expensive fraternity. Every morning Ned was fired with a wild ambition to get Tom on the ground and every morning Tom, recognizing the zeal in his eye, held him off with straight, strong punches which, mufflers or no mufflers, hurt. And being hurt made Ned's determination increase; his punches improved in power and accuracy. Tom Belcher would sweat and grunt and duck until, provoked too far, he would finish the round by putting Ned down with a smart cross-buttocks. Ned, black and blue from heavy falls, watched like a hawk to get Tom equally at his mercy, and failed.

'But he's a professional, Ned. What do you expect? I bet you could get Railton down, or Rupert.'

Jackson could get Belcher down without any trouble. He showed Ned how it was done, proving that Belcher was in fact heavy and slow. Ned watched, sore and angry, and tried again. Belcher complained that Ned took it too seriously. August laughed, and doused Ned down with a cold sponge. Ned's left eye was closed and his cheek split. Her Ladyship was not amused. Immaculately turned out as he was by his long-suffering valet, nothing could disguise his black eye.

'I can see I shall have to take all my outings by night. I shall be the laughing-stock of Bond Street. I suppose my son has put you up to this? You needn't bother to deny it. It seems to me that he sets you up in all the nefarious pursuits he can no longer follow himself.'

It seemed so to Ned as well, particularly where driving the curricle was concerned, where his own ambition to stay in one piece conflicted with August's judgement of pace.

As the days went by August grew noticeably shorter-tempered, which Sam attributed to too much of Amelia Amherst and maternal pressure to announce a betrothal.

'She must be mad,' Ned said.

'His Lordship doesn't help himself by finding someone more suitable,' Sam said stiffly. Sam currently disapproved of Ned for the same reason as her Ladyship: his preoccupation with getting Tom Belcher on the ground. 'The gentlemen don't get themselves so marked after a visit to Mr Jackson's. I don't know what his Lordship's thinking of, taking up so much of your time with it.' Ned knew exactly what August was thinking of: the hour at Jackson's place each day was an escape from scheming women. August enjoyed it and Ned, in his painful fashion, enjoyed it too, aware of how much his skill was increasing. August was happy there, and with his horses, and with the rest of the social round he grew increasingly impatient.

'We are wasting time, Ned. I think we should go home and attempt the wager. The horses will never be fitter.'

'No, my Lord.'

'I want some fresh air. I want – oh God, I want –' They were on their way home from the Amhersts and August, slightly drunk, hard-pressed by the matchmakers, was desperate for Sarah, for time, for his life. Ned could feel it; it did not need to be put into words. At times on the box there was a current between them; Ned could not have described it in words at all; it was a perfect accord, strangely keyed-up, instinctive. He knew that August felt it too by the way he spoke – or, even, did not speak; perhaps just a word, a hint, as it was now, left hanging, as if it was all too much for him to *say*. There were times, as now, when his spirit flagged, when he seemed to Ned frighteningly vulnerable, watching the horses with hollow, desperate eyes. There was no time for him, a basic commodity for a young man, and nothing in his life was resolved, scarcely even started, only the sweetness touched on and instantly soured by the responsibilities he must shoulder by his death. When he was crowded by events, as now, fresh from an Amherst family consultation, he came back to the horses and had Ned drive them very fast through the dark streets, their hooves throwing sparks off the cobbles, their bearing-reins let off. He would sit forward, holding the fingers of his left hand as if it were on the reins. He said once, 'I can feel my right arm, you know, as if it is still there, on the whip. It is ridiculous – and the sleeve empty. I can put it out, touch your knee, and you know nothing. People say, "I would give my right arm for –" whatever it is. They don't know, they just don't know. And it wasn't necessary – I saw it. They cut the sleeve up and I thought he was going to bind it together, and then he took this knife out of the kitchen drawer. I couldn't believe it. There was no one to stop him Sam wasn't there. Sam wouldn't have let it happen.'

But now he was saying, 'I can't marry her, Ned. It's no good, not even for convenience. I can't do it. I want to go home.'

'Marry Sarah,' Ned said.

'God that I could! My mother would stomach it if she had to, but Dr Redbridge – never. And his reason is so good I cannot press it. He is a good man. Let's go home, Ned.'

'Now?'

'Yes. Drop my mother and collect Sam and we'll go home tonight. We'll rest the horses for a couple of days and then try the wager. I can't look on Amelia again.'

'No.' Ned agreed. He instinctively eased the horses, thinking of the work ahead, and August sat in silence, apparently consoled by his change of plan.

'Don't say anything to my mother.'

They drew up at the front of the house in Conduit Street as usual and August got down and went into his house with his mother. Ned waited for the footmen to get back, then drove on round into the mews. The grooms came out, yawning, to take the horses, but Ned, getting down, told them of the change of plan. The reaction was not unexpected.

'He must have gone off his head – *now*! Are we to go too?'

'I think so. He wants to try the wager.'

'Gorblimey! Never a dull moment.'

Ned fetched his working clothes and few possessions and put them in the boot; Sam came out, swearing; a box was put on board; the grooms hastily got ready and shortly afterwards August, changed out of evening dress and into travelling clothes, climbed up, rather wearily, on to the box. The men got inside, and Ned, not without a feeling of relief, eased the team out of the small mews yard, watching the spark of iron on cobbles, breathing the now familiar dank evening smell of open drains and stagnant water. The night was cool and fine, a bright half-moon to show them the way, and Ned shared Ironminster's thirst for the serenity of their own acres, the homeliness of their own yard. The horses moved steadily, at their best at the end of the day when their over-abundance of energy was worked off. Ned was happy, looking forward to the softer ground of the open road after city stones.

'We won't press them,' Ironminster said, looking at the watch in his waistcoat pocket. 'I'll time them, but no matter if they take a couple of hours. We'll be home soon after midnight. And pleased to be there.'

The journey was quiet and easy. Ned took the route past the

Redbridge home, because it was the shortest. A light was burning in an upstairs window. August said softly, 'Dr Redbridge is in London. I saw him this evening. Alone.'

August was silent for a minute, and then:

'When we get home, Ned, leave the horses to the boys and put Apollo to the Stanhope and come to the door for me.'

'Yes, my Lord.'

Ned was moved out of his content into a deep and bitter humour. He had waited before, in the stillness of the woods, through the heavy summer afternoons, and must now wait again through the night with only his thoughts for company. He did as he was told, ignoring the curious looks the boys gave him, harnessing Apollo in silence while they rubbed down the team and set about preparing straw beds and filling hay racks. They did not dare question him, recognizing his mood, save young Harry who asked: 'Is it true that we're going to try the wager?' Ned led Apollo out of his stall and replied, 'It's what we've come home for, so I've been told.' But driving up to the house he wondered if that was the truth, or whether Ironminster's glimpse of Dr Redbridge up in town was the real reason for their coming home so precipitously. Ironminster shared no confidences now, sitting silently beside him on the ride back to the Redbridge home, very tense and pale, the pallor accentuated by a black velvet coat. The road was soft and quiet beneath Apollo's steady hooves.

'You'll have to wait for me, Ned,' Ironminster said, half apologetic, his only words. Ned drew up outside the house and Ned saw him admitted, the door close behind him. Had she known, had she been waiting? Ned, trying to be phlegmatic and servant-like, pictured the reunion and bit his lip to stop a genuine groan from puncturing the night's silence – he felt ill-used, bitter, almost tearful at his miserable role, as unexpected as it was painful. He had no defences in this sphere; there was no way of stopping his imagination working, damping his own jumping desires and jealousies, and blotting out the vivid, dreamlike memory of the lovely Sarah with her bare brown arms softly freckled like the bantams' eggs: the misery was acute. Ned, if he had been prepared for Ironminster's outing, would never have guessed the sharpness of its effect on him. He was quite unable to sit still, staring patiently into space, but was obliged to get down and walk up and down, stamping his cold feet in their shining London boots on the verge, clenching his hands like a maniac. What a role! The lowest servants got no worse than this, even discounting the personal misery: the prospect of boredom was wide open, the night dead and dark, the moon obscured, his body tired and hungry and full of these cravings for a lady as unapproachable as the withdrawn moon itself.

After the first half-hour his spirit flagged and numb weariness glazed his emotions. Apollo stood on three legs, dozing; the lights on the gig gleamed through the misty dark. It was three hours to dawn, the lowest ebb of the night's cycle, still, womblike, damp and silent. Ned, deadly tired, led the horse to the doctor's stables and unharnessed him and made him a bed in an empty stall, then, unwinding only the highest revolutions of his smart cravat, he wrapped himself in a convenient horse blanket and lay down with Apollo in the straw. Even so, he could not sleep; or, if he did, it did not seem like it; half-thinking, half-dreaming – the thoughts, or dreams, were un-kind and uncomfortable, sour as the chilly night air, lunatic as the screams of the barn-owl hunting over the thatch. Ned was not used to his mind being disturbed.

'I thought you'd gone home.'

He must have slept for Ironminster was standing there, prodding him with his foot. It was barely light, the rising sun shrouded by mist; Ned saw cobwebs in the doorway suspend-ing glittering drops of dew, Ironminster's face amused . . . He was as cold as a clamped turnip, stiff as a corpse. They drove home at a sharp trot, in silence, strangely isolated by the milky, autumnal stillness, the sun swimming unseen over the hollow where the lake was invisible: everything, even their thoughts and humours, undelineated, unreal, divorced from the sharpness of real life. Ironminster said nothing, save – on parting – 'Have the team ready at two o'clock. We'll give them five miles on the turnpike, ready for Friday.'

And Sam, questioning Ned over breakfast, drew his own conclusions. 'We don't get shaved at midnight and change into black velvet to go shooting rabbits, that's all I know. God help us all when her Ladyship finds out what's going on.'

But Ned thought that was the least of their problems.

*   *   *

'Well, they'll never go better, Ned. Friday it is, at first light. Sam is coming. I've sent a message to Andrew and we shall pick Miss Redbridge up at the gate. And whichever groom you want – that makes a complement of six. I think we stand a very fair chance.'

'Yes, my Lord.'

Ned, taking a pull at his leaders as they approached the turning for home, was excited at the prospect ahead, more so than he would have admitted. Even now, on a familiar exercise run, he felt an extra dimension in the routine, tautly aware of every detail as if his senses had been honed. It was true that the horses were at the peak of their form, not a flaw or blemish to be found, and all in tune with each other, sharing the work, knowing the job without his having to do all their thinking for them. Their long steady trot covered the ground as fast as many a team cantering and their fitness made it seem effortless. Ned, holding them for the hill ahead, was actively enjoying them, watching them, feeling them, pleased with the firm, peaty lane and its prospect below, wheeling down in a long galloping curve to the village green and the North gates of Threadgolds. The trees were yellowing and the air sharp and clear.

'Come,' Ironminster said. 'Let them gallop.'

The hill wasn't steep enough to be dangerous, but it was blind at the bottom, a group of cottages and trees concealing the last bend where another lane joined and the road went over a bridge over the village pond and across the green. Ned preferred the horses in hand for the bend, for there was no stopping until the other side of the bridge if they were galloping and had the weight of the coach behind them. But Ironminster liked to spring them and give a blast on the horn to clear the road; then it was just a matter of accurate steering to clear the bridge and let them run themselves out by the Threadgolds gates. If he was alone Ned did it his way; with Ironminster he did as he was told.

He eased out the reins and spoke to his leaders. He felt them pulling, quickening, but he had to hold them carefully to keep their traces slack enough. If Esmeralda, the near-side wheeler, felt herself being towed along she would start to kick. Ned knew her little ways, and preferred to please her. The lane started to roll away beneath the pounding hooves, and Ned sat back, bracing his legs against the footboard, pitting his strength against Starling and Nightingale. There was a science to galloping, a hairline between safety and disaster, and he liked to ride it his own way, whatever Ironminster might be shouting in his ear. He felt the wind quickening past his face and the great pulling of the muscles of his shoulders; his body braced and quivering and exhilarated and the horses spread to the gallop below him. God help anyone who might be in their way! Ned, having done it many times before, never tired of the pure excitement of springing the team down such a hill as this, long and just steep enough to give weight to the coach. The smell of hot horses and leather and the sharp autumnal air was like wine – he had never known this in his old days of over-laden public stages. Galloping downhill then was a sure way to die, to spread the passengers all over the road. Esmeralda's ears were going back. Ned took a stronger hold of the leaders, steadied as best he could for the bend into the bridge, and simultaneously saw disaster. Ironminster beside him said, very quietly, 'Oh, Ned, we've done for them,' and put his left hand out instinctively towards the reins. A hay-wagon was standing in the middle of the lane, blocking the bridge, its team of horses apparently having backed it there out of the side turn-ing, for they were standing skew-on across the road, of too jaded a breed to stand a chance of galvanizing into action and moving out of danger. There was no way round them.

Strangely enough, in that moment, although Ned could see that it was disaster for them all, horses, coach and men, it was Ironminster he felt a great pang of compassion for. Not that there was anything he could do for him, other than steer the horses for the least sickening of their options – and even for that there wasn't enough time for the reaction to be much more than instinctive. He could see clearly what was going to happen, as plain in his mind's eye a fraction before it actually took place as if he were a bystander observing – and by God! that he had been a mere spectator! He stood up, flinging his whole weight on the near-side reins – enough to take the leaders clear of the stone parapet of the bridge, but not poor Sunbeam who took it on his shoulder and was smashed stone-dead before he ever had time to see it coming. The coach, cracking its pole with a noise like gunshot, took off as the bank

99

fell steeply away below and turned a complete somersault, catapulting its two passengers violently into the air. Ned had a glimpse of threshing hooves below and heard the horses screaming, then hit the bridge head-first, his beaver stoving in and crushing down over his eyes. Falling into the water, blinded, he wasn't sure if he was dead or alive, but the rush of water up his nose and in his ears stung him into such violent, instinctive action that the doubt was soon resolved. Up till then, he hadn't known he could swim, either, but self-preservation saw him into shallower water, choking and spitting, tearing at his jammed hat and stupid cravat, desperate to get at the horses. He could only see two of them, his sight regained – the two leaders kicking frantically in water up to their withers, a great muddy churning boiling up around their terrified nostrils. The coach was upside down, wheels spinning, and the other two horses were pinned underneath, whether alive or dead he could not tell. Ironminster was staggering up the far bank, shouting for help to some running villagers.

Ned, tearing off his heavy coat, plunged out towards the nearest horse, Nightingale, his feet sinking into deep mud, his shins torn by old metal rubbish. The water was up to his armpits, stinking black at the disturbance. Miraculously, Nightingale was still on her feet kicking like one possessed and held by God only knew what under the water. Managing to un-hook one trace, Ned was knocked over, a stinging front hoof scoring his thigh, threatening to trample him under. He reached up desperately for her head, caught her bridle and with his free hand scrabbled for the knife he carried in his belt. The reins were caught fast in the wreckage of the coach. He slashed at them, cutting them through, shaken like a rat for his pains, and Nightingale heaved herself free, throwing him aside, stag-gering up the bank with black mud pouring off her torn flanks.

The accident had by now attracted most of the villagers, and several men and youths lined the bank shouting advice and climbing out on to the up-ended coach. Ned, knowing that few of them wanted anything to do but gawp and stare and point, was appalled by the task of getting the rest of the horses out. Starling was half-down, apparently unable to free his hind legs. Ned, the noise of the impact still in his ears, didn't think Sunbeam was worth considering, but somewhere under the coach, where blood and froth and bubbles broke on the surface, the gallant Esmeralda was pinned – drowning, if there was still life in her.

Ironminster was suddenly there, sliding down the bank and galvanizing the gawpers with a sharp, urgent voice.

'Enough men to lift the coach! Get into the water – a guinea for every man who helps get the coach off those horses' backs! Quickly – there's no time to lose –'

He was soaking wet and had blood trickling down the side of his face. Ned struggled towards him.

'Starling – is held. I fear for his back legs. They must be – very careful, moving the coach. Nothing sudden –'

'But fast, Ned, for the mare. See if you can free her. She might get up if they can ease the coach.'

The depth of the water made it difficult to know what had happened exactly. Ned eased himself round Starling, who was calmer than Nightingale and unable to kick because of whatever was holding him, and started to explore for the mare. He wasn't used to water and nobody else was volunteering for the job of freeing her, although several of the youths were now down in the pond and getting their shoulders to the coach. Ironminster was directing them.

'Find her head, Ned – if we can lift it clear we'll have more time.'

Ned could feel flesh with his feet, moving and trembling. He had to go down, shuddering himself, feeling with his hands, blind, choking, terrified. He could feel her collar, and her mane – but he had to come up, spluttering, heaving for air. The black, thick water terrified him. But she was moving.

He gulped, nodded, at Ironminster.

'Can you get her head, her bridle?' Ironminster was down beside him, very cool. 'If you can pull her head as soon as we lift the coach –'

Ned had one foot on her neck, one leg sinking deep in the slime. He knew where her head should be – a froth of bubbles still broke the surface. No time to lose now, she must be losing consciousness. 'A rope – yes. Here. They've brought one.' He took the end of the hairy coil and forced himself under, almost wishing there was some one to push him down and hold him there till the job was done. The roaring black darkness disorientated him completely. It was all he could do not to panic, more conscious of himself than the poor wretched mare, although his hands had found her mane again and, groping, her head and bridle. He had to move his feet to reach her and the mud held him, something sharp and agonizing hit his leg – he was drowning . . . panic . . . oh, God! He slipped, the water was going down his throat – he couldn't breathe. He reached up for air, gulping and spluttering.

'Ned, the rope –'

Hands reached out, ready to take it. Ned shook his head, gasped a mouthful of air and went down again, moving his hands feverishly over the horse's flesh, finding her throat, dragging at the rope to pass it under and unable to find the end with his other hand. It jammed, he tore at it, the awful bubbles breaking and bursting round his head. The horse lurched beneath him, her head moved, and he was able to find the rope and pull. He threshed for the surface, found it, choked, fell under again, his foothold going from under him, but hands pulled at him, grasping him under the armpits. The rope was pulled through his hands. He saw Ironminster's face, shouting, and the concerted heave of shoulders under the coach.

'Help her, Ned, help her!'

Find her head, her bit. She was threshing about with what he could feel was her last and only remaining spark of life, not strongly like Nightingale but with a pathetic, instinctive will to live. He got his hands round her head and pulled, got down and pushed his shoulder under her throat, heaved till he thought his back would break. His head and hers broke the surface together. The rope was tight round her neck and the helpers pulled all together and Ned was knocked over again, sure this time that if the mare didn't die he would. All his bones and muscles had turned to water, infected by their new environment; his lungs felt like Ironminster's own. Somebody pulled him out, dragged him up the bank together with the mare, and he found himself lying beside her, seeing the convulsive twitching of her ears, her eyes closed, her nostrils dilated, filled with blood. He put his hands out and pulled gently at her ears. 'Ezzie, come on, Ezzie, you musn't die. Not for us. Not now.' He rolled over and got to his knees, talking to her, leaning over her and rubbing her ears and her neck, freeing her from the rope. Her skin looked new-born, wet and steaming, but blood was running in thick streams down her chest and shoulders, mingling with black mud in the grass.

'She's breathing,' Ned said to Ironminster, not getting up, exploring her wounds with his fingers, and finding the bone bare, flesh hanging loose in lumps like butcher's meat. 'Get needle and thread. Some pump water.' He wiped his hair out of the way with the back of his hand, smelling the mare's blood. There was blood everywhere. He felt sick with disappointment. Her eyes were open, terrified. He talked to her, undoing her girths, the hames, easing the collar up her neck.

'Starling –?' He glanced up and saw the black gelding standing on three legs on the edge of the bank, head down, shaking.

'Off-side hind-leg – cut to ribbons.' Ironminster's face was bleak. 'Nightingale is fair, Sunbeam dead. Esmeralda –?'

'Oh, Esmeralda –' Ned could feel his own tears hot, running down his cheeks, but no one was to know amongst the pond water and the mare's blood. He started to put her together, with men sitting on her to keep her still, probing with his fingers, gently pushing back the flaps of hanging flesh and stitching it as best he could with the peasant woman's best thread. He had done it before; his father had done it; horses in collisions got dreadful injuries, spiked on shafts and poles, it was common enough. But to Esmeralda . . . God, it was awful, he couldn't believe it had happened, pausing to wipe his nose with the back of his hand. His sleeve was torn and hanging in ribbons. So were his breeches, his white thighs and God knew what else showing through, steadily darkening with all the pints of Esmeralda's blood. His fingers held and pinched and slithered through the mess, the thread sliding and knotting and holding, running out, tied off . . . start again. And what good would she be afterwards? If they ever managed to get her home.

And Starling? Ironminster was kneeling beside him. 'Is Starling all right?' Ned could not stop to look.

'Carry on. Nothing urgent, like this. But bad enough, Ned – on the hock. It'll take weeks.' The worst place.

It struck Ned then, and he glanced at Ironminster: 'You should look to yourself, my Lord.' Ironminster was in much the same state as himself.

'Oh, Ned, does it matter?' Ironminster was on the edge of tears.

'Yes. Here, hold this, just here. No, here. You should have

Sam to you. That's it, it's all right now. Go and get dry, my Lord.'

The other horses should be taken home. Ironminster was seeing to it. The grooms had come down from Threadgolds, informed of the accident; the farm men were dragging the remains of the coach out of the water, Sam was taking charge of Ironminster. A mist was sobering the late golden sunshine and the white ducks were coming back to the pond. Ned, very tired and suddenly very cold, swilled the last of the clean water over Esmeralda's wounds.

'Get off her,' he ordered. 'Let her up, if she'll come.'

She might not bleed to death, for his handiwork, but it wasn't a pretty job, nothing to be proud of. Only, if she got to her feet and stood, he would feel something was achieved, that he hadn't laboured entirely in vain. She was trembling and twitching and groaning, scraping the grass for a foothold with the last remains of her strength.

'Help her, help her,' Ned ordered, and the men got their hands round her, straining and coaxing, while Ned stood at her head, pulling on her bridle and using his most persuasive voice, as if it were the wager itself at stake. She staggered up and they leaned on her to hold her, stroking her and steadying her until her legs stopped shaking.

'Get her moving. She can – she must –' Even if she only got home to die, Ned was determined she should get there. He didn't want to linger any more in the mess of blood in the grass, with Sunbeam's tragic body hauled out of the water behind him, lying stark on the bank, the boys stripping off his harness. Splinters of coachwork and glass were scattered everywhere, more like an explosion than a mere accident. The hay-cart had gone; the road was empty. He walked at Esmeralda's head, watching the quaking of her wounds bending and opening to his inadequate embroidery, coaxing her poor staggering legs, splaying like those of a newborn foal. It was a long walk, achieved, Ned felt later, more by his will-power than the mare's, coaxing and talking and pushing and holding, following the miserable trail of blood already left by the two leaders gone on ahead. It was gone dusk by the time they reached the stable-yard, and all the household not already helping turned out in silence to watch the sorry procession, leading the way with lamps. Deep beds of straw were ready laid down. The maids had filled the water-buckets, the cook had made gruel and the fire was stoked up in the harness room with hot water ready. Harry, the youngest groom, was crying. Ned told him roughly to be quiet. He got Esmeralda into her stall, saw her buckle down into the straw, and did not believe, in spite of all his effort, he would ever see her get up again.

He leaned back against the partition watching her in the lamplight, exhausted, feeling himself trembling with fatigue.

Mrs Burns the cook shooed everyone back to the house and came to Ned briskly, holding out dry clothes.

'Some brandy would do her good,' Ned said, 'And later some eggs mixed up with milk, warm, and some whisky. Can you make it and send it down?'

'Yes, and for you too. Get cleaned up and dried, Mr Rowlands, before you start on anything else, or you'll end up sick as her.'

'I've the other horses to do.'

'Yes, in good time. Do as you're told. The boys can cope for five minutes.'

She was a bossy old bag, used to getting her way, and Ned wasn't sorry for it afterwards, stripping off the tattered remains of his clothes and bathing the mud and blood off him in the wooden tub she prepared in the harness room. Quite a lot of the blood was his own, he was surprised to see. She sponged him down and dried him off and rubbed stinging ointment in his cuts.

'We could use you out here. You're wasted in the house,' he said.

'You've the devil's own cheek, but I've got fond of you,' she said tartly. 'His Lordship's got Mr Arnold to see to him, but I thought you looked as if you could do with a bit of mothering. I'll make you a drink and you'll admit you feel a lot better for it. You ought to get married, Ned.'

'Are you making a proposal?'

'Get on with you! I've trouble enough. But you're ripe for it, and wasting out here. If you were married his Lordship would put you in the coachman's cottage – very nice it is. And you could have all this laid on every day of the week.'

'Yes, well, I've no time for courting just at the moment. We'll talk about it later. You tell me how to go about it.'

'I'll tell you who to choose.'

Ned pulled his breeches on, not answering. She handed him a clean shirt, warmed at the fire, and he hurried the rest of his dressing, not anxious to be enlightened as to the lady of her choice, whom he could very well guess. They were as bad in the servants' hall as Lady Ironminster in her drawing-room. He pulled a groom's smock over his waistcoat and smacked the old woman's backside in parting, not sorry for her ministrations, even if unimpressed by her propositions.

'Send up the eggs and brandy as soon as you can. The wife can wait a bit.'

Attending to first Starling and then Nightingale sobered him again, and kept him until almost midnight. By then, when the lamps were dimmed and the poor wreckage of his team was patched and soothed to the best of his ability, he was too tired to think about his supper, but a message came to say that it was waiting, and that his Lordship wanted to see him. He would have had it otherwise. Now that the stable was quiet and everyone gone but old Pegram who would sit up with him through the night, the sorry, flat disappointment and plain tragedy of the day's work came to him with fresh impetus. Sunbeam's empty stall gaped; the heavy, laboured breathing of the wounded mare, and the awkward, painful stirrings of the two leaders, cut and bruised and swollen-legged, were a sad requiem to his proud achievement. His feelings were very different from the self-congratulatory glowing satisfaction he normally experienced on his goodnight look-round. The timing of the accident worried him. At the back of his mind he was suspicious.

He went to his room and found a neck-cloth and his black coat, and went up to the house. His body was sore and stiff, aching all over from the contortions it had been put to, and he thought that if he sat down to his dinner he would never get up again. Better to go up to Ironminster first.

But Mrs Burns, waiting to serve him, said otherwise.

'He said to eat first. Sit you down now, and Matty will wait on you, then we can get off to bed. Once you start going over the ground upstairs, we'll never be finished till morning.'

Ned knew he wouldn't be anyway, but was too tired to argue, too tired even to be nice to Matty. She waited on him silently, and he remembered Mrs Burns' advice, mothering him, and thought of Ironminster loving Sarah, and none of his thoughts added up to anything at all, even when Matty, taking his plate, contrived to touch his hand. He got up and went slowly upstairs to Ironminster's room and found him alone, sitting by the fire, dressed in his night clothes. He was breathing heavily, his cheeks flushed, his chest swathed in Sam's precautionary woollen bandages. Ned paused at the door.

'Come in, Ned. I want to talk to you.' August got up and poured some brandy out of a crystal decanter on the table. 'Here. Sit down.' He held out the glass and gestured to a comfortable velvet chair beside his own at the hearth. A single branch of candles burned on the mantelpiece, and in its light Ned could see the telltale glistening of perspiration on August's face, the painful dilation of his nostrils to the shallow breathing. The sight of the symptoms moved him to a fresh bitterness, for his own disappointment at what had happened could not be a fraction of Ironminster's own, who had so much less time to see it put to rights.

'I want you to say, honestly, Ned – you must have thought about it by now – if you have any ideas about that accident.' He paused very slightly before the word accident. Ned was watching him, and knew what he meant.

He considered his brandy very carefully.

'Yes.'

August stared into the fire, not saying anything.

Ned was cautious of his phrasing. 'I think – it might have been – meant.'

August remained silent. Ned watched him, feeling his way. 'They must have heard us but they never sent a boy to the bend to warn us. And it was a Mole End wagon.'

August nodded imperceptibly, not looking up. 'And how did they know?' he asked.

'I think they were told.'

'Who by?'

'I'd rather not say without being sure.'

'Can you make sure?'

'In the morning, yes.'

August straightened up slowly, and looked at Ned. 'I have to decide, you see. I've been thinking about it, whether we fight back or whether we –' He paused and shrugged. 'Look at me. When I say "we" fight back, you know that *I* can't do a thing, physically. But if I thought that you, Ned, were prepared to do – be, that part of me – the right-hand man, as Andrew put it – well, then, it might be different. Things like this can't be settled with words. You have to play the same game as they play.'

Ned said, carefully, 'I wouldn't do anything to their horses.'

'No. But because *they* did it that way, Ned – that's why I feel I'm damned if they'll get away with it. We can't be beaten there. We can't sit here and accept what they've done to us, and watch Rupert take that wager and do nothing about it. Only it depends on you, Ned.'

'How?'

'First, to find out exactly what those men were doing with that wagon, who put them up to it, how they found out. They were acting for my cousins, I'm sure. We can only do that by bullying – no good politely asking. I know that carter. If you're game, we'll call on him in the morning. I can do the talking and you can do anything else that might be necessary. And after that, if it's as we think – we won't let it rest there, Ned, believe me – not as long as I know that you will back me up.'

'I will.'

'It might be more than is strictly in the line of duty.'

'Yes. That's no matter.'

'And to get a team on the road again, Ned, as soon as we can. We'll go to Tattersall's for the wheelers, and Vidler's for a new coach – or to repair the old one. We'll look at it in the morning.'

'Yes, my Lord.'

'We'll drive them off the road again, Ned. If I think that, I can keep on going, you see. If we're beaten now, I feel it's all up with me. I wouldn't have the will. But it really depends on you. Without you it's impossible.'

Ned swallowed his brandy down, in need of it. In effect, Ironminster was saying that his life depended on him. He proverbially lived by will-power, and he needed his purpose in life. If it wasn't to be Sarah, to see him out in peace, it was to be doom to all Savilles, and go down fighting. It fitted, if it wasn't too late. Ned, over-tired, wondered whether he was exaggerating the position, but seeing August get up and stand silhouetted against the candlelight, he felt he recognized the strange, lonely courage that occasionally, as now, needed stiffening. It didn't need sympathy, or admiration, or even acknowledgement, but just, in its off-moments, a mute promise of support. Ironminster's predicament was common enough; lucky, indeed, that he had such care and comfort to rely on, but his attitude to it, his public carelessness and his inner, private desperation – Ned did not think the word too strong – was rare in Ned's experience. And the desperation, Ned suspected, was only revealed to the few intimate people who did not count because they were outside his circle of friends. They were servants: himself and Sam. There was no sign of a private, spiritual resignation, which Ned thought might have been a comfort at times, but only of an aggressive determination to ignore the condition which, when it sometimes faltered, left him in a state of mind which Ned could only guess at, and preferred not to consider. Sam might have shared more, in the long hours of the night – he did not know – he was only aware of sharing a lot more than he had ever bargained for with Lord Ironminster and of such a subtle, private and onerous character that he wondered, as now, whether he was seeing the situation correctly. Nothing of this, to obscure the issue farther, was ever put into words. It was just a bond, evoked, as now, by what lay beyond the actual conversation. But Ned was perfectly aware of what he was being asked to do. He was to be the physical partner to Ironminster's spirit, for as long as the spirit held out.

'Yes, my Lord,' he said. 'I'll do whatever you want.' Which was as committed and generous an offer as any he was likely to make in all his life, and made without hesitation. He appreciated the significance of it as well as Ironminster, who held out his hand. Ned reciprocating, put out his right hand and changed it deftly to his left, to match August's.

August laughed.

'Well done, Ned. That gives me heart. I wanted to know – it makes all the difference. Go and get some sleep now, if you can, and I'll see you in the morning, early.'

Sam appeared at the door and asked if he was needed, but Ironminster dismissed him. Ned left the room and went downstairs with Sam, Sam snuffing out the last candles as he went.

The house was dark and quiet. Ned felt conscious of a heavy responsibility having fallen, but also of a tentative, nervous pride that it should be so.

'What did he want?' Sam asked.

Too difficult to say. Ned shrugged. 'About the accident. He thinks it wasn't one.'

'Do you?'

'Yes, very likely. We're to sort it out in the morning.'

'He should stay in tomorrow. Today's little excitement hasn't done him any good.'

'He's set on getting on the road again – to beat the Savilles.'

'No, that's his way. But he hasn't the strength any more, if he'd only acknowledge it. It'll be work for me, I can see.'

And me, Ned thought.

'He thinks he can still do what he did before.'

'Before what?'

'Oh, when he was at Eton, and at Oxford later, he had his own drag then, you know, and even as a boy he had a team of ponies. Used to tear round the park like goats, his father laughing his head off. He was all right in those days, only small, mind you, but the energy of ten. Then at Oxford he caught pneumonia – some damn-fool escapade on the river – he nearly died then, and afterwards – well, that was the start of it, the lungs affected. That's why his father bought him the curricle, thinking the drag was too much for him. And see where that got them! But he still pretends he's the same, that it's only the arm that stops him – and he makes himself worse, not resting up.'

'He doesn't pretend all the time.'

Sam, in the light of the last candle, glanced up at Ned, surprised. Then he said, 'No. You're right. He doesn't. To-night, for example, he won't.'

He blew the candle out.

Ned, going back along the drive to sit with Esmeralda, thought: 'I'm not the only one who won't sleep well tonight.'

8

IN THE morning, after miserably sharing Esmeralda's agony through the night, it was through no loyalty to Ironminster that Ned took punishment into his own hands, but purely to avenge the mare. He caught the boy Harry by the scruff of his coat collar and dragged him kicking and crying into the harness-room. Here he locked the door, thrust him hard up against the wall and reached for a coiled hunting whip.

'Now tell me, before I beat the hide off you, what was your part in this sorry business? Who was paying you to spy, to carry messages? Who did you run to, when you saw us leave the yard yesterday? Who did you tell, the night we got home, that we were to try the wager?'

With one hand he held the boy down hard over a saddle-horse and with the other he started to beat him with the crop. It came easily enough, sick as he was with his night's work, and fresh from bathing Starling's flinching legs. The boy was hard and strong and wriggled like a puppy. Ned knocked his head against the wall until he begged for mercy.

'Tell me then. I've more against your masters than I have against you, you poor snivelling little toad.'

'I didn't –'

Ned struck him again. 'I saw you. I saw you coming out of the Mole End covert when I came home with Apollo in the morning. And you saw me, because you dropped down to hide. More fool I that I didn't ask you then what you were up to. Now tell me!'

Having been in the boy's position many times himself in the past, mostly at the hands of his father, he knew exactly how much force to deploy, how much self-pity he must provoke to extract a confession. It didn't take very long.

'I told Pettifer!' the boy howled. 'He paid me to tell him!'

Pettifer was head groom at Mole End.

'To tell him what?'

'Anything! Anything to do with the wager. He made me!

And he'll beat me too when he knows I've told you!'

'I'm glad. I shall tell him myself. You told him we were home, first? Is that right? I'll bet that was a shock to him.'

'Yes, I told him that.'

'And you told him we were trying the wager today? And that we were driving out at two o'clock yesterday?'

'Yes.'

'And what did he say he was going to do about it?'

'He didn't tell me anything. He just growled and swore and gave me a shilling.'

'Well, I shall beat you now, because of what you've done to our horses, and because you're a sly toad and you need reminding, and afterwards you're to go away and never set foot near Threadgolds for as long as I'm here, else I shall beat you again.'

He picked up the riding-crop and gave the boy as much punishment as he thought he deserved and then threw him, howling, into the yard. Shortly afterwards Ironminster came into the yard, muffled up and coughing, his face drawn. He was obviously in a very bad mood, and bitterly impatient with his state of health. He examined the horses, heard Ned's tale of Harry, and ordered him to harness Apollo to the Stanhope.

'We'll see these carters and then, if it's as it seems, I shall go to London to see James and Rupert. And I want to see Andrew as well, and Railton.'

Ned would rather have stayed with the horses, but didn't dare say so. He ordered Apollo to be put to, and drove Ironminster to the carter's cottage in silence. The family was at breakfast, the man having been out in the fields since daylight, and were plainly terrified at the sight of Ironminster, who rapped at the door with his cane, kicked it open and walked straight in. The man and his wife and two grown sons all got up in confusion and gaped at their visitor.

'You're the man who caused the accident to my coach yesterday. Who put you up to it?'

'Oh, my Lord, I can explain –'

'Explain why you gave us no warning? Explain why you didn't move when you first heard our horn? Come then –'
Ironminster crashed his cane down on the table with such

force that the porridge bowls all jumped up in the air. Even Ned, having expected a display of authority, was impressed. 'Let me hear your explanation! Or should I ask Pettifer? Do you hear me?' This last, as the man was too frightened to say a word. The great gawky sons shifted their feet and looked at the floor. They were as big as oxen and Ned hoped he wasn't going to have to take on all three – but Ironminster's performance was so brilliant that it seemed it would prove sufficient.

'It was a – a mistake, my Lord.'

'A mistake? To kill one and probably two of my horses – yes, the mistake was in killing the horses and not their master, isn't that true? And bad enough, in any case. My horses don't deserve that, not of anyone. Not of anyone, Mr Turner, least of all from a paid man like yourself.'

Ironminster's quite genuine scorn was as searing as Ned's whiplash had proved earlier. The poor bribed carter was shaking with fright.

'Who paid you?'

'W-we had orders, my Lord.'

'Orders from whom?'

'I – I don't know, my Lord.'

'You're a fool but not fool as all that. Tell me your authority, else I shall turn you over to the magistrate. Hurry, man, damn you – it's murder we're talking about, not an accident. Was it from Pettifer?'

'Mr Pettifer said – said word came from Mr Saville, from Mr Rupert.'

'He told you that? He told you to block the bridge, orders from Mr Rupert?'

'Mr Pettifer said to use the hay-wagon –'

'Mr Rupert, no doubt, merely said – do it – a very fine gesture between cousins, I'm sure you will agree. I hope it gave you joy, Mr Turner, to kill my horses. I wouldn't do the same for yours, whatever I was bid. You will hear more of this. Meanwhile good-day to you. Finish your breakfast. You've told me what I want to know.'

He could say no more for lack of breath, Ned noticed, leaving as abruptly as he came, leaning on the gig outside while a fit of coughing convulsed him. Ned waited, tactfully drawing up Apollo's girth by a hole, until Ironminster managed to climb up, and then they drove back to Threadgolds, August hunched and grim, quietly choking into his handkerchief. Ned felt flat and depressed, anxious about what was being hatched. He didn't want to go to London and leave Esmeralda and Starling, and Ironminster seemed in no condition to travel, although Ned could quite see how anxious he was to share the news of the Savilles' latest infamy with his friends.

'I suppose we'll have to travel in the phaeton, if there's to be room for Sam. We can use Apollo and Hyacinth, and put them to the curricle when we get to Conduit Street. One of the grooms can travel up on the stage, and we can leave Pegram in charge here.'

'Yes, my Lord.'

The stable-yard was in a gloomy mood, and Ned's fresh orders did not improve the atmosphere. Hyacinth was a grey mare used by the house for shopping and messages and Ned did not look forward to driving her in London. He went and packed his clothes and put the box ready in the phaeton, sponged Esmeralda's wounds which were still bleeding badly because she kept threshing about, dressed Starling's swollen hock – the most ominous impediment to seeing the team on the road again – and went for his breakfast.

'Breakfast!' Mrs Burns snorted. 'Dinner more like! There's cold mutton and some cabbage. I can't do better, seeing as your hours are so funny. Mr Arnold wants to see you. I hear you're off back to London.'

'Yes, in the phaeton, no less.'

'That'll please Sam!'

Sam registered cold disapproval with the whole proceedings, and the sedate and boring journey was made in total silence, Ironminster sunk in deep thought, feverish and impatient at Ned's side. Ned could only guess as to the real bitterness of Ironminster's feelings on the affair, but he had an uneasy feeling that some dire retaliation was in his mind. When they arrived in Conduit Street, Ned put August and Sam down at the front door, and was then told to take a message to Railton's town house in Maddox Street.

'Fetch a footman,' August ordered Sam.

Sam had opened the door; Ned saw the head butler, and

Lady Ironminster, outraged, waiting in the hall; saw August's face, pinched with pains both mental and physical, as he held up the envelope with Railton's name scrawled on it.

'Be as quick as you can.'

'Yes, my Lord.'

The footman hurried out and got up, taking the envelope from Ned. 'Why a phaeton, for Gawd's sake? Has his Lordship gone off his head?'

Ned explained, easing the horses out into the traffic, touching the reluctant Hyacinth with his whip. The footman was impressed.

'Gawd's strewth! What a to-do. Her Ladyship's been in a terrible temper, and now him as well.' He rolled his eyes, and wiped his nose with a white-gloved finger.

Lord Railton, they were informed, was not at home. He was taking tea with Lady Archibald. Ned sent the footman back to get the address, and drove to Lady Archibald's. Railton came out into the street to see Ned, looking very pretty for tea with the ladies, hair beautifully curled, a perfect diamond in his cravat, but not at all concerned with decorum – 'Wait one moment, Ned, while I get my coat. My carriage isn't coming back till six, so I'll ride back with you.' On the way back Ned explained what had happened.

'My God, but what has August decided to do? This would be a calling-out matter, if only – well, better as it is, perhaps. Rupert is very bitter about losing Miss Redbridge's affections to August – that is what lies behind it. Are we to call on the Savilles, then? What a splendid prospect!'

They called on the Savilles later, when Andrew Field had joined them, driving in Railton's carriage. The following morning, early, they all went round to Bond Street to Mr Jackson's gymnasium. Ned, stuck with driving her Ladyship in the carriage to Windsor for the day, did not know what they were up to, and wished heartily that he could be given orders to go home. He did not trust Esmeralda with Pegram, and was afraid for Starling's hock getting mucky and the boys not being patient enough to give it the care it required. Her Ladyship was tart with him for not being as smart as she liked, and he spent the day waiting about, bored rigid. When he got home, there was a message to say that Ironminster wanted to see him in the house, after dinner. Railton and Field were still with him, presumably to dine, as their horses were in the mews, and Ned was curious and slightly apprehensive as to what they could want him for. When he went to the kitchen for his supper, Sam could not enlighten him.

'All I know is that they're in a high good humour, his Lordship and all, quite different from yesterday.'

Ned went upstairs when he was bid, smoothing his hair and straightening his coat. The women had left the table and gone to the drawing-room, and the three men were sitting with the port and brandy in front of them. As forecast by Sam, they seemed in very good spirits and Ned was aware as soon as he entered the room of a very positive atmosphere of excitement. Ironminster, although coughing a good deal, looked much better than when Ned had last seen him, his colour heightened and his manner brisk. He sat at the head of the table which the servants were clearing; the room was brightly lit, velvet curtains drawn across the tall windows and a bright, hot fire burning in the marble fireplace. Railton was standing with his back to the fire. Ned had a sense of being examined minutely as he came before them, the conversation halting at his entrance. He felt, unaccountably, very nervous, almost afraid.

'Give Mr Rowlands a drink, and leave us,' Ironminster ordered the servants. 'Sit down, Ned. Sit by the fire.'

Ironminster's voice was no longer sharp, but almost cajoling. Ned did as he was told, taking his glass from the waiter who then, with the other servants, left the room. With the click of the door there was a short silence, broken only by the comforting fluttering noise of the burning logs in the hearth. But Ned did not feel comfortable.

'Ned, we've a proposition to put before you.'

Yes, he had guessed as much, and remembered, with a sad, regretful amazement, his own voice saying, 'I'll do whatever you want.' It had caught up with him now, and he knew he was going to live to rue the promise. Whatever the proposition, the thought of it had cured Ironminster's malaise. He looked like a boy again, the excitement spilling up, and Railton and Field were grinning.

'You can refuse, of course, but I don't think you're that sort of man. In fact, I think, after the first shock, you will warm to the idea, Ned – it's so splendid. Think of it – my cousin, Rupert Saville, has admitted that he gave the orders to stop our team going in for the wager. It seems he needs another few weeks to get his team fit and the thought of our attempting it – winning it – before him was more than he could bear. And I think – although he didn't admit this much, of course – that he would also have liked me to have broken my neck. You will agree that all this is sufficiently dastardly to retaliate in kind – physically, I mean, Ned. One would ordinarily consider calling him out, but you know it's impossible for me. You remember the conversation we had last night, Ned? That's why I feel we can count on you. What we have done is – we have asked Mr Jackson to arrange a prize-fight. We will challenge Mr Saville. Mr Jackson thinks it's very fair, and will generate a great deal of interest, and he doesn't think that Mr Saville can possibly refuse the challenge.'

Ned looked into his glass of port, feeling slightly sick, the blood pounding in his head. The ambiguous 'we' did not deceive him for a second. It wasn't Ironminster or Field or Railton who were going to face Rupert Saville, but himself, naked in a ring, with Ironminster's very life at stake. He could not bring himself to make an answer.

'We haven't gone into it without a great deal of thought, Ned, don't think that. We have only gone into it convinced that you will win.'

'Did Mr Jackson say so?'

'Mr Jackson thinks it's a very fair match, very equal, with a good edge in your favour. As soon as it is made public, he thinks the betting will be very heavy, and that the support will be tremendous. Which will make it, you must see, a most public and resounding trouncing for the Savilles, a far greater victory than anything we could contrive in private.'

'But if not –'

'If you won't agree to fight?'

'If I fight but don't win?'

'Very unlikely, Ned. There is enough risk, yes, to make it a gamble, or no one would be interested – but not enough to bother you. We've all seen Rupert fight –'

'We can tell you all his weaknesses, Ned,' Railton put in. 'I've sparred with him myself, and he's no Belcher.'

'And Mr Jackson will train you, Ned. It's all agreed, if the challenge is made and accepted, that you're to stay in London and train with Mr Jackson and Captain Barclay.'

Ned drained his port, and Railton filled his glass again. 'Drink up, dear lad. You must see that it's impossible to refuse.'

Ned knew that he couldn't refuse, but wasn't as sure as they were of winning. He also saw that, however the fight might go, it would be a fight to the bitter end, and the end could be bitter indeed. He didn't know how brave he was, after all, never having been tested. And the whole burden of the contest would lie in the fact that he would be fighting, not for himself, but for Ironminster. For himself he would have accepted. For Ironminster – the responsibility was appalling ... but Ironminster, having hatched the plan, seemed to have taken on a new lease of life. Ned regarded him doubtfully, wishing desperately that he could have thought of a different way of equalizing with his cousin.

'You know I can't refuse, my Lord.'

'I'm not forcing you, Ned. Come, look happier about it, else I shan't be happy either. You're not afraid of him?'

'No, my Lord, only afraid of not beating him. Then you would be as public a loser –'

'But I'm the loser now, Ned. It would make no difference in that respect. And we don't expect to be the losers, Ned. You mustn't approach it like that. Two or three weeks with Captain Barclay and you'll be a real professional.'

Ned had heard of the training schedules of the enthusiastic Captain Barclay, with its obligatory doses of physic and ten-mile walks before breakfast, and wasn't heartened by the pro-spect. He wanted to say that he had been hired as a coachman; he wanted Ironminster to understand that he wasn't frightened of fighting, only frightened of how much depended on the result. However much Ironminster might say it would make no difference, Ned knew that it could, indirectly but no less cer-tainly, be the difference between Ironminster living and Ironminster dying.

Perhaps Andrew Field, always more gentle and thoughtful than his friends, guessed what was in Ned's mind, for he said, 'Don't take it too seriously, Ned. The consequences are of no matter to you. You just hammer him as best you can – remember what he did to your horses, and forget the rest. You've got right on your side – and the crowd will be for you.'

'Yes, that's all, Ned. The family politics are no concern of yours. You are just my sword, so to speak, or my pistol, had I two arms. No responsibilities.' Ironminster was laughing again. 'Think of it, Ned – surely you would rather be one of Barclay's stable, lodging with Tom Cribb, for the next week or two, than trailing my mother out to Windsor and Roehampton?'

Another glass of port and Ned began to think so too. He had been a long time out of tavern company, and was in danger of becoming as stiff-necked as all the liveried tribe. 'Think of it as a holiday,' as Railton said. Ned began to fancy himself a hero. He might prove so good that prize-fighting would become his living, and Tom Cribb his sponsor.

To celebrate the decision, he was liberally plied with the bottle ('Make the most of it, for Captain Barclay will have you on water!') and dispatched to Bond Street early the following morning with his box of clothes and a bad headache. Mr Jackson agreed with Ironminster to organize and publicize the fight, having already had word from Rupert Saville that he accepted the challenge, and Ned was delivered into the charge of the formidable Captain Barclay, after which Railton's 'holiday' became a poor joke in Ned's mind.

'Give me three weeks,' Barclay told Jackson. 'A fortnight if you must. We shall start work straight away.'

Ned was allotted a small bare room in Tom Cribb's famous tavern from where, in the evenings, he could hear the roistering of the sporting fraternity below while he was supposed to be in bed. By dawn, when they were just turning in, Ned was pitched out by the Captain to complete his first ten miles before breakfast, stumbling reluctantly through the awakening demolition and building sites across Piccadilly Circus, to the ribald shouts and encouragement of the men just starting work. On past the end of Conduit Street (where Ironminster was no doubt still slumbering peacefully) and into the green fields and cow pastures beyond Portland Place: the body would start getting into its rhythm, its complaints forgotten, and by his side the indefatigable Captain would explain: 'Legs, boy, legs – you'll win or lose by how long you can stay on them. It's stamina we want. We can't get enough of it.' The Captain had once walked a thousand miles in a thousand hours. Ned quite often felt as if he had just completed the same feat. Back at the Union Arms, his glowing fatigue would be abruptly banished by some buckets of cold water thrown over him and a pummelling rub-down by an affable bruiser with towels as rough as gravel; the subsequent raging hunger meanly treated to a couple of raw eggs and a dose of the famous physic. After that he could rest for an hour with his hands soaking in a mixture of vinegar, alum and horse-radish concocted by the Captain – 'To harden your knuckles, boy – we want 'em as hard and as thick as your head.' And when he was nicely on the verge of dozing off, it would be up and run to Bond Street to the gymnasium for the afternoon, to spar for a couple of hours and discuss tactics with Mr Jackson. Ned found it hard to believe it had all happened, so sudden and catastrophic was the change in his habits.

Ironminster came to watch him spar. Barclay and Mr Jackson apparently thought him capable of preserving himself against quite considerable opposition, for it was not the amateur young toffs he was matched with, but young aspirants to Tom Cribb's crown who were often far more experienced than Ned and anxious, in front of a noble audience, to impress. Ned was extended and came near, at times, to wondering if he would survive to meet Rupert Saville.

'The last day of October, Ned. It's all arranged. Midday, at Threadgolds, we hope – but the place won't be made public until the morning, in case of trouble.' August was referring to trouble with the magistrates, who were supposed to ban any matches in their area but, as often as not, came to watch. Ned was aware of the unspoken risk that – if he was unlucky – he could be sent to prison for a few weeks for breach of the peace, but preferred not to think of it. There were troubles enough for the present.

'You've lost a lot of weight,' Railton commented. 'Saville's still quite pudgy. We watched him this morning.'

'He's with Mendoza, in Tottenham Court Road. There's not the same atmosphere there. Not nearly so professional.'

'Easier, you mean?'

August laughed. 'You'll be glad for Captain Barclay's cruelty the day of the fight.'

'All you coachees carry too much weight,' said the Captain. 'All those hours of sitting in the cold. The body pads itself in self-defence. And your legs are your weakness – not used to doing any work.'

Ned glowered at him, remembering the feel of the four horses down their last long hill to disaster. His body had worked hard enough then. The Captain was untying his mufflers for him after the sparring session, looking for signs of damage. Ned sat breathing heavily, stung and tingling and impatient, wishing he could get back at the man he had just been parted from. He liked fighting, if not the training, and the urge to hammer his opponent came easily. Having accepted the situation, he hadn't thought again about obligations to Ironminster. He knew now that he wouldn't be nervous, faced with Saville, but only anxious for his own satisfaction to beat him: Ironminster could not possibly feel more keenly than he did himself. And not only Saville. He felt the same whoever they faced him at.

'He might not have the science, but he's got the spirit,' Jackson told August. 'Stamina could well decide it, against Saville. And that's what Captain Barclay is working on.'

'Perhaps tomorrow you will tell Captain Barclay that Ned can take his practice run in the direction of Tattersall's, because I'm hoping to buy a pair of wheelers in the morning, and I want Ned to see them first. About eleven o'clock. D'you hear that, Barclay?'

'I daresay I can spare him for an hour,' the Captain said tartly. 'We can make it up later.'

'He'll need your stamina to handle this couple,' Railton said. 'They're said to be rare fizzers – the property of Lord Holland, who wants to live longer than seems likely behind these two.'

Ned looked up. 'A pair of bays? White blazes?'

'Yes.'

'I've seen them.'

'What do you think?'

'Very handsome. Might not be sensible enough for us. Wheelers need sense.'

'They know their job, given proper handling.'

Ned opened his mouth to say more but was stopped by Barclay's cold sponge on the back of his neck, turning his words into a gasp. Railton laughed. 'We treat our horses better, eh, Ned?'

Ned, with the prospect of an evening walk round the orchards of Kensington and bed at nine after a meagre supper of almost raw steak, was bound to agree.

The following morning he walked down to Hyde Park gate with Captain Barclay, and met Ironminster in the stables to examine the pair of bays.

'We cannot wait for Esmeralda to heal – she'll be a year or more. New wheelers and it will only be a matter of waiting on Starling's hock. Nightingale is quite fit already. The hock is doing nicely enough. We've got to keep Rupert on tenterhooks, Ned, even after you've dispatched him with your fists.'

The rows of busy stalls, thronged with buyers, the nervous animals tossing their heads, the clang of iron hooves on cobbles echoing in the cavernous roof, gave Ned a sense of familiar well-being, on home ground. Here, with the horses, he was in command. The bays were perfectly matched, a pair of blood geldings, fine but very nervous. One of them lashed out several times while Ned examined his legs.

'The boys will have to look to it, if we give this one a home. Does he do it in harness, I wonder?'

'They're risky,' Ironminster agreed, 'But I like the look of them. Lots of heart. I think they've been badly handled – you could cure that easily enough, Ned.'

'It's not always cured,' Ned said. Ironminster knew it, but wanted them. Ned, unless he found a positive blemish, did not think he was going to escape having to cope with them. He couldn't. He looked in their mouths.

'They're not young. Nine-year-olds.'

'They'll see me out,' Ironminster said carelessly. 'I shall bid for them. If you wait you can drive them back to Conduit Street to Railton's curricle. You can run behind, Alex, with Captain Barclay.'

'I shall ride groom. I can't run as fast as the Captain.'

They were in very high spirits – even higher when the pair were knocked down to Ironminster at two hundred guineas, not a high price for their looks and match. Ned had thought August had been joking about putting them to Railton's curricle, but he was required to strip the harness from Railton's pair in the livery stables and use it to harness the new horses. The kicker nearly killed him before he got its crupper on; Railton had to hold up a foreleg before it could be managed. Railton's curricle was a ridiculous confection of feather-weight spars and springs, very high and thoroughly unroadworthy, eminently unsuited for a trial of two high-spirited and likely dangerous horses.

'I'm not dressed, my Lord,' Ned pointed out hopefully. 'Perhaps Lord Railton should drive them?'

'I wouldn't dare,' said Railton.

'Oh, come, Ned. I'm not her Ladyship, for heaven's sake. Of course you shall drive them. Alex can hang on the back if he wants and Ned shall return for you, Captain.'

'Certainly not. I shall walk,' said the Captain.

For once, Ned would have preferred walking too.

'They should be to something a good deal heavier, my Lord.'

'Well, they're not. Are you afraid?'

Ned, annoyed, started to thread the reins into his hand. He wasn't afraid of any horse, but the lunacy of trying unknown beasts to a curricle down Piccadilly appalled him. Railton, as groom, held them while August and Ned climbed up. It was like being in a bird's nest up a tall tree. Ned looked down dubiously on the horses' backs. They carried their heads very high, and were pawing the ground to go, setting up sparks.

'All right, my Lord!'

Ned doubted if Railton would get aboard, once he let go, but managed to curb the horses sufficiently for the feat to be achieved. It became apparent at once that they were frightened by the curricle and its lack of stability behind them, for they took off like birds from covert, racing out of the yard and cornering into the road so fast that the curicle went round on one wheel. Railton hung out to balance it with his weight like a Roman charioteer, and several ladies talking on the pavement screamed and ran for their lives.

'Perhaps it's as well you're not in livery, Ned. Better to be anonymous on a day like this.'

He was holding on firmly with his one hand, but Ned felt as if he was sitting on a cloud, with nothing to brace himself against. To keep the horses from swerving was imperative else the curricle would go over; Ned wondered that Ironminster wasn't reminded of his father and chastened, but – quite the opposite – the excitement cheered him enormously.

'For God's sake keep us all in one piece, Ned. You've to live to meet Rupert, remember –'

'They're fast enough!' There was no doubt there. The trees of Green Park flew past; they overtook a drag and a pair of tilburys, but Ned could not stop them in time to turn up Bond Street. They had mouths like iron. When he managed to convey his message about stopping they started to prance, half-rearing, and he was forced to get them forward again before he had a leg over the traces.

'Oh, confound it, Ned, we're going to land up in all the new building! Turn into Sackville Street.'

They were already holding up the oncoming traffic by being on the wrong side of the road and causing a crowd to collect, and Ned was terrified of cornering too fast and turning the outfit over. But there was no way of slowing them in time and he decided to take it wide, trusting in providence that nothing would be in their way. Best when it was hard to stop to concentrate on steering, with a few prayers remembered for good measure. He signalled with his whip and saw the people on the pavement start to scatter, a hat flying in the air. The horses started to turn, trotting very fast and pulling like maniacs, covered in a white sweat of alarm. A milliner's delivery carriage, very sedate, was coming down the street towards them and Ned brought his whip sharply up to his off-side horse to veer it up to the pole, wincing as the curricle gave a violent lurch. The left-hand wheel hit the kerb-stone and rode over it, and the nearside horse went up the pavement and almost through the shop-front of a jeweller. With a trio of ladies right ahead, standing as if rooted to the pavement, Ned had to be very quick to correct. Railton, hanging out to do his balancing act, and managing to raise his beaver to the ladies at the same time, was caught off-guard by the rapidity of the curricle's change of direction and flew off into space as they bumped into the road again.

'Stop, stop!' August bawled. 'We've lost our man!'

It wasn't possible to stop for almost a hundred yards, by which time Ned felt in as much of a lather as the horses. Without a footman, even standing still was a full-time job, the two horses jiggling and prancing and backing and turning, frightening everybody in the road and on the pavement alike. Railton, his breeches split and his white knees showing through, liberally splattered with gutter-water, sprinted after them and swung up again behind.

'Drive on!'

The curricle moved forward with a convulsive jerk, the pair rearing into action at Ned's merest indication. He prayed hard for a clear passage into Vigo Street, cornered once more on one wheel and cantered on under the trees that overhung the road from the gardens of Burlington House.

'Take us straight into the mews, Ned,' August said anxiously, 'We don't want to cause a confusion outside the house.'

'Her Ladyship might care to go shopping –?' Ned was grinning.

'Oh yes, I'm sure – right through the shop-doors.'

The horses' flying manes were decorated with the golden sparks of fallen leaves, yellow and red. Ned, smelling the gardens and dung-heaps and thinking of the horses at home, to match this wild pair, was infected with the same abandon as their Lordships, and equal excitement at all that lay ahead. No one could say life was dull, whatever else. He laughed, judging their entry through the archway into the yard with an intuitive eye, and summoning all his newly-improved strength to pull up before they went straight through the stable wall.

'Well done! Well done!'

August and Railton jumped down and ran to the horses' heads and the grooms all ran out to see the new excitement and shake Ned's hand and ask after his life with Captain Barclay.

'We've all got money on you, sir! Six to four they're offering at Ladbroke's –'

'I've staked a thousand!' August declared, 'Railton here stands to lose his new French cook to Francis Tilbury if you lose, and even her Ladyship has wagered an emerald tiara to James's set of gold plate!'

'There's as much interest as if it's a Championship – seeing as how it's a fight to settle a difference. And the Captain himself says it'll be good. He sends spies up to Mendoza's –'

Ned climbed down into the gossip, feeling his feet touch the ground again, and reality take hold. He tried to pretend that the talk didn't concern him, but it was hard to show indifference. He wasn't an actor, amongst his many parts. Thinking about it coolly, faced with the eagerness of his friends, he knew that the match was the most important thing that loomed closely in a great many lives, not only his own. Not least in Ironminster's. It didn't do to dwell on this fact, if he was to remain calm.

9

B Y THE day of the fight, Ned was fit and restless and keyed up, feeling very strange and tense, and glad that there were people looking after him like a prize race-horse, handling him, telling him what to do, soothing him. He had convinced himself that he was too keen to fight to be nervous, but the feeling was worse than plain nervousness; it was almost impossible for him to keep still, to relax. He could not make ordinary conversation or listen to what was going on round him, only think of what lay ahead, bitterly anxious to get started. The coach-ride to Threadgolds seemed interminable. They would not let him drive, nor even sit outside, but made him sit by the open window and rest and fill his lungs with air. August and Railton and Mr Jackson rode with him, and Barclay and half the members of the Pugilistic Club outside, and on the road with them a monstrous stream of fight-goers stretched away ahead and behind in all manner of vehicles, as if it was a championship. Ned had expected nothing like this but, the way he felt, it seemed quite unimportant. He hardly noticed. The day was very cold, with a heavy frost hardening the ruts.

'But by midday it will be splendid for your match,' Mr Jackson told him. 'Splendid fighting weather, air like wine. But keep warm now. Warm and quiet. Save all your strength.'

They wrapped blankets round him but would give him nothing to eat or drink. He felt dried out, spare, on edge, constrained by the jolting dark interior of the coach. August and Railton, very excited, were eating chicken out of a hamper and even the professional Mr Jackson was quietly anticipatory, glancing at the watch in his waistcoat pocket. He was to act as referee. Railton and Sam were to act as Ned's seconds. The fight would continue until one man was unable to get up, and how long that would take there was no way of knowing.

'You must watch out for that blow we were talking about, Ned. Under the ear, to fracture the blood-vessels.' Railton tossed his chicken-bone out of the window. 'They say Rupert has been working on it. It's new.'

'Nothing's new,' said Jackson. 'Leave him.'

Ned stared out of the window. By tonight he would no doubt be in a quite different condition but at the moment he felt as presumably his overfit horses felt faced with the exigencies of Piccadilly when they wanted several miles of galloping space to work off their impatience. He could not stop shifting about, biting his finger-nails (which tasted of horse-radish and vinegar) and stretching his legs first one way, then the other. Never had Railton's horses covered the ground so slowly. Ned thought he could do it more quickly running.

The Threadgolds trees were yellow, black skeletons showing through, the ground mashed with thick, damp leaves. The carriage did not make for the house, but away beyond the coverts to the farm, where Ned had never been before. The drive which gave on to the North gates and the village was a winding mass of carts and pedestrians, like a procession. Ned watched it, no longer surprised. He scarcely felt that it concerned him. A thinning mist glazed detail; the park was dim and shimmering, breath making webby clouds into the breath-coloured sky, the horses steaming. Ned could feel the moisture in his nose and on his eyelashes, as if it was still dawn.

'How do you feel?' August asked him, anxious, smiling.

Ned could not reply. He didn't know.

Their carriage got held up by a winding queue of vehicles and people. There were people everywhere. It was like a hanging. Ned had seen a hanging or two and didn't like it. August put his head out of the window and shouted to the coachman, and the horses moved on, outriders forcing a way. A lot of people called out to them and peered in the windows and thumped on the roof, all very good-humoured. Ned leaned back and shut his eyes, not wanting to be involved, and Railton threw out some more chicken bones and wiped his face on a napkin.

'We're not late. We're in nice time. Half-past eleven, is it? Saville's coming from home, so there'll be no hold-up there.'

The ring had been marked out with posts and ropes behind the big threshing-barn and was already thickly surrounded with spectators. The farm wagons had been pulled out to make grandstands, creaking to their unusual burdens. On the far side of the ring Ned saw the Saville drag with its team of greys, cloths thrown over their backs.

Faces crowded round, pressing against the windows, but the officials brought by Mr Jackson, in their liveries of dark blue and buff, quickly cleared them away and opened the door.

'Come.' Mr Jackson touched his elbow.

Ned got out, surrounded closely by his team, the redoubtable Sam appearing at his shoulder, grinning with excitement. Ned had asked for him to be a second, having great faith in his mending skills and no less in his mere friendship. A face veered out of the crowd, pushing hoarsely against an official.

'Ned! Ned! Your father's got five pound on you – he sent me to tell you –'

It was his younger brother Robert, sent packing before Ned could get a word to him. Ned strained after him, shouting his name, but was hauled back by several hands.

'It's my brother!'

'You can see him afterwards. He won't run away.'

Their father wasn't a betting man . . . five pounds! Ned felt it more keenly than Ironminster's reputed thousand, not to mention Railton's cook, and was assailed by a desperate pang of hopeless homesickness and a sudden longing for his mother, no doubt brought on by the precariousness of his situation. His family . . . he hadn't given any of them a thought for months.

'No time now, Ned. They're all here, don't you worry, your brother, the Pope, the Archbishop of Canterbury –' Sam's little grey eyes gleamed with anticipation. 'Forget 'em for now, lad. It's only Saville you've got to worry about.'

Sam was unbuttoning Ned's coat. Ned didn't feel he was ready, the breath coming fast and the sweat of sudden fright greasing his palms. God Almighty, he must be mad, making an exhibition of himself before all these people, for no cause of his own!

'I don't –'

'Keep quiet. Save yourself.'

They were at the corner of the ring, its waiting empty square the only space for miles. It looked virgin, desirable. Ned couldn't wait, forgetting his mother, remembering the curling black hair on Saville's chest (Railton had told him about it). He started to jig with impatience. 'You're barmy, Ned!' Sam was laughing. Over his shoulder Ned saw Ironminster leaning on the ropes watching him, his face very white, with the familiar spots of colour flaring over the cheekbones. He was no longer laughing and talking, but completely alone, although surrounded by people. Ned, seeing him, felt his way into the required state of relaxed determination; it came easily, suddenly, so that he felt very fit and calm and perfectly ready to face Saville. Sam took his neckcloth and waistcoat, and then his shirt, and Ned felt the cold on his tense body, and felt very alone. The crowd had been hounded back, and now fell quiet, posted by Mr Jackson's liveried men. It was so quiet for a moment that Ned heard a cow lowing sadly away in the park, lamenting its slain calf. He climbed into the ring and walked slowly across the grass to the scratch, where Mr Jackson was waiting alone, familiar but unsmiling. It was very cold. Ned could feel the goose-pimples coming up on his bare flesh. From the other corner Rupert Saville, looking much larger than Ned remembered him, approached with similar caution, dressed in dark purple drawers and lilac stockings, regal to Ned's unremarkable drab. They faced each other and shook hands. Rupert's hand was as cold as his own, Ned remarked. It seemed a long time since he had fought with bare hands; the hard clasp of bony fingers emphasized the seriousness of what they were about. It was a quite different business from fighting in mufflers.

'There will be half a minute to get back to scratch after a fall. No hitting or grasping below the waist, no unnecessary dropping.' Jackson frisked them both down the thighs, smiled, said, 'Good luck, gentlemen. You may proceed,' and stepped back.

Ned had time to take in his adversary. It seemed, in fact, that they stood there for some time considering each other, very much aware of what was at stake. Rupert was heavier and thicker than Ned. Ned saw the thickness of the muscles on his torso, rounded and rippling like sculptored Greek muscles, and the fanlike pattern of fine black hair across his chest. His neck was very thick and strong (one day it would be heavy and jowled like his brother's) and he held his head high and imperiously – vulnerably so, Ned noted, and acted on it. His first quick punch to the haughty jaw landed, bone stinging on bone with a sharp reminder of what it was to be ungloved, but before Ned had time to contemplate any more of Saville's beauty he was equally reminded of its strength by a quick reply to his diaphragm which hurt – already! Ned, frightened, flung back, to show that he hadn't felt it, and they both milled in wildly, forgetting science, angered by the first blows. Ned, aware of hurting already in a lot of places, and breathless, remembered that his mentors thought that stamina would see him through – how long did it take, by God, hurling punches like this? It seemed that they hadn't been at it more than ten seconds, and he was already panting and stinging and grunting and not at all sure of what was going on . . . surely he knew more than this? It was nothing like it had ever been in the gymnasium, where he remembered it as warm and friendly and the punches padded and not made with malice. These punches were like knives, and there was blood all over his hands already, although where it came from there was no way of knowing. Rupert had blood on his face. Ned hoped it was Rupert's own. He flung him off desperately and withdrew, considering, trying to control his breath. He was supposed to be very fit – but Rupert's splendid chest was heaving too. He no longer held his head high, but tucked it down, and his imperious expression had changed to one of mean anger, the thick, handsome lips tightened with pain. Ned knew he ought to have more control of what was happening, but perhaps this was what made amateurs what they were – he didn't think Rupert had controlled what had happened there any more than he had. They circled each other cautiously and Ned decided to be more clever – concentrate in hitting one vulnerable place, an eye possibly. Having decided this, he then missed a lighten-ing move on Rupert's part and received a blow to his own eye that nearly put him down. He staggered back, dropping his hands, and Rupert followed, flailing madly at his head and landing most of his blows, for Ned was too muzzy to protect himself. He came up against the ropes, ducked sideways and Rupert's hand whistled over his shoulder. Ned, not too far gone to realize that Rupert was momentarily off balance, straightened up in time to barge him completely through the ropes, where he landed on his back. Jackson came up and directed them to their corners for the required half-minute. It had all seemed to Ned very quick indeed, and very painful.

'Eight minutes,' Railton said. 'That was clever, getting him down like that. You needed a breather.'

Eight minutes, Ned thought. No wonder he was short of breath.

'Just sit and breathe,' Railton said. 'Breathe deeply.'

Only thirty seconds to rest. Whose blood was it? Sam was dabbing at him with a towel. Perhaps it would be better not to know. Sam was frowning. Ned took breaths right down into his lungs.

'Come on,' Railton said, and pushed him to his feet and back out into the ring again. Saville converged on the scratch, not with any great eagerness. No doubt he was thinking, like Ned, that it was the longest eight minutes and the shortest thirty seconds he had ever experienced. Ned, looking carefully, saw that Rupert's sponged face was revealing a small cut on the cheekbone. He should try and get that opened up, and with luck it might swell enough to affect the sight. At the same moment, before any punches had been exchanged, he felt a warm trickle of blood down his own cheek. Some of it was his own, then. Equal so far. And remember the nasty idea Railton had broached – something about blood vessels under the ear. He might try that himself. Someone had to start. All this time they had been circling cautiously, fists up, waiting for the other to start the action. Seeing his moment Ned led out straight and fast with a blow to Rupert's ear that, judging by how much it hurt his hand, must have rocked the Saville brains. Saville let out a loud, anguished grunt, almost a howl, and flung back at Ned in his wild and dangerous manner, blow after blow which Ned managed to parry for the most part, before succumbing to a stinger high up on the cheek. He felt himself swung round, but was in no danger of falling. He moved back and let Rupert come after him, realizing how wildly the man fought and hoping to catch him as he had the first time. He ducked anxiously, saw Rupert stumble after a miss and managed to get his elbow round the back of Rupert's neck and get his head in a lock under his arm. With his free hand he pummelled at what parts of the body he could find, but the situation wasn't very advantageous. Rupert retaliated with a grasp round the abdomen which forced Ned to let go, but with his freed hand he forced Rupert's head up with his palm against his nostrils and caught him a splendid blow across the throat.

Rupert went over backwards, falling heavily.

'He fights like a mad bull,' Railton said. 'No science at all but – by God – don't be caught by one of his swings. How are your hands?'

Ned stretched them out, palms down. The knuckles were red and sore but not yet bleeding.

'Good man. Off you go.'

Having taken the measure of each other and warming to the occasion, the fight, in a sense, was only just starting. Ned had a feeling of settling down, of having learned what he was up against. First blood had been called, the first, instinctive fears vanquished, the temper warmed, the body sharpened. Perhaps this feeling, of eagerness, excitement even, of cool, avid desire to hurt his opponent, was the fighting spirit, the 'bottom', so admired by followers of the sport. He felt coldly determined to fight until it was no longer physically possible, and not for any high ideal – Ironminster was now as far from his thoughts as his own mother – but because it was the only purpose in his life, sharpened by the preliminaries into a zeal he hadn't known before that he possessed. Whether Rupert felt like this as well, Ned had no way of knowing, but he certainly displayed an equal determination. Toe to toe they stood, watching, weaving, hitting, ducking, feinting, hitting. Rupert's wildness, perhaps born of nerves, had calmed into a more dangerous accuracy, but Ned felt he had the edge on him in speed, in seeing an opening, a slight advantage in reaction. But Rupert, with more weight, packed a heavier punch. Ned started to go down under them, although never losing his senses, merely glad for thirty seconds recovery. His knuckles opened up, and he assumed, although he could not see himself, that he was in as nasty a state as Rupert, with blood flowing from eyes, nose and mouth.

'Very equal,' Barclay judged. 'Good boys, both of them. A very nice fight, very nice indeed.'

Mr Jackson, eyes on his watch, nodded in agreement. 'I've seen worse championships.'

'It's like animals,' Matty said to Mrs Burns, her eyes full of tears, her teeth biting into her muff as she held her hands up to her mouth. 'It shouldn't be allowed. It's all wrong.'

'It isn't allowed, dear.' Mrs Burns comforted her. 'But there – you can see – Mr Strange, the magistrate, he's sitting in the wagon there. He's got ten pounds on Mr Saville, the silly old fool. Don't cry, lovey. You'll have your Ned Rowlands to look after when they take him home, if you're lucky. I doubt he'll be out driving much for a week or two, whether he wins or not.'

'He's my brother,' Robert Rowlands told all assembled round him, and they all congratulated him and pushed him nearer to the front, until he was right beside the Ironminster corner.

'He's my brother,' he said to Sam. 'I'm Ned's brother.'

'Well, I hope your head's as thick,' Sam told him. 'Keep out of the way.'

The sun was coming through, although it was now after-noon, very faint and warm-breathing and not dispersing the late October mist, through which the distant cows kept on lowing.

'It's getting dark' Ned said to Sam.

'No, you fool. Wipe your face. I bet it's darker in Saville's corner. Take some water.'

He forced the bottle between the swollen, split lips. 'Only a mouthful. That's enough. Take deep breaths now. You can still see all right, can't you? Your right eye's all right. Saville's is worse by far. Get up now. It's time. Get moving.'

Ironminster's face was now more grey than white. Railton, glancing at him, handed him the brandy flask reserved for Ned.

'I didn't know it would go like this,' Ironminster said to him.

'So well?'

'I thought it would be easy.'

'For Ned? August, it's a splendid fight. You're too involved to see it. I've never seen a crowd enjoying themselves so much, really getting their moneysworth.'

'He can throw in the sponge. You mustn't stop him, Alex, whatever the outcome.'

'You're talking rubbish. There's no thought of it.'

'But if it goes worse for him, it's for you to judge, Alex.'

'He's no thought of it yet.'

'They're both very tired.'

'He'll go up to scratch a lot more times yet.'

Ned was beginning to understand what Captain Barclay had said about legs. It was his legs that felt so weak. The punishment to his head and body did not bother him, but his legs were drained and slow. But Rupert was slowing too. He knew they were getting near the end and, although they were falling a lot, the falls were more from weakness than any power to the blows. He wanted to finish it decisively with a good one, but so did Saville, and they circled each other, shaking their heads to flick the blood away, blundering in heavily if there was an opening, but only managing to maul and mangle and push. Ned had a strange feeling that his strength was still there, if only he had the will-power to summon it. Three times he put Rupert down, but each time he made it back to scratch, pushed by his seconds, at the last count of Jackson's second-hand. At the next encounter, they lay off, circling, by mute consent recovering strength. The crowd was utterly silent. Ned, wiping bloody eyes with yet bloodier knuckles, felt that very soon, somewhere, he would see his chance. He felt that he had the edge on Saville. Did Saville feel it? A fraction of a second's lack of concentration . . . Ned saw Saville's hand coming, ducked, but not in time. It was as if the sky had fallen on him, with the sound of thunder in his ears, splitting his skull. He could feel himself falling, but not only to the ground, surely . . .? It felt as if to Hades. He clawed frantically with his hands, reaching up, searching for air, for light, for sense.

'Keep still! Keep still!'

He didn't know where he was, only that he must get back on his feet. Something held him down.

'Open your mouth, you fool! Ned! Ned!

They were hitting him, slapping him. Water trickled into his mouth. No, it wasn't water any more. It was firewater, seeping agonizingly into his cut lips. He struggled, swallowed, choked.

'Get up! Move, move!'

He wanted to, more than willing, but his legs, his Captain Barclay-trained legs, would not work. They dragged him out to scratch, the crowd no longer silent but screaming encouragement. Rupert's seconds were there too, Ned noticed. It was a gang-fight, all six milling in the centre of the ring.

Mr Jackson spoke sharply.

'Thirty seconds! Clear the ring!'

Ned shook his head, managing to stand, swaying, searching for Saville. Rupert, to his speckled vision, was a monstrous weaving pillar of mottled hues, red and purple, the curling black hairs on his chest marbled with blood. Ned put up his hands, reaching, pushing. He wanted to lean on Saville and hammer him, but his hands were like butterflies to the red petals of Saville's splattered face. They leaned on each other, pushing and clawing and feeling the rasping breath snoring, bubbling. They both fell together, crawled apart.

Sam ran icy water over him. The crowd roared. Matty had run away, sobbing, alone, but Mrs Burns sat munching currant buns, enjoying every moment of her afternoon off. Dr Redbridge, attending in a professional capacity, for the end of the bout, stood by his gig, dispassionate, not filled with love for his fellow creatures. He thought Ironminster was probably more in need of immediate medical care than either of the participants in the fight, but Ironminster was not his customer.

'Time, gentlemen!'

Ned stood, arms hanging, summoning up every last ounce of his failing strength. Having come so far, it surely must be his victory . . . he needed not the strength of his body but the last breaking thread of his will-power, for he knew when the next black cloud fell it would not clear in thirty seconds; it would hold him in blessed oblivion for an hour. He lifted his hands, stepped back to avoid the great mangled paws reaching for him, and in an instant saw his opportunity clear and shining as a mountain stream. He felt cold and certain and utterly convinced, then and for ever, that he had been visited by a miracle. His vision cleared, his judgement was perfect; his fist came up and with a blow compounded of every last despairing fibre of his virtually beaten body, he caught Rupert full on the point of his jaw, felling him like an oak-tree struck by lightning, spread-eagled on his back with his eyeballs turned up in his head in undoubted cold unconsciousness.

Mr Jackson came up with his watch closely held, raising up his other hand against the unholy outbreak of the crowd, and waited in his small island of still silence for the official expiry of the thirty seconds. When it was passed he smiled at Ned, held out his hand, closing his own enormous grasp very tenderly over the agony of Ned's pulped fist, and said, 'You've won, Mr Rowlands. I congratulate you on a very fine fight.' In all the swirling screaming hubbub that was now spilling towards them, it was a very intimate, private, passing moment of – for Ned – utter and perfect fulfilment, never to be shaken by the bestiality of how it was won. He never wanted to fight again, but to feel that moment, he would not have missed a single minute of the ordeal – neither that already passed nor that yet to come – before he resumed life again as the coachman he was supposed to be.

IO

SAM, once a campaigner in Spain under Wellesley, serving the late Lord Ironminster, rubbed Ned's wounds with salt despite his screaming, and laid raw beef over the slits where his eyes were. The broken hands he spread with lard and leaves of woundwort and wrapped in linen bandages. Dr Redbridge, arriving from Mole End to examine Ned some two hours later, dosed him heavily with laudanum and said he could do no more.

'He's in better shape than the loser, if that's any comfort to the household. You may send for me if he becomes delirious. I shall call tomorrow in any case.'

August was standing looking out of the window on to the drive, where the lamps of the doctor's gig made blurred pools of light in the foggy dusk. Redbridge, putting away his bottles, said, 'It would pay you, August, to stay quietly at home while this fog is about. These excitements don't suit you.'

'No.'

August turned round to the light. He looked much older than twenty-three, the doctor observed, particularly at this moment.

'I ought to be celebrating downstairs with the others,' he said. 'But I don't very much feel like it. I think the fight took almost as much out of me as it did out of Ned.'

'Not surprising, under the circumstances.'

'I didn't know what I was asking.'

'You have a spirit that inspires devotion.' The doctor spoke drily, yet with perfect sincerity. August did not know how to reply. He felt feverish and hard-pressed and desperate again, in the way that he was used to revealing to Ned; he thought the fight would have resolved a whole lot of things but after the diversion, the excitement, was over, it was, as always, plain that his path, whatever he might do, was not deviating one inch from its gloomy, rapid course to extinction. Ned's courage, at that moment, altered nothing. It had made August deeply ashamed. His hands trembled. Perhaps he was a little bit drunk.

'I wish things might have been different.'

Redbridge, touched, fumbled back in his case for some opium pills.

'I wish it too. Take these – you need something.' On the Saville port he was perhaps slightly mazed too. The irony of offering August pills for his perfectly sane contemplation of the inevitable was not lost on him. August was possibly stronger than any of them. Both of them, afraid of what they had revealed, searched for cheer and normality.

'You mustn't worry about your coachman here. He'll soon get over his trouncing. Sooner than Mr Saville, who has no victory to cheer him.'

'Rupert fought well. I admire him for it.'

'The result hasn't improved the Saville temper. Rupert, in his stupor, was muttering vengeance.'

'Not another fight, I hope?'

'No. I think Mr Field's wager was on his mind.'

'The wager is what started this fight in the first place. Thanks to Rupert, I no longer have a team. I have four horses, but we haven't tried them together yet.'

'I don't think these hands' – the doctor gestured towards the bed – 'are going to hold reins easily for a while. Rupert has two broken fingers, which will take time to mend.'

August was interested. Redbridge's news had cheered him better than his pills. 'Time enough, perhaps, for our horses to learn each others' ways? Ned's bones aren't broken.'

'You hold that advantage then.'

'The roads are deteriorating, though. It could only be done in the right conditions. A lot of wind to dry the mud, or perhaps the frost.'

Dr Redbridge laughed. 'You feel better for my news? Let's hope your man here has as fast a recuperation! Is Sam in charge of the nursing? Someone should sit up here tonight –'

'Yes. We'll fetch Matty up. She's a splendid nurse, I can vouch for her when one has a fever – so much prettier than Sam.'

'Excellent. I will call and see him again in the morning then. I can let myself out, my Lord.'

'No, sir, I will come down with you.'

Matty, sitting before the embers of the fire during the long night, listening to Ned's drugged breathing, remembered another fire and an earth floor, and Ned in the part of nurse, a far more reluctant nurse than she was now. She had grown ten years since then, she felt. Her animal terror had repulsed Ned. She had never forgotten his impatience, his anger and his tenderness. The night he had brought her from London on the brown mare it had been the same, and the dark afternoon of the coach accident and the dreadfully wounded Esmeralda: she would not have loved him if he had been what he seemed, if she had not seen the unexpected compassion.

Not that it made him a good patient, not a fraction as enduring as his much-practised Lordship. He complained bitterly: he could not see, he could not breathe through his swollen nose nor eat with lacerated lips and tongue; he could not use his hands. There was a ringing in his ears and his head throbbed constantly; his body ached all over; his legs were seized with violent cramps.

'And you the winner!' Matty murmured. 'How lucky that you weren't beaten! You'd have good reason to complain then.'

But it hurt too much even to talk. Ned, not quite sure where or what he was, who tended him, whose were the voices he heard, whose hands working over his multitude of pains, forcing foul liquids down his throat, found it hard to equate his condition with victory. He wasn't certain what had happened, and did not remember the end of the fight, nor Mr Jackson's congratulations nor anything thereafter.

'Do you remember me, then? Matty?' Matty was happy with her role, and Sam laughed at her devotion.

'Would you do it for me?' he asked her, bringing Ned's dinner on a tray.

'No.'

'Do you hear that, Ned? She's got you where she wants you. You'd better watch out.'

'Yes, that's what I'm afraid of.'

'He's getting better fast. He can see the danger he's in. Eh, Ned? He's talking sense now. He'll start running soon, Matty, and you'll have lost your chance. Give him this now, and don't get it on the sheets.'

Matty laughed. 'I shall run after him.'

Ned, improving, was in no position to disregard Matty's charms and was not, in fact, averse to being comforted in the wakeful small hours by Matty's thin warm arms round him, cradling his head on her breast.

'Is this how you nursed his Lordship, then?' he asked her. 'Getting into bed with him?'

'Ah, no, poor fellow. It's what he needs. He needs Miss Redbridge in his bed.'

Ned, seeing the moonlight shining in bright fenestrations flung across the bedroom wall, remembered the night he had waited. He said nothing, spiked with unutterable pity for Ironminster, barred from his Sarah.

'She came to see you,' Matty said.

Ned was startled. 'Miss Redbridge?'

'She was with his Lordship. She was sorry for you, almost in tears. But you were too busy groaning to notice.'

Ned was indignant, annoyed. It was not the picture he would have preferred to make for Miss Redbridge. Matty laughed at him. He shifted away from her, but her arms brought him back. His condition was his only defence.

'You are hurting me.'

'Ah, there!' She laid her cheek against his. He had the beginnings of a red-gold beard between the scabs and bruises over his face, which she stroked tenderly. His sores glistened with Sam's woundwort ointment. He could not help smiling at her devotion in face of such detractions.

'I think I am getting better,' he said, knowing it by the way his blood was stirring. 'I shall go down to the stables tomorrow.'

'They won't let you. You can't work yet.'

'I want to see the horses.'

'I don't want you to get better.'

'Those are kind words! Do you want me all scabby and swollen for ever?'

'At least you're here, all scabby and swollen. When you're fit and handsome you're away out all the time. You're not going back to London, are you?'

'I hope not.'

'Do you like being a coachman?'

'Most of the time. Not when it means waiting about.'

'They are nice to work for here. I told you – that's why I love you. Because you brought me here.'

He was silent, remembering her with her eyes like stones, waiting for him in the gutter. He had so nearly left her.

'Where did Kit find you?'

She kissed the swellings round his eye, very gently. 'I was walking along the road, and he came by. He was nearly as handsome as you. I liked him.'

'Where were you going?'

'Nowhere. I was running away, and I had no money and no food and I was frightened. He was kind.'

'Where were you running away from?'

'The parish put me out to a dressmaker in Bermondsey. He was horrible. He starved us and made us work all night.'

'Have you no home? No parents?'

'No. Well, everyone has parents, but I don't know 'em. I was brought up in the workhouse, but they put you out at ten. I worked in several places, till the dressmaker, then I couldn't stand that and I ran away. I don't know what would have happened without Kit. And then you.'

Ned watched the moonlight, feeling her caresses, gentle as butterflies. He had never had much time, ordinarily, to consider the human condition, and he was soberly impressed by his own luck, hearing Matty, thinking on Ironminster. Poor Kit. Poor Sarah Redbridge.

'I was frightened of you,' he said. 'They said you bit.'

'Not nice people.' She kissed him again.

'Truly, do you nurse his Lordship like this?'

'No. I just do what Sam says. It's quite different. Besides, he's not like you. He never complains, however bad it is.'

'I'm not complaining,' Ned said softly.

'At this moment, why should you? But you will.'

He did, endeavouring to get dressed with Sam's help, feeling as weak as a new-born foal, and as feeble on his legs. His head ached at every move and he could see everything twice over. He thought he could easily cry.

'That blow that put you down – that's what did the damage. Shook you to the bottom of your brains. But think what our friend Mr Saville must be feeling, if it's any comfort.' Sam was both brisk and gentle. 'It's only three days. It's very soon,

Ned, to be moving. Sit here by the fire. I'll fetch you Ironminster's dressing-gown.'

Which was how Ironminster found him shortly afterwards. Ned attempted to stand up, but was glad to be waved back into his chair.

'So soon, Ned! That's splendid. I didn't think to see you on your feet for a day or two yet.'

'I'm not, my Lord. That's the trouble.'

'Out of bed. It's a start. More than Saville. He's got two broken fingers, Ned, did you know? Won't be on the ribbons for a while, according to Redbridge.'

Ned felt sick enough to consider exactly what part of his own anatomy Rupert had broken his fingers on. It could have been any one of a number of places, the way he felt. But he wasn't so far gone that he did not recognize the edge of decisiveness in the way Ironminster spoke. He was planning something, Ned felt: another of the eternal panaceas for his own condition. Ned had begun to recognize the way August kept himself going.

'I understand he's set on beating us to winning Andrew's money, Ned. Even more so, since losing this round to you. We mustn't let him, Ned.'

So that was it. Ned saw the task before him.

'Get our team going before Rupert's fingers mend? Is that it? But the roads –'

'The roads are the same for us all. There's just a chance we might do it – not a good one, I grant you. But not for Rupert.'

'And Starling? I wanted to get up to see him – but I wasn't as good as I thought. His hock looked as if it would take time. More time than our new horses.'

'Well, I've looked at him, and I feel quite hopeful. It's gone very nicely. He walks out sound already. The joint wasn't hurt. Esmeralda, of course, is out. She's alive, but that's all one can say of her. She might be better put down. You can decide.'

August got up and walked to the window. He stood looking across the park, very thoughtful. Ned waited, aware that on August's whims his own fate was decided. Not, he hoped, as painful a fate as resulted from the last little diversion.

'Alex and I had an idea . . .'

August turned round slowly, saw Ned's expression and laughed. 'I'm sorry! You look nervous. I can understand –' He came back to the fire. His eyes, catching the firelight, sparkled in Ned's unclear vision; Ned felt rather sick. 'It will be difficult, making plans, you understand. So much will depend on the weather – if we can do it at all. But the same for Rupert. We were thinking –' He paused, uncertain. 'It depends on what you think, because you will have to do it.' He then had the grace to add, 'Again.' And smile.

'Do what, my Lord?'

The warmth and fevour in August's voice was unmistakeable. 'Think of it, Ned. Rupert will be out to do it as soon as he is ready. The weather will decide it. How about if, as soon as he decides to go, we go too, at the same time? Give him the road, let him make the pace most of the way, and then – to beat him – go past.'

Ned shut his eyes against the feeling of sickness. 'Easily *said* . . .' Difficult to do. 'If he won't let us –'

'We can force him.'

'He will use his whip on our leaders.'

'He cannot go against the rules of the road. It is a match on the public road. There will be a referee.'

'It will be a race.'

'Perhaps.'

'It could be done, if we are good enough.'

'Oh, but why not, Ned? Of course we're good enough.'

'And how do we know when he starts? Do we have to keep all ready, day and night, harnessed up, ready to go?'

'He spied easily enough on us, Ned. We can use his tricks surely? Even the same boy – what was his name? He can be our spy. We'll find him.'

'I beat him hard enough. I doubt he'll come back.'

'Oh, yes. It can be arranged. Or another, it makes no difference. Sam can work it out. Besides, we'll know when to expect it, if the weather is suitable. It might never be, of course, if the winter is wet.' A note of regret damped August's excitement for a moment. Ned opened his eyes and looked upon August's irrepressible enthusiasm for what was difficult, dangerous and doubtful, and felt a lot better.

'I don't see why we shouldn't try it like that. We could give your cousin an anxious ride, whatever happens. He won't like it.'

'He'll be beside himself with rage. That will be worth it alone.'

'We don't know how those horses go yet.'

'No.'

Ned could see August taking stock of his condition and working out how long it would be before he was back at his job. He was too considerate to inquire, in fact was embarrassed by the implications of wishing him a speedy recovery. 'You mustn't think I —'

'You cannot wish me sooner back at work than I wish myself,' said Ned. 'I'm not at home in sick-rooms.'

'Would that I could say the same! But thanks to me we've well-trained nurses in the house. Sam tells me that you are receiving the best – the tenderest – of care —' August was laughing. 'Not, I gather, from him alone.'

Ned scowled, wishing damnation on Sam. August said, 'Don't be angry. I've few enough secrets from you, God knows. I only hope your affairs might bring you greater satisfaction than mine. I can tell you, Ned, I'm glad to be back here, safe from the marriage-mongers up in town. I shall avoid all Amhersts like the plague in future. I shall not stay in London again.'

At this apt moment Sam knocked on the door and announced that Miss Redbridge had called and was waiting in the morning-room.

'Bring her up here, Sam,' August said. 'Serve coffee up here, and try to avoid my mother.'

'Yes, my Lord.'

Ned straightened up uneasily but August said, 'Be still, Ned. It is you she has come to see. She is very concerned about you.'

Ned would like to have believed this assurance, but his vision was not impaired so badly that he could not see whose well-being Sarah was truly concerned with. In a heavy brown cloak, the hood thrown back and her hair dishevelled by the wind, her cheeks glowing, she was a tonic more powerful than any of Sam's draughts.

'Oh, Ned, what good progress you are making! Up so soon – you were scarcely conscious when I saw you last.'

Ned, remembering Matty's words, felt the blushes rising

again – hidden, he hoped fervently, by the scabs and stubble.

'I'm not convinced it was a good idea of Lord Ironminster's, even with your winning. So much suffering – even on your part, August –'

'You've been listening to your father, Sarah,' August said, smiling. 'Ned knows our grievance against the Savilles. You never saw our horses dragged out of that pond. We've settled a score – it's finished now, and Ned will be mended sooner than Esmeralda.'

'I wasn't forced.'

August laughed. 'There, you hear him? Not physically forced, but in every other respect –' August shrugged and made a face. 'Ned is used to our ways now. To be fair, I only ask him to do what I would be glad to do myself – would have been glad to do, a few years back. I fought often enough at Eton.'

'There, Ned, I'm sure that's great encouragement! What he got up to at Eton is legendary. Have you heard? Do you know what's in store –?'

'You are mocking!' August took her cloak. 'Ned believes me, eh, Ned? We have to have something to look forward to, besides the accounts, the year's price for corn and the complaints of our tenants. We mustn't be bored, must we?'

The bitter implication behind his words was softened by a wry smile. But, recognizing self-pity, he quickened again into genuine pleasure at Sarah's company, pulling up a chair before the fire close to his own. Sam brought the coffee and served it and Ned, strangely included in the circle, was witness again to the intimacy that existed between August and Sarah. Their being together was so content, their spirits apparently untouched by the dark conditions of their relationship, that Ned was struck even more deeply by August's resilience. Pity was out of place; instead, Ned felt envious of August's astonishing capacity for happiness. August, for all his doomed prospects – or perhaps because of them – was likely to encompass a normal lifetime's experience of both joy and sorrow in a quarter of the span, which Ned began to appreciate was not necessarily to make him a subject of compassion. By the time he had departed to escort Sarah to see the new horses, it was Ned who, aching and dizzy, retching miserably into a bowl held by the brisk and efficient Matty, felt in dire need of sympathy. Beside such a triumphant happiness, it was his own immediate future that seemed far more in need of encouragement. August required nothing from him save his physical strength but at that moment, by comparison with Ironminster's riches, Ned knew he had nothing to offer.

11

'I DON'T know as how you let his Lordship saddle us with these two brutes, I'm sure, sir,' was Pegram's greeting to Ned when he resumed work in the stable-yard. 'The boys are all scared to go near 'em. You look, they haven't been properly groomed since they came, but I can't do nothing about it. Wicked around the hind-legs they are, I'm warning you.'

Having examined Starling and grieved over Esmeralda's scars, Ned was not feeling particularly happy by the time he came to the new wheelers. Nor was his mood improved by Matty arriving with a message from her Ladyship to say she needed the carriage.

'Pegram can drive her. Tom and Miles, get Apollo and Hyacinth ready, and Pegram, you go and get some proper clothes on. If she doesn't like it, she should have put her orders in earlier, tell her.'

Matty giggled. 'Shall I tell her? Do you mean it?'

'If she asks, Pegram can explain.'

'She's going to visit Mr Saville to see how he is. She thinks it's her duty. She's taking me, as her maid.'

Ned raised her eyebrows. 'Really?' But Ironminster had probably not told his mother that the coach accident was Rupert's doing. He contrived to tell her very little, Ned knew. He smiled. 'Maid, eh? Is that promotion?'

'It's not as good as nursing,' Matty said meaningfully.

'You keep your eyes and ears open over there, and see if you can find out what they're planning next. We'd like to have some warning next time. Or if she leaves you in the carriage, make friends with one of the boys. It could be useful.'

He grinned, taking the horse off Pegram and turning it round in its stall.

'What's it worth to you?' Matty asked softly.

'A kiss,' Ned said, pinching her bottom.

When the carriage had departed with the reluctant Pegram, Ned got the new pair harnessed to the phaeton with the help of the grooms, not without considerable difficulty. Driving them was equally difficult, although Ned was not displeased, for they were an extremely powerful pair which promised well for Ironminster's plans. Back in the stable-yard, he was not surprised to hear from Pegram that her Ladyship wanted to speak to him. He tidied himself up and walked up to the house, and was told her Ladyship was taking tea in the drawing-room. She was alone, being served by Matty, whom Ned would gladly have wished elsewhere.

'I understand you're employed as a coachman here?'

The visit did not appear to have put her in a good mood. 'I must say, one would hardly know these days that we possessed such a servant. Certainly for the last few weeks we haven't. But I understood you were now recovered from your little digression into pugilism and that we could avail ourselves of your services once more? Isn't that right?'

'Yes, my Lady.'

'Well?'

He mumbled something about having to work on the new horses.

'His Lordship chose them, I suppose?'

'Yes, my Lady.'

She sighed, and the anger visibly subsided. 'I suppose you are not to blame. His Lordship gives you a difficult time here. But what you do for him gives him his only real, abiding pleasure in life, so I must be grateful rather than otherwise. I am quite happy with those horses, the grey and the chestnut, but I like you to drive me, Ned. I like to be smart, and I'm afraid old Pegram isn't up to standard. So remember – I shall try and give you more notice.'

'Yes, my Lady.'

'Very well.'

He withdrew, annoyed at having his time wasted, but Matty contrived to excuse herself before he had crossed the hall, and ran after him, catching his arm.

'You owe me a kiss!'

Ned had not bargained on his flirtation with Matty continuing after his return to work, and certainly not on her flinging herself on him in the middle of the hall only thirty seconds from Lady Ironminster herself.

'For heaven's sake –'

'You promised! You said – if I made friends with one of the grooms at Mole End, you would pay me with a kiss –'

'Wait a minute! You work fast! Is it true? How friendly?'

'Kiss me and I'll tell you.'

He pulled her to him and kissed her briskly.

'Oh, Ned, that's no payment! It's worth more. You must keep your word!'

She lifted her face up and slipped her arms round his neck, pressing herself close, and he kissed her – not unwillingly – as she desired, which took quite a long time. They were interrupted by the sound of footsteps coming down the stairs and drew apart abruptly, but too late not to be seen. Ironminster was laughing, not at all censorious.

'Do you miss your patient then, Matty? He's mended too soon for you? Sooner than Mr Saville, my mother tells me.'

'Mr Saville's still in bed, my Lord.'

'Perhaps you should tell his Lordship what you just told me,' Ned said to her. 'About making friends at Mole End.'

'I did. I did what you said. His name is Tom Garnett and he wants to see me again.'

'What's this then?' Ironminster asked. 'Tom Garnett is a good lad. His mother used to be cook here once, till Alice Saville poached her from us.'

'I told Matty – as she went visiting there with her Ladyship – that it might be useful if she made friends in the stable-yard,' Ned explained. 'It could help us to know what's going on.'

'Oh, very shrewd, Ned. A bit risky for you – Tom Garnett's a very presentable lad these days – eh, Matty? He wants to see you again?'

'He said so.'

'Will you agree?'

'If Ned wishes it.'

'That's devotion for you, Ned. It's a good idea, I agree. By all means see what you can do. I hear you had some trouble with the new ones today, Ned? My mother wasn't overpleased at being fobbed off with Pegram. But you got them going?'

'Yes, my Lord. Very well.'

'As soon as the coach comes back we'll try them as a team, eh? We can use Apollo if Starling isn't ready. We don't want to waste time.'

'Yes, my Lord.'

Ironminster went to join his mother in the drawing-room and Ned accompanied Matty back to the kitchen, feeling slightly put out, although for no reason.

'This Garnett fellow – what's he like?'

'Tall, well-built, curly brown hair, fine features, blue eyes, a nice mouth, broad shoulders, clean, well-dressed.'

'Is that all?' Ned was now distinctly put out.

'It's your idea,' Matty said, grinning.

'Only to find out things. Not – not to let him –'

'Let him what? Kiss me? He might want to kiss me without my having to ask him! What would you say to that? Or lie down on his bed without saying that I hurt him –' She wasn't smiling, suddenly, but was quite fierce and angry. Ned felt astonished, hurt.

'But, Matty, you're –' How could he say it? She was a dear child; he wouldn't do that to her. It wasn't like that between them. Was it? He never gave her a thought when she wasn't there. Is that what was wrong, why she was so angry? For she was definitely angry.

'I won't bargain kisses with you again, Ned. I don't want favours from you! Yes, I will go with Tom Garnett, and I will tell you what he says, but not for kisses. So remember that!'

She turned abruptly and hurried back towards the drawing-room, leaving Ned feeling bewildered. Perhaps it hadn't been quite such a good idea of his after all, although he still wasn't sure where he had gone wrong. Being friends with a girl was very difficult; Ironminster himself, of so different a background and changeable in his moods, was simplicity itself; one understood him without his even having to put it in words. But Matty . . .

But Matty was, in her new role of spy, the only way of knowing what the Savilles were up to. Ned, having set in train the system, was obliged by its success to go on encouraging the liaison. Ironminster was entranced by the news Matty brought home, and gave her a guinea each time she reported to him, with encouragements which Ned found distinctly distasteful. So did Lady Ironminster.

'Really, August! As employer, you are supposed to be concerned with the girl's moral welfare, not giving her time off to go courting. She'll end up with child, then what will you do?'

'Arrange a wedding,' August said equably.

'To whom?'

'Whom she pleases.'

'I thought there was something going on between the child and Ned?'

'Yes, and this was his idea, Mother. I suspect that the idea offended her and that she is pursuing it so warmly in order to make Ned jealous. Isn't that how the female mind works?'

'It seems likely, yes. And is Ned jealous?'

'I haven't asked him, Mother. He isn't visibly so. But I would have thought he was perfectly capable of winning any girl he chooses, competition or no. I'm hardly likely to sympathize with one so remarkably superior to myself on that count.'

'What a silly thing to say. You only have to lift a finger for any number of suitable girls to give their ears to marry you, as I never tire of telling you.'

'Yes, and what hens to want such a bargain! You know who I want, Mother, and cannot have, and so the subject is closed. But this little ruse of Ned's – apparently Garnett sees Matty in the evenings and they walk in the woods, and the poor lad has very little conversation beyond his work and his employers, and so we learn all their aspirations. Apparently they think that with the winter here, and our difficult new horses, we aren't contemplating the wager again until next year, whereas they are going to spring it as soon as Rupert's fingers are mended – probably at night when there is a good moon. So far the roads have kept fairly dry – of course, if it starts to rain heavily, we can forget it. But it's promising, Mother, full of splendid possibilities. Field and Railton are praying for it to happen. If all the conditions are right, they will be over, ready and waiting.'

'And you'll make a race of it?'

'Why not? The horses are up to it. Garnett says they are feeding theirs twenty pounds of oats a day. Who says they're not in earnest?'

'Oh, I've no doubt –' Lady Ironminster shook her head. 'You've been keeping very well lately, August. You take care and wrap up well when you go. The excitement is bad for you – gets you in a sweat, and that's when you catch a chill. But keep me informed – I think I'll put a couple of hundred on you, very discreetly, of course . . .'

A distinct coolness developed between Ned and Matty.

'Tom told me today, when we lay in the hay-shed, that Mr Saville has started driving again.'

'What else did he tell you?'

'That's the only thing he told me that concerns you.'

Ned felt a violence rise within him, which he had to stifle. He had met Garnett at the blacksmith's and found him a disconcertingly pleasant young man, almost as handsome as Matty had made out. For some reason Ned found him intensely irritating, his very amiability offensive. He supposed he must be jealous, but he didn't know why, for he didn't think he desired Matty. But, strangely, although he couldn't understand her wiles, he felt that he knew her very well; he had a proprietary feeling over her. He resented Garnett very much.

'I didn't tell you to lie with him,' he said furiously.

'We talk there. It's warm.' She smiled, as if recollecting pleasant memories. She was only a little thing, but very self-composed, with an underlying formidability which had taken her from the gutter to her present position. Perhaps it was this that drew him to her, a sort of respect. She had rough, red, working hands, very capable, but the skin of her cheeks was as soft and pink as a child's, and she had very long eyelashes, golden-red, which he found himself examining minutely. She did not look at him. He was drawn, disconcerted. He wanted to remind her that he would pay her for her information with a kiss, but he didn't dare.

When Sam sensed the reason for Ned's ill-humour, he was hugely amused, which did not help. Ned could do without his baiting, already on edge with keeping the horses at the peak of fitness, ready to go at a moment's notice, yet having to follow an ordinary routine. The new team was nothing like as reliable and well-tuned as the old one, and took all his skill to handle, but it was very likely faster, and certainly wilder, the two leaders infected by the crazy pair behind them. The rain was holding off and the moon was waxing.

'Mr Saville is now driving without any pain and has been talking about the gooms acting as out-riders, to clear the road,' Matty reported. 'He is looking for a referee, whose word Mr Field will accept, and he's been to see the magistrate to have the time of the start witnessed.'

'All very proper,' said August, eyes gleaming.

Ned had to keep the horses harnessed at night, and himself in his livery, even in bed, for they were taking no chances. Matty could not see Garnett every day, and James and Rupert were setting no definite date, but depending on the weather.

'And we can judge the weather as well as they can,' August said. He kept in touch with Field and Railton through the pigeon-lofts, and they came twice, and a boy was set to watch the gateway out of the stable-yard at Mole End, but nothing happened.

'Tom says – Tom says the blacksmith is coming in the morning to check all their shoes,' Matty reported, coming into the stable-yard very late, when Ned was shutting up. The moon was just on full and the night clear and still, a week short of Christmas. Ned stood with his hand on the door, seeing his breath hanging, and through it Matty's upturned face, flushed and pleased and – and – how did it strike him? – *aroused* . . . her eyes were brighter than the wretched stars above her head. Ned was so angry and so frightened by his anger that he stood like a stone, afraid of grabbing at her like an animal.

'Have you just come from Tom?'

'Yes.'

'From lying with him?'

'I only tell you what you want to know, nothing else. That was the bargain. I am doing exactly what you want.'

She looked up at him, very defiant. Without her maid's clothes on, her hair springing loose in a wild red-gold halo round her face, her expression so changed from the tenderness he remembered when she had nursed him, she looked like a stranger to him. He did not understand her any more; she seemed so set on baiting him, as if she wanted to make him angry. He shrugged, hating what she was suggesting.

'You'd better tell your news to his Lordship,' he said coldly. 'It looks as if we shall go tomorrow night.'

'I'm going to ask him if I can come too. Miss Redbridge is going. And Sam. Sam is only a servant, and has done less than I have to help.'

'It won't be a comfortable ride. We could well all land in a ditch. And tempers will be running very fierce, I've no doubt.'

'I've seen more bad temper in my time than Miss Redbridge. He owes it to me, after all I've done.'

Ned wanted to ask her what she had done. He shot home the last bolt and locked the door. From the direction of the village the sound of the church bells practising for Christmas echoed across the park, very sweet and comforting, but Ned felt as forlorn as he could ever remember. He saw Matty up to the house, as manners directed, but did not go in, not wanting Sam's eyes taunting, nor to see Matty in candlelight, taking off her cloak. He went to bed and lay trying to think of the job in hand, all the difficulties that faced him to win Field's wager. They were so many that the line of thought was no more comforting than thinking about Matty. He lay with his hands behind his head, watching the moon's shadows on the damp-stained ceiling, thinking of Matty lying beside him, and the coachman's cottage that Mrs Burns said he should have. But dammit! He didn't want to get married! He was going soft in the head! He didn't know what he wanted; he only knew that he wished he was in Garnett's shoes – or even that he was back with his pains in Ironminster's guest-room; he would arrange things differently, given the chance again.

But come the morning and there was no thinking of women and regrets. The boys were set to spy on Mole End, and reported much activity, friends calling. James visiting the magistrate once more, the horses exercised only gently for half an hour, instead of their usual two. August sent for Field and Railton, who came at once, giving Ned four extra horses to see to on top of his own. Miss Redbridge came at teatime, ostensibly to play chess. Ned fed the horses early and lightly and had them harnessed, cleaned and lit the lamps on the coach, and changed into his livery. He had his supper early, on edge, and Sam reported that his Lordship and friends were all togged up ready to go, drinking hard and in fine spirits.

'And I can tell you,' he added, 'there's one of us who would rather stay at home. Just you remember, Ned, wager or no wager, I don't want to be killed tonight.'

'I'm not likely to do anything stupid. We'll have a lady on board, for a start.'

'Young Matty wants to come too, but Ironminster won't let her.'

'I should think not indeed. It's not a ride for ladies.'

Sam grinned. 'Matty wanted it as a reward for –'

Ned got to his feet. 'If you say anthing offensive, I'll smash your teeth in, Mr Arnold.'

Sam put his hands up in mock terror, laughing himself stupid. Ned despised him bitterly.

Lord Ironminster sent word for the horses to be put to. Ned fastened everything himself, double-checking, and had the horses' rugs put on. He put on his box-coat and gloves, and stamped up and down the yard, waiting. There was too much frost for his liking, the ground likely to be hard enough but too hard for the horses' good. What they were attempting was dangerous and foolish; he knew it and so did Ironminster, but that was the attraction. It had been dark for four hours but it was only eight o'clock; they could be in London by ten and in bed by midnight with any luck, like an ordinary day. But Ned had a feeling that this was to be no ordinary day. He felt tensed up and irritable, very conscious of how much depended on his skill. It wasn't going to be easy overtaking a coach that didn't want to be overtaken – although he wasn't likely to lose his job by trying on this occasion. He would have been happier without Miss Redbridge on board; he suspected that Ironminster might regret her presence too, when the moment came.

There was a quick scrunching of footsteps on the gravel and Sam appeared, running. Ned grinned, glad to see him losing his dignity.

'You're to start – collect 'em at the house. The Saville coach has just left.'

The boys whipped off the rugs and Ned picked up the reins,

threading them into his hand, not hurrying. Sam climbed up to go back to the house, and Ned climbed up after him and settled himself, nodding at the boys to let go. They all shouted 'Good luck!' and the horses plunged away, anxious to be moving after the cold wait. Ned felt their power, and his doubts dissolved, excitement taking its place. Damn the lady – if she wanted to come surely it was because her life was so dull? This ride wasn't going to be dull, whatever else.

He pulled up at the front door and Railton went to the horses' heads. Miss Redbridge was handed briskly inside. Ironminster climbed up beside Ned, and Andrew Field got up behind, Railton joining him when everyone was in place. Ned eased his reins again and Ironminster said to him, 'We should be in time to see them start. We'll wait inside the gates until they're away. I think we've plenty of time. One of the farmboys was watching their yard gate, and he came back on a pony at a gallop, so they can't be much ahead of us.'

Ironminster's face in the moonlight was chalk-white. Ned wondered spontaneously what he would do if they won the wager tonight – what the next exploit would be? No doubt Railton would help him think up something. Field was more serious, holding his time-piece in his hand, and very likely to lose five thousand pounds within the next hour or so. Enough to sober any man, Ned thought, but he was smiling. Sam was the only gloomy person aboard, hunched down under a horse-blanket and nervously watching the drive ahead. The gravel was bound with frost, crunching like glass. The horses would be knocked up for a fortnight after this, Ned thought, their legs hammered, and it would be all work, bathing and bandaging and walking out. He took a pull at his leaders, feeling the wheelers getting edgy, Brimstone letting fly once or twice but not in real earnest, thank God. To stop to untangle traces would put paid to their chances, once started.

'Steady on,' Ironminster said.

Beyond the gates of the park a small knot of people were gathered, mostly on horseback. Their surprise at the appearance of the Ironminster coach was evident. Ned drew his horses into a walk and stopped them just inside the gates. Ironminster remained silent, making no sign, and one of the men on horseback rode through the gates and pulled up beside them.

'Are you going far, my Lord?'

'To London,' August replied.

The man frowned and was unsure of what to say next, but while he hesitated they heard the sound of hooves on the road coming from the village, and the man turned his horse and rode back to his friends. Ironminster was laughing. They watched them all debating; then the Saville coach drew up outside the gates in a cloud of frosty breath and jangling of chains and bars: as splendid a team, Ned had to admit, watching closely, as any he had seen in London, and perfectly matched – also, far more tidily handled than they used to be. Rupert was learning. He had James beside him on the box, and a full complement of his cronies, rather noisy and excited. When they saw the Ironminster coach waiting, there was a stunned silence. The man who had spoken with them no doubt conveyed what he had learned of Ironminster's destination, and after some hurried conversation James bawled across to them without ceremony, 'What are your intentions, August?'

Ironminster said to Ned, 'Go close to them.'

Ned eased his horses forward and brought his coach up alongside the Saville coach so that August and Rupert could have shaken hands, had they wished it. Remembering the last time he had shaken hands with Rupert, Ned glanced across at him and caught his eye, a very angry eye. The two brothers, side by side on the box, looked very alike in that moment, certainly in their thunderous expressions, heavy jaws stuck out, overlapping their high cravats, almost bull-like in the impression of brute strength and anger.

'What are you about, August?' James asked angrily. 'You've been spying on us, I take it? What are you planning?'

'To drive to London,' August answered smoothly.

'Well, don't baulk us, I'm warning you. It's no coincidence you've chosen this moment, I can see. Well, we've Mr Simms as witness here as to what we're about – he'll tell you – we've outriders too, and time-keepers waiting for us in Aldgate. The road is ours and we shan't brook any interference. I'm warning you now.'

'The road is public, James. We shan't interfere with you in any way at all, unless you make interference *your* prerogative. You may start first, by all means. Mr Field himself can witness your time from the gates.'

August was very calm, smiling, which incensed James all the more.

'Damn you, August! Believe me, you'll not get past us – you won't be able to keep up with us! Drive on, Rupert! We're starting now, Mr Field – look at your time-piece – eight thirty-five, exactly, I believe.'

'Correct!'

'We'll give you five minutes, James!' August called out. 'Hold them Ned! Let them get away. We don't want to be rubbing our noses on their tailboard.'

Rupert eased his reins and the four greys moved off sharply, with much halloing from the passengers. Two riders went on ahead, and the rest of the spectators drew back out of the way, muttering and excited. Ned held his horses motionless, feeling their immobility trembling in his fingers, the arrested power as if on a thread, watching the short, eager clouds of their breath on the air, the glitter of terrets and buckles and brass in the flooding moonlight. Every blade of grass, every stone, stood out sharp and clear, the trees frosted over as if in perpetuity. Ned could feel himself sharpened, aware of every detail, very nervous. Nobody spoke on board, waiting on Andrew Field's time-piece which he held in his hand, its face perfectly legible in the moonlight. August, muffled up in a dark caped coat whose collar reached the brim of his beaver, smiled at Ned, nodded when Field touched his shoulder, and said, 'Let them go, Ned. We shall do it – I know we shall!'

They went away very smoothly, the wheelers drawing into their collars a fraction before the leaders were given their heads – the manoeuvre which Rupert had learned at last, Ned noted – and going straight into a very fast, level trot, perfectly balanced.

'You're used to time-keeping,' August said, 'You're back at your old job again. I shall leave it to you.'

'It's a rare stage that will travel at this rate.'

Strange, Ned thought, but there was never any real doubt in his mind that he would accomplish this feat that August's heart was set on. Rupert ahead was no more than a nuisance and possible danger in the overtaking. The horses – *his* horses

– were all fire and steel, invincible. He talked to them, encouraged them, saved their strength, extended them, held them, loved them; he never for a moment contemplated failure. It was everything, this ride, the consummation of all his work for August. The petty Savilles were no impediment at all. They passed them before Stratford, without even having to use the whip, for the greys were done, driven wildly, nearly on their knees. Ned didn't even spare them a glance, heard the tumult of laughing, jeering, shouting, jubilation, and kept his eyes strictly on the road, fearful now for making a safe passage at such speed through the villages, where straying donkeys, cows and drunks were likely to upset them all into perdition. August at his side was quivering like a strung wire, feverish and breathless, his dark coat spotted with the horses' white lather. Field's time-piece gave them four minutes from Bow church, but there were coster-carts coming home and a load of hay being moved. Screams and invective pursued them: a hail of stale vegetables, and dogs barking ... legs slipping and sprawling and the reins carving white ribbons of foam off the horses' necks. Ned peered ahead, swearing, feeling as if he were holding up four horses with his own arms, his heart as bursting as theirs. 'Two minutes, Ned!' August cried out. Ned thought it was going to kill August, but if they made it he would die happy. Two damned drunks running, a bottle thrown and splintering. Railton threw one back, and his hat in the air, crowing, 'A whole minute to spare! Your money, Andrew!'

'My lovely money!' Field shouted back.

August started to laugh, and then fell to coughing instead, hopelessly, while Ned was starting to pull up. The horses and August were all as bad as each other.

'Into The Bull, Ned. We must get him down!' Railton said, holding August in his arms.

Torches flared, anxious faces looking up, wondering what the hurry was: the familiar expression of the coaching-yard, of dour obsequiousness. The horses' backs were steaming; the first spots of rain falling would surely hiss, Ned felt, as they landed on those sweat-black backs. He was steaming too. He could feel the drops of moisture hanging on his nose and eyelashes, running down his temples under the brim of his beaver. He turned and smiled at Ironminster, and Ironminster, blood on his lips, smiled back. Ned dropped the reins and picked August up bodily and climbed down with him on to the stones. Railton and Field, with their practised, casual tact, gave him an arm each, laughing.

'The shock's too much for him, eh, August? He needs brandy –'

Laughing, half-anxious, half elated, they were all extraordinarily excited. The enormous relief of achieving the difficult thing they had set out to do, after so many days of uncertainty, was tempered by August's condition and – Ned felt very certain of this – the incipient meeting with the defeated Savilles. For himself, the prospect pleased him, with a sharp sense of justice having triumphed. He felt tense, very tired and yet not at all ready to relax. He felt as if he was just starting something, not finishing it. He wanted the chance to grin at Rupert and let his eyes linger on the exhausted horses; Rupert was defeated, again. August, ill and exhausted, was the victor, the flame of exhilaration in his feverish eyes. His expression warmed Ned with loyalty.

'Come, let's get inside and show Saville we've had time to drink two pots while we've waited. Will you join us, Ned?'

'I must see to the horses first, my Lord.'

The grooms were eager, impressed by the achievement and scenting large tips. Ned watched them, revelling in the feel of the soft, cold rain on his face, watching the horses' breath like pink smoke clouding the torchlight: scrape of iron shoes and smell of sweaty leather . . . shouts and running feet out of the way and the archway darkened suddenly by the bulk of a drag and sprawling, staggering horses. Curses and swearing, and the grooms' smiles . . . Ned saw them, grinned, and the Savilles saw him grinning.

'Blast you, Ned Rowlands, and your confounded spying tricks!' Rupert swerved his leaders viciously, and Ned had to move smartly out of the way. He saw the two Saville faces against the archway, side by side and equally venomous in expression: for a moment, strangely, he saw a family resemblance to Ironminster: the impression was of strength. Yet Ned knew in that moment that Ironminster had a strength beyond anything the cursing Savilles would ever know. He felt fiercely proud of what he had done for August, and stood watching as the staggering greys came to a halt, pouring sweat, hollow-flanked, straddling with exhaustion. His own horses by comparison, although tired, walked to the stables unconcerned. He smiled again, and James Saville watched him. Ned touched his beaver to him and walked away to supervise the stabling. He hadn't known such gratification since the fight; even then, hadn't had the chance to savour his triumph as he did now, examining his horses in the warm hay-scented stables, the lantern light casting flaring shadows onto the roof. He was in no hurry; he wanted no part of the confrontations in the inn. His job was accomplished and his place was in the stable. He stripped off to his waistcoat and did the grooms' work, preferring it that way, until his animals were comfortable and starting to feed, then just as he was finishing he went to the harness-room to see if he could get a drink off Ben, the old horse-master. Ben, glad of an excuse, poured him a rum, but before they could drink, a boy put his head round the door and said, 'Mr Rowlands? There's a man asking for you, in the lane at the back — says it's very important.'

Ned was surprised, but went out to see who it was.

Afterwards he could never understand how he could have acted with such complete lack of suspicion. The gate gave into an unlit alley. He went through it like a lamb to the slaughter. It shut with remarkable promptness behind him, the bolt slid home, and in the darkness he sensed rather than saw the figures converging on him, smelt the gin-laden breath and the reek of unwashed human body even above the native stench of drains that ran down the alley. The sudden fright acted in his veins like a stimulant; he did not think, he moved purely by instinct, dropping down on one knee as the two attackers sprung for his head. Their enormous hands, clenched up like horny battering-rams, hit the wall above him, and he rolled out from under their boots, as quick with pure panic as they were cumbersome with drink. But the pain of their contact with the wall stung them to a quick and bitter reaction. Ned wriggled sideways to his feet just in time to avoid the boots, lashed out to the nearest face and felt a lovely contact, bony and squelchy together. The other man got him round the neck but, Ned, primed by his bouts with Tom Belcher, was able to twist round and turn the hold to his own advantage, throwing the man without much difficulty flat out on the cobbles. He reached for him, picked him up by the shoulders and slammed his head back hard on the stones. The man bawled out like a stuck pig.

By the time these few seconds had passed, Ned, so entirely successful, slightly breathless but no longer panic-stricken, was able to assess the situation: there were only two men, obviously paid thugs hired to do for him, for he knew neither of them. But somewhere in the darkness there was somebody else. His eyes, accustomed to the gloom, saw this figure crouching down beyond the gateway, tense with what Ned presumed was ambition to see him mashed.

'Not if I know it!' he thought, and got up to parry the next onslaught, quite confident now that his comparatively professional skill would see him through unscathed. These bruisers, massive and brutal as they were, were no match for his ability. One of their blows could well kill, but they were pathetically slow and drunk, and quite incapable of making the blows connect. Ned almost laughed as he dispatched them, darting in with lovely crunching punches which presently had the two of them bawling for mercy, staggering to their feet and departing rapidly down the alley.

'And now –' Ned turned to the third figure who was now turning to make off after the others, but he was not much sprightlier than they, in spite of not having seen any action, and Ned was able to catch him up and spin him round by his shoulder against the wall.

'Don't touch me!'

Ned, keyed up, almost laughing, saw James Saville's face, mottled, flabby, the gooseberry eyes popping with dismay, and hit it hard without even stopping to think. The man had no bones, like a stuffed cushion. He reeled back, hit the wall with a crash and slithered like blancmange to the ground. Ned just stood there, waiting for him to get up again, happy to have had the satisfaction – the excuse – for doing what he had wanted to do for a long time. God, what a pig the man was, gloating over Ironminster's disease, with his greed, his pathetic snobbery! Ned enjoyed seeing him fall, enjoyed having dispatched the ill-chosen assassins, enjoyed seeing poor Saville's drunken botched plans come to nothing in the sewage of the alley. He prodded him with his foot.

'You swine! You tried to get me killed, to hurt Ironminster! What wouldn't you stoop to?'

Ned bent over him, presuming him felled more by drink than his own strength.

'Come, you old fool. I'll get you sobered in the horse-trough.'

He put a hand under the man's shoulders to pull him into a more comfortable position and found a strange warmth flowing unexpectedly where he expected to encounter only cold stones. He paused and looked at Saville's face again. Although it was too dark to make out properly, Ned was struck by the utter stillness of the figure. Was it his imagination, or ...? Ned lifted his hand and saw that it was dark, and all his white cuff was dark too. He put his arm under the man's shoulders again and rolled him over, using all his strength, and his knee as well, and now saw what he thought was – God's truth! He touched it with his hand, cried out, felt the vomit rising. God Almighty! He was crouching there, suddenly stone-cold and shaking with the horror of it, the great blancmange spewed open on the stones, the eyes staring up into the rain like polished marbles, cold in their sockets. The shock of it was like the sky itself falling, hardly to be accepted.

Ned sat back on his heels, breathing heavily, trying to take stock. It was utterly deserted in the alley, silent save for the trickling of water in the central gutter. Ned was cold as ice and trembling uncontrollably. He had killed Saville, there was no doubt of it. Keyed up from his opening bout with the hired thugs, he had delivered Saville a killing blow with all the irresponsibility of a boy catapulting a sparrow. The stupid soft skull had hit the wall and split open. Saville, in the space of one second, had passed from his useless life into an even more pointless death, leaving Ned with the consequences. Ned, sitting there, his sleeves and now his knee breeches covered with Saville's blood, slowly took in these consequences and was appalled. Not only appalled but frightened, as frightened as he had ever been in his life. He was hard put to it to keep himself steady, get up, set his teeth to stop them chattering. He needed help. He needed Ironminster. Badly. He needed him as badly now as Ironminster had ever in the past needed him.

Soft, cold rain was falling, greasy with smoke. The smell of London smoke, sulphurous, of drains and dung-heaps, was fresher than the smell of Saville's blood. Ned crept back down the alley to the gate, not looking back. He wouldn't have much time, if the others knew what James had been up to. They would be waiting for James back in the inn. Ned knew he had to get word to Ironminster, or Sam, but he dared not show himself to anybody, all covered with blood. He slipped the bolt and went back into the stable-yard. It was busy enough, a post-chaise going out, boys leading out horses and luggage being handed up. Ned, keeping his back to the flares, went round to the front of the inn, caught a boy by the arm, waiting to earn a penny holding horses, and said to him, 'Go inside and tell Lord Ironminster or one of his party to come out to the stables. It's very urgent.'

'I can't go inside!' the boy yelped. 'They'll throw me out.'

'Tell Mr Nelson!' Ned hissed. 'He won't throw you out if you ask for Lord Ironminster! He's in there.' He was holding the boy's arm so tightly that the boy squirmed. 'Here,' he groped in his pocket and found a sixpence. The boy's eyes opened very wide. Ned found he was still trembling. He walked slowly over to where their coach had been parked under cover, climbed up on the box and picked up his driving-coat which he had left there. He put it on again, covering his stained breeches and cuffs, and immediately felt a lot more confident. Perhaps it wasn't all as bad as he feared . . . self-defence was a strong plea. He went back into the stables and pretended to be seeing to his horses, but in spite of the stab of optimism he found that he felt sick and weak as a girl. He had to lean against the partition; his gorge kept rising with nausea at the mental image of what lay out in the alley.

It was Railton who came, curious, cheerful.

'Ironminster's not very well – best for him to rest, if he can. Is something wrong? I was going to send Sam, then I thought – well, you don't know – strange message . . . What is it, Ned?'

He peered at him closely, and his expression changed.

'Is something wrong?'

Ned found it almost impossible to say.

'I – if you look outside – no, oh God! Better not. It's – it's James Saville –'

'What's he up to? He's in a mad rage – I've never seen anyone so foul! It's really made our evening, seeing him like that. Has he been out to see you? Ned, for heaven's sake, what's wrong with you –?'

'I've killed him.'

'What d'you mean? Killed who?'

'Saville.'

'You're not serious! God dammit, though, you look as if you are – you're not saying you've killed Saville?'

'Yes, I am. He set some men on me, hired louts – I saw them off, and then I hit Saville. I didn't mean – I thought –'

'Where was this?'

'Out through the back gate, in the alley.'

'Nobody saw?'

'Not a soul.'

'Are you *sure*?'

'Yes!' Ned felt close to sobbing. He pulled the skirts of his coat aside and showed the bloodstains on the pale breeches. 'His brains are all over the alley.'

'*Jesus!* You really did –?' Railton winced and the animation left him. 'I can't say I'm sorry, but – oh, Ned!' He looked at him with a strange expression, which Ned diagnosed as pity. 'This is difficult. Tell me again, tell me exactly how it happened. He's still there? Nobody's seen him yet?'

'No, we'd have heard the commotion if they had.' He told Railton the story in detail. 'It wasn't even self-defence, in fact, for *he* wasn't going to attack me – he was too damned scared.'

'And there's not a mark on you, Ned,' Railton confirmed, examining him closely. 'Only that blood, which is pretty incriminating. I think it might pay us to disappear quietly, what do you think? Luckily we made it known we were only stopping for an hour. I think perhaps I'll slip back inside, send Sam out to you with orders to put to, and we'll all fade silently into the night before anyone finds out what's amiss. The horses have had a bit of a rest – what do you say?'

'I'd like to get away from here, yes.'

'Don't worry, Ned. He might not be found for some time. And there'll be no one to pin it on you, once we've got you a change of clothes. Sharp now, I'll go and ease the others out, and you start getting these rugs off. We can be away in ten minutes.'

It wasn't so easy, Ned kept thinking, going about the routine ... Rupert Saville would know what his brother had been up to, surely? Any minute now he would start wondering why he was being such a long time. The head groom knew that he – Ned – had been called out into the alley, so did the boy who had brought the message. These were the people Rupert would find to give evidence; he would pay them handsomely. Ned had no doubt that the hunt for the murderer would be thorough indeed.

It was strange; Ned had never considered himself a coward, nor easily given to fear, but now, even as their party came out and climbed aboard, all apparently in fine spirits and blessed by the landlord himself, smiling and bowing, everyone exchanging cordialities, he was possessed by an almost paralytic fear. The finality of what he had done was numbing. The departing of the coach from the yard, with its attendant stir, the lights, the smell, the ostlers' faces looking for their tips, cracked into sour smiles, the urchins dodging hooves, the road cleared for them with shouts and cursing – it was all so utterly familiar, the pattern of his life, that he could not believe anything was different. Yet, going through the ritual, he was shaking with abject terror. Anyone noticing him would be assured that he was a murderer, for he could feel his lips trembling; he could actually feel the pallor in his face and the staring in his eyes. He could only act out of habit, his mind completely divorced from the job in hand. If the horses had been as fresh as usual, he would have driven straight through the wall opposite. As it was, he pulled them up in the middle of the road, not knowing which direction to turn in.

'Home, Ned, home,' Ironminster said.

It was an instinct, perhaps, but Ned was glad of it. Ironminster looked drawn and ill.

'It's true what Railton said? You've killed James?'

'Yes.'

'I've wished him dead many a time, but you mustn't suffer for it.'

Railton leaned over from behind and said, 'He wants a

change of clothes. Without the bloodstains, there's nothing to incriminate him.'

'The boys knew,' Ned said. 'A message came to say go and see someone in the lane. They saw me go.'

'They won't speak against you.'

'They will for money.'

'We can pay money too if necessary.'

Ned watched the road ahead, too frightened to think about it. He didn't want to hang, especially for James. He thought he would have to go away, a long way away, and he didn't want to do that either. But better than hanging. Anything was better than hanging. Rupert would be bent on getting him . . .

'Ned, believe me, we have a lot of influence between us. You'll not swing for James, I'll see to it.' Ironminster spoke quietly, and with great conviction.

He added, 'It's the best thing that's happened to James all his life,' and smiled.

'There's no sign of any excitement behind,' Railton said. 'We could well be home before they find out what's happened.'

Ned doubted it somehow. Rupert must already be wondering what was keeping his brother. He surely knew what he was up to? Or had James acted on impulse, half-drunk, bribing those louts? In which case, if the grooms kept their mouths shut, there would be nothing to connect the murder with him. The louts could have killed James. Ned began to feel a little more optimistic. The horses, rested for an hour, were not so tired that they could not keep up a steady trot. The road was dark and quiet and it was still raining. Ned, now that the first shock was over, began to feel the blood circulating again. He hadn't *intended* to kill James, and James had certainly intended to kill him. If there was any justice in the world, he would surely be spared.

The mood on board was very different from the outward journey, no one saying very much, chastened by what had happened, half shocked, half excited. August was obviously very tired, strained by the rough journey, and sat in his hunched, painful way, elbow on knee. Ned, soothed by the familiarity of watching his horses' backs, found he was already accepting what had happened, the numbed incredulity giving way to a grim awe at the ease with which he had taken a human life, not untouched by pride. At least he had chosen the right gentleman. Regrets were purely for his own predicament; not on anybody's part was there regret for James's departure.

'There's a light behind us,' Railton said suddenly.

Ned kept his eyes ahead, while everyone else craned behind.

'You're imagining things,' Field said. 'Or perhaps in a house – we've passed a few.'

'No – moving, I'll swear. On the road.'

There was silence for some time, Ned consciously keeping his mind from wandering off the job in hand. Then, simultaneously, both Railton and Sam said, 'There it is!'

Without being able to help himself, Ned picked up his whip.

'Come, it could be anybody,' August said to him.

'It's late,' Ned said. He sent the horses on, not forcing them, but making them lengthen their stride. The fear surged in him again, shaming him.

'Just keep going steadily. There'll be plenty of time to work out a way of outwitting them. Their horses were wearier than ours.'

'They might have fresh ones.'

August did not answer. Ned found it impossible to believe that it could be anyone but Rupert Saville behind him. From what the others were saying, they suspected it too. Ned spoke to his wheelers, sharpening their pace, and Starling and Nightingale quickened instinctively. They passed through the Romford turnpike, wasting as little time as possible, and August tipped the gate-keeper handsomely to delay the following vehicle. They were making good time: in any other circumstances Ned would have been congratulating himself on the magnificent performance of his team, to recover from such a pounding after a mere hour's rest to work so doggedly again.

'If whoever it is turns off the turnpike at the Threadgolds corner, then we shall know,' August said. 'Then we must decide what to do.'

The Threadgolds corner was still five miles from home.

'With luck we won't see him again,' Field said.

For some time nothing was said. Ned went on pressing the horses harder than he would have wished, but helping them to the best of his ability, aware that the silence was a tense,

instinctive agreement not to air the fears in all their minds.
Ned supposed he was grateful, frightened by the panic that he
could feel lurking in his guts. He wasn't as cool as he would
have wished, and it wasn't easy to appear to Ironminster as
bold as somehow Ned thought Ironminster expected him to
be. Or was August, under the silent frown, frightened too?

The road was very dark and the following light was sharp,
dancing intermittently through trees and hedgerows, travelling
fast. They came to the Threadgolds corner, their horses tiring
rapidly and blowing off streamers of foam, and Ned eased
them into the lane and sent them off downhill at a canter. All
eyes were on the road behind, save Ned's. And nobody listened as sharply as he, sick with foreboding.

'If they turn this way,' he asked Ironminster, 'What then?'

'You'll have to leave us.'

A fugitive then. Ned felt the indignation rise, choked with
self-pity and the gripping fringes of panic.

'Don't be afraid,' Ironminster said. 'I shall go with you.' He
turned round to Railton. 'The keeper's cottage at Fairoaks – do
you know it? Where Foxy Franklin lives? It's a mile off this
lane, from the ford.'

'No. What of it?'

'It would make a good hiding-place.'

Before the ford, the lane breasted a slope, which com-
manded a backward view.

'We shall see them from the rise if they're coming,' August
said. 'Slow down a little.'

But there was no need.

'Yes, by God, and not very far behind!'

'All right, Ned! As fast as you can, and pull up by the ford.
Then you and I shall take to the woods, and Alex can take the
ribbons.'

'And what in heaven's name are we to say to Saville when he
catches us?' Railton asked urgently. 'We're not going to have
long to make up a story.'

'Oh, you'll think of something, I'm sure. Sam can send a
boy to Fairoaks with his other livery and breeches and in the
morning Ned will turn up and brazen it out. Then you and
Andrew can go back to London and pay those boys well to say
Ned wasn't in the alley. If Rupert has already paid them, pay

them more. Start pulling up, Ned. The path is by that big oak.'

'And what about you, August? What shall we say about you? Can't you stay with us?' Railton was already climbing over into the front seat.

'Ned will never find Foxy's without me,' August said shortly. 'And I must take Miss Redbridge too – she cannot be mixed up in this. She said she had gone to visit an aunt, if you remember. Rupert might have seen her at The Bull, but I told him to forget it, and I'm sure he will, whatever the other business. But she mustn't be found with us now.'

August was already climbing down, pushing Ned before him. Railton took the reins out of Ned's hands, threading them through his fingers, muttering blasphemies. Sam had got Sarah Redbridge out of the coach and was slamming the door behind her, leaping up aboard again even as Railton started moving. It was all achieved with scarcely a stop. Ned felt the soft ground beneath his feet and saw the dark tunnel of the track plunging into the woods, saw August take Sarah's hand and start to run, heard – already – even as the thud and rumble of their own coach receded, the urgent pounding of hooves approaching. He ran headlong, frantic, sprawling in deep, waist-high bracken, crouching still as the following coach came fast down the hill behind them in a great splattering of mud and stones – a mixed team of lathered, heavily-breathing nags, wildly driven, stumbling into the water with such lack of control that one of the leaders all but fell. It was appallingly close. Ned instinctively put his head down, holding his breath. The swearing was indubitably Rupert Saville's. There was a tangle in the ford because of the leader, the wheeler colliding and a great jerking and jangling of bars and traces, then the coach was away again, wearily, the sound of hooves and shouts and general excitement receding. Ned got up and moved out on to the path where Ironminster and Sarah Redbridge presently joined him, and they stood listening for a moment, feeling the panics recede and the lovely peace of the empty night take over. After all the emotions of the past few hours, Ned felt the peace and the silence almost as a blessing, a tangible comfort and relief from his fears, and was quite content to stand there letting it all sink in, feeling the aching of his arms and the stiffness of his fingers cooling and unwinding, the night air no longer cutting into him, but soft and damp on his face. It meant a great deal at that moment, after all that had happened and the hazards still ahead, and, even as he started walking, he savoured it, and then wondered if this was the instinct of a man in danger of being hanged ... he wasn't normally an admirer of nature's moods. Confound it! He was almost too tired to think any more, and better not to think on such defeatism.

Ironminster, leading the way, didn't set a rapid pace, and Ned could see that he was in a very fragile state and breathing badly. But useless to comment on it. Sarah was tactful enough not to remark on it, and made her way without any feminine fuss at all, nimble as a pony. Ned understood why August had said only he could find the way, for the paths criss-crossed in all directions and August, even in the dark, never hesitated at any of the many intersections, walking on steadily. Once, Ned surmised, he had come these ways hunting, or as a boy on a pony, or shooting, or birds-nesting, and he remembered them like an animal, not stopping to reflect. Ned felt easier now, confident in August's authority. Things might not be so bad, if he were lucky.

The cottage was deep in the woods. It was in darkness. August knocked on the door, shouted, and then lifted the latch and went in. For all its apparent delapidation outside, the room inside was snug enough when revealed by a candle that Sarah picked up from the table and lit from the embers of the fire: primitive but warm and clean and welcoming. Sanctuary was the word that came to Ned's mind, with both its warm and its chill implications; from all the haste and excitement of their journey, the sudden quiet and harbour of the gamekeeper's den was comforting in the most elemental, spiritual way.

August said: 'Gamekeepers work at night. I daresay we shan't be disturbed till dawn –' He then made a shrugging, despairing gesture and sat down abruptly in the chair before the fire, leaning forward in the familiar, painful fashion. Sarah glanced at him, then went to him and gently began to help him off with his coat. Ned stirred the fire and put fresh logs on, then took the coat and beaver from Sarah. August was in a bad way.

'I think you should use the bed, my Lord. We can move it up near the fire.'

It was only a straw mattress with some woollen blankets, although clean enough. Ned started to pull it across the floor, wishing Sam had come with them, and propped one end of it up with their box coats, remembering how Sam propped his patient up with pillows at home. He helped Sarah to remove August's boots and loosen his neckcloth and between them they got him into the makeshift bed and made him as comfortable as they could, which still left a good deal to be desired. He was shivering, yet his forehead and cheeks were burning. Ned put a brick in the embers to warm for his feet, and Sarah sat beside him and rubbed his cold hands.

'There's nothing much we can do until Sam comes,' she said. 'I think he'll feel better when he's warm and rested.'

Optimistic, Ned thought. But optimism wasn't to be scorned. If he hadn't so much to occupy his mind, he might well have felt embarrassed by this intimacy with Miss Redbridge, but uncommon situations seemed to abound in Ironminster's way of life. This was merely part of the pattern. He stood by the fire, staring into its comforting flames, but finding little comfort, feeling far too restless to lie down and go to sleep, which was Miss Redbridge's sensible suggestion

'You go to sleep,' he countered. 'I can watch his Lordship.'

She did not reply, and he supposed that she was happy enough to tend August when he needed her, as Matty had been happy to nurse him; it was something a woman liked, he supposed, to have her man helpless and in her power – although, God knew, he wasn't perceptive where women's minds were concerned, if understanding Matty was anything to go by. She had loved him when he was ill, but back to health and strength – that was another matter. Would she love him as a murderer? It was a condition where Tom Garnett would find it impossible to compete. On that score he held advantage. But his confusion over his feelings for Matty were of second importance to his present purely selfish feelings for his own skin. He would not feel at ease until he had got rid of James's incriminating blood, and he doubted, even as he made an effort to compose himself for sleep on some old sacks against the wall, that he would find release from his fears in blessed unconsciousness. His mind was working like a windmill and getting nowhere, his head ached and he was raving hungry, and all he could do was pray for Sam to hurry.

He was right. Sleep did not come. It came to August after a couple of hours of exhausting coughing, and then to Sarah, curled up with August's head in her lap. Ned made up the fire without waking them and lay down again, wondering what had happened when Saville had caught up with Railton and Field, what story Railton had concocted to explain Ironminster's absence. He thought of his horses and their brave performance, wished he had been there to see them made comfortable for the night; thought of James's dead eyeballs and shivered in his sacks; listened to the owl in the oakwoods and the mice in the thatch, the barking of a dog-fox far away, intent on its own careless existence . . . He wanted to hear footsteps softly padding across the clearing – not the gamekeeper's, but Sam's: Sam with his fresh clothes, and news of confounding Rupert Saville with clever alibis. He lay watching the firelight making patterns on the ceiling, uneasy, longing for morning, a fresh light to put a new countenance on what had happened.

The fox called again. Or dog – it sounded like a dog howling. But no one lived near enough. The gamekeeper's dog wouldn't howl. The mournful noise was no comfort to him, clear and sad through the stillness of the forest. It reminded him . . . it sounded like a dog hunting, but deeper in tone than a foxhound. He lifted his head to hear it again, heard the short, painful rasp of Ironminster's breathing, a log fall apart in the hearth, then the dog again, nearer, purposeful somehow. Confound the animal! Its noise was unnerving, the way it echoed.

He sat up. The idea did not come to him in a flash, but quite slowly, with the most awful dread. And as slowly as it came, so with equal certainty he knew he wasn't mistaken. He had heard that noise before and now he knew what it was. It was a hound following a trail. And the trail was his. There was no element of doubt in his mind. Rupert Saville was not likely to have been deflected from his course by any flippant words of Railton's, and it wouldn't have been hard for him to deduce that the Ironminster coach had stopped at the ford to put somebody down. He had his own bloodhounds; Ned had seen them at exercise, great melancholy beasts with slathering mouths and drooping eyes.

Ned knew then, without any doubt, that it was all up with him. He got up quickly to go to the door, paused to see if August and Sarah were still asleep, and saw August's face in the firelight, eyes open, watching him. He was in a bad way, breathing painfully, the perspiration shining on his cheek. He did not move and Ned went to him, leaning over to speak without waking Sarah. He did not know who, at that moment, he was the most sorry for: himself or August. And because it was so poignant a moment to say good-bye, he avoided it, smiled instead, and whispered, 'Sam will come soon. You'll be all right. I'll lead them away from here.'

Did August know? He was bright with fever, fighting for breath. Perhaps they were both near the end of the road, if things came to the worst, but there were no words for such dire considerations under the circumstances: only a glance exchanged, a mixing of love with despair, and panic with sympathy: no time to analyse feelings, but only to run. Ned turned his mind from the turbulence of emotions to the strict agenda before him: to draw off the bloodhounds from the cottage before they laid their slathering teeth into his backside. He ran wildly, for there was so little time, and – as time ran out – because he was terrified. Emotions now needed no analysis; they were elemental, primitive, to suit the situation. To be hunted was a medieval doom, akin with simple, feudal remedies for wrong-doing, like burning alive and stoning to death, and the fear it provoked was equally uncomplicated. Ned did not expect mercy, and did not receive any. With lungs bursting, crying out, he ran blindly through thickets and clearings until his constitution could stand it no longer, which moment coincided with the arrival of the first hound who bowled him over like a rabbit and sank jaws heavily into whatever threshing part he could get hold of. Ned struggled and kicked for his life, rolling over and over in soft peat and leaves, mouthfuls, eyefuls, clutching with his hands at the slippery, loose-coated malevolence but powerless to contain it. He had never guessed at such horror, the weight and the bone and the muscle bearing him down for the questing of the unimaginable teeth. Ned didn't want to see, but the hound's saliva flashed like phosphorescence in the dark, stars in his eyes, and he screamed and screamed as the dog's fangs sank and held and he could no longer do anything about it. But the men came with long ash-poles and beat the hounds off and beat Ned too for good measure – or bad aim – until he stopped writhing about and lay still.

When he came to he was in chains, lying in a cart, and a very pretty winter sunrise was struggling through the trees.

12

NEWGATE was familiar enough on the outside, its grim granite walls bounding the meat market a mere stone's throw from the familiar rattling terminus of the Royal Mail coaches in St Martin's-le-Grand; Ned had passed it dozens of times all his life, never giving a thought to the wretches inside, merely a shiver at the sight of the gallows before one of the doorways, to be avoided on a hanging Monday when the crowds gathered and it was impossible to push a way through. But now, alighting from the hackney carriage with his guard, the gallows had a more pressing interest: one inspected it with hypnotic attention, straddled against the clear, cold sky, a more than usually vivid imagination adding the human interest. They said it took an ordinary-sized man several minutes to lose consciousness, and ten to fifteen minutes to die; a wise victim got his friends to hang on his legs to hasten his agony. Ned knew he would have the opportunity to prove or disprove this hearsay within the next few months, unless Ironminster and Railton were successful with the influence they boasted, and his confidence in them wasn't enough to stop his steps faltering miserably before the grim doorway. Two days to Christmas, and the air was frosty and sharp, the market faces cheerful; a fresh-cut cartload of holly went past, triggering happy childhood memories in Ned's mind at the very moment of entering under the Newgate archway . . . it was unkind and almost his undoing. He had to make a great effort to walk on, stop himself from behaving like a girl.

Having prepared himself for the worst, he was still unprepared for what met him: first the stench, which made his stomach turn over. He held his breath, passing on with his escorts down a dark, icy passage, then gradually came to realize that the smell was inescapable, permeating every corner of the vast, heaving, evil building: the smell of human filth. Merely breathing was the first punishment.

'How much can you pay?' he was asked. 'Are you going in

the Master Felons? Thirteen shillings and sixpence a week? What've you got on you?'

Ned had nothing on him, not even a sixpence.

'Common Felons then, until your master pays up. Or was it him you murdered?' The turnkeys were grinning. 'And you won't have your irons off unless you can pay for it. You need friends, lad, when you come in here.'

God Almighty, but that was the understatement of all time, Ned thought, taking his first glimpse into the Common Felons' ward through the bars while his jailers unlocked the door. No good weakening, flinching, thrust into the horde of eighty or so fellow prisoners, the bullies of which set upon him even before the turnkeys had finished advising him, frisking through his pockets, banging his head against the wall. He fought furiously, using the handcuffs like knuckledusters, going down under such a weight of stench, drunken breath and malevolence as he thought would see him out before he ever got to the gallows. But the welcome was more habit than ill-intentioned, an excuse for relieving the utter boredom of living out one's life in black, hopeless squalor, and Ned, having been quickly initiated into the same hopeless state as themselves, was allowed to recover himself after some unpleasant grovelling, during which he was relieved of his boots and his neckcloth. He would have lost his coat too but for the handcuffs which prevented its removal – a bonus to make up for their inconvenience, for the prison was cold as charity, the walls running with water, the stone flags with liquid slime. After the tussle someone brought him some gin in a tin cup and pushed it up to his lips, and he wasn't sorry to gulp it down for its burning comfort to body and brain – the only comfort either was likely to receive in this stinking hell-hole.

In the first half-hour he was therefore introduced to both the degradation of the life he would be forced to live in Newgate and to the only relief from its horror, which – in its turn – sank one still deeper into degradation: he could see the effects clearly enough in his companions. By the same evening his old life was already a dream, as far removed from present reality as to be on another planet. Fed only on a hunk of rock-stale bread, water and gin, he took his sleeping place on the wooden bench, pressed close between a pair of horse-stealers, and felt their lice take joyously to the fresh pastures of his own body. Unable to either sleep or scratch for the wretched irons, he lay listening to the unholy cacophony of snores, moans, distant lunatic screams and laughing, sobbing, praying and mere muttering, to the incessant drip of water and echoing footsteps, watching the black dark, thick as a blanket over the eyes, wondering how it was possible to exist in such a sink for more than a few days. Yet some of them had been there for six months. He guessed, prayed, that someone from Threadgolds would seek him out in a few days' time and pay out the fees that would at least see him out of irons and into the so-called privileges of the Master Felons side: a few days in his present state would no doubt make those privileges glorious indeed. Meanwhile he must endure to the best of his ability. He could well imagine that in Newgate one could easily die of despair.

They were the longest days of his life. He existed. He fought against the bullies, he fought for his wretched food; he learned to sleep in his fetters, shivering cold and starving hungry, waking to a worse nightmare than the one of his unconscious. He kept himself as clean as he could by the half-frozen trickle of water to be obtained from the pump in the exercise yard where they were allowed for an hour in the morning, and from where the peals of the Christmas bells of all the surrounding city churches sounded joyfully across the drear spiked walls, provoking the most unholy stabs of homesickness as painful to the spirit as any of the more obvious miseries. Back behind bars the miasma of filth quickly embraced once more the shrinking flesh, no respite to be found from the total squalor save through getting drunk, which was accomplished easily enough. Ned lost count of the days, and began to despair of deliverance. He asked the turnkey if anyone had inquired of him and received only a mocking answer. But surely they must know where he had been taken, he thought! They wouldn't *leave* him . . . Sam would come. They couldn't get him out, but they could come and talk at least. Visitors were in and out all day long, thronging the place, women and screaming children. He stood at the bars searching their faces, sickened by the atmosphere of degradation.

It was Lord Railton who came, eventually. He held a handkerchief to his face and was wrapped in a black cloak so that

Ned didn't recognize him immediately. He was speaking to the turnkey, who was behaving in a notably sycophantic manner, which attracted Ned's attention. He went closer, saw who it was, and felt such a violent surge of excitement and relief that he was quite incoherent as he went up and grasped the bars. He put his head against his hands, hiding his face, close to tears.

Railton was visibly shaken. 'Ned! God Almighty, Ned, I'm glad I've found you!'

The turnkey was holding out his hand. 'I shall have to have the money first, my Lord. It's very crowded just now in the State side. It will be very difficult to find a place. Three guineas, if you please, my Lord, half a guinea for a bed, a guinea for easement – the irons off, my Lord – a guinea for –'

'Dammit, man, it's more than the best inn in the city! Come on, confound you, open the door.' Railton poured a small stream of gold into the turnkey's hand which made the man hurry to do as he was told, bobbing and grinning and muttering. He let Ned out and Railton grasped his arm.

'You must forgive us, Ned, for being so long – but there's a reason. I will talk to you when we are alone – if this idiot can find you a decent lodging. God, how you stink! What a hole! I've never visited here before, although I was warned what to expect. The stench is enough to cripple a fellow.'

He buried his nose in his handkerchief once more and they followed the jailer through dark passages and bleak yards and several barred and locked gates which had to be laboriously undone and locked up again, to a corridor with separate cells opening off, where a consultation took place with a couple more jailers and they were eventually let into a cell which boasted a bed with a straw mattress, some dirty blankets, a table and a chair. It was lit by a small barred window high up in the wall.

Railton looked round critically and said, 'What do you say, Ned?' – as if he had any choice – and Ned smiled bleakly and said, 'Paradise.'

Railton said, 'I'll send a man in with some things for you – bedding and fresh clothes, some boots –' glancing at Ned's bare blue feet.

'And food,' put in the turnkey. 'We don't feed 'em here, you know.'

'That doesn't make it much different from the Common side in that case,' Ned said. He was used to an empty stomach now, and the lethargy that went with it. He sat down on the bed, feeling himself trembling with both weakness and the relief of seeing a familiar face, knowing that he was no longer abandoned. With much goading from Railton the turnkey then removed the handcuffs – 'You can't have the leg-irons off else we won't know you from a visitor' – and left them alone, leaving the door unlocked.

'Thank God I can speak with you. I was beginning to think we would never get the chance,' Railton said. He sat astride the chair, leaning his arms over the back of it and regarded Ned with pity. Ned avoided his glance, fingering the sores on his wrists. In spite of being delivered from the nightmare of the Common Felons' department, he did not feel as cheerful as he expected; in fact, the knowledge that his companion was shortly going to get up and walk out into the busy everyday street, leaving him behind, was as painful as any of his experiences since murdering James Saville.

'The reason we've been so long, Ned – it hasn't been easy. Ironminster has been ill near to death, and we had to wait until we knew which way it was going. If he had died, you see, things would have been rather different. And he was as near it as makes no matter.'

'He's better now?'

'He's improving, yes. To spite Rupert. If he had gone, Rupert would have inherited, and been grateful to you, I daresay, for removing his brother. I doubt if he would have pressed the charge, or – if it had come to court, he wouldn't have tried too hard to get you hanged. It would all have been different.'

'But now he will?' Ned drew the obvious conclusion.

'Yes. He's got some very good lawyers to prosecute. He is even more furious since August started to get better – having come so close, you see, to coming into the fortune. He's been scampering around madly collecting his evidence, hiring attorneys and perjurors. He's setting us a pretty problem, I can tell you. But nothing for you to worry about, Ned –' he added somewhat hastily and, Ned thought, over-optimistically, considering what had gone before. 'We are cleverer than he is, and we shall defeat him in court, having recourse to equally clever lawyers and rascally witnesses. We aren't sure yet how he is intending to prove that you did murder James, and until we know that we can't really set about unproving it. But you've no need to worry,' he repeated, frowning slightly. 'He has a very hard case to work on, you know.'

'And so have you,' Ned thought, but said nothing.

'We'll keep you informed, Ned. Now Ironminster has rallied we can concentrate all our efforts on getting you acquitted. And meanwhile I'll see that you get good meals sent in every day, and whatever else you want. Here, I'll leave you some money, and then perhaps you can get some washing facilities and the service of a barber or whatever else they have for sale in this god-forsaken hole – and my man will come in with fresh clothes and bedding before nightfall. Whatever we can do to make it easier, Ned – God knows, you didn't deserve this! Winning that wager meant a good deal to Ironminster, you know – we told him, if he was going to die, at least he'd be dying happy, with that behind him.'

There are too many of 'em in danger of dying, Ned thought. Thinking of Ironminster stirred him unhappily: when Ironminster went, life would be extraordinarily empty and joyless. Did Railton feel it too? If he – Ned – were still alive to remark on it, that is . . .

Ned felt even more uncertain about his future after Railton's cheerful summary of the situation than he had felt in ignorance. Locked in by the turnkey once more, alone, he felt no happier than before his deliverance, in spite of all the advantages Railton had acquired for him. His body, no doubt, was happier, when its fresh clothes and boots arrived, and the hot dinner in a basket, but his mind was far from relieved of anxiety – more the opposite, to learn that Rupert Saville was searching so aciduously for vengeance. How on earth were they going to explain away his guilty flight home from London, and the hiding in the woods at Fairoaks – hardly the behaviour of an innocent man? They needed more than lawyers: they needed novelists with fine imaginations. Strangely enough, away from the brawling mass of rotting humanity in the Common Felons', he was more afraid of being hanged. From there, it could well have been deliverance; now, considered in the silence of his own stone cell, it was a very awful prospect, a grotesque ending to what he now realized was, up to the present, a very happy life. Lying on his bed, insulated from the stinking straw by Railton's fine linen and goosedown pillows, he found himself thinking of Matty. He kept seeing her spirals of red-gold hair springing out round her angry face. Would she be sorry if he hanged? Would she come and watch him? Would she be sorry, seeing his legs kicking in the air, sorry she hadn't been kinder to him? His melancholy thoughts were interrupted by the biting of the fleas that preferred him to the mattress. He rolled over, groaning and miserable, scratching, swearing, an agony of boredom, self-pity and frustration bringing the tears to his eyes. Going dusk, five o'clock perhaps, and the long, long night ahead with its eternal symphony of moaning and snoring and sobbing and dripping, less urgent and close here than in the Common Felons, but no less chilling in one's solitude . . . in solitude one could weep too, and there was no shame, only a relief of a kind, and eventually exhaustion and sleep.

The weeks drew on. Outside it was almost spring, but the soft air did not penetrate the stone walls of Newgate. Newgate still smelt of excrement, however much one paid for one's cell.

'The date is fixed for the trial, Ned,' Railton came to tell him, inhaling snuff in large quantities from a tortoiseshell and silver box. 'Ironminster wants to come and see you, but we're preventing him, for fear of infection. He's still not very strong, and a dose of typhoid would do for him. But I think our laywer will wish to see you.'

'And I will wish to see our lawyer, too, if I'm to speak the same story as everyone else.'

'No, Ned, you don't say a word in court, apart from "Not Guilty". It is all in the lawyers' hands. Just don't look too surprised at what they say, that's all. The prosecution avers – if you can believe it – that James sought you out in order to offer you the post of coachman at Mole End. What do you say to that? He sought you out in a private place, to have a confidential conversation. We knew that Rupert wasn't going to confess that James sought you out in a private place in order to do you in, but we were somewhat surprised, to say the least, at the audacity of his excuse. So you can understand that we feel free to make some fairly audacious excuses ourselves.'

'It's all to be lies in court?'

'Largely, Ned. The truth won't do for Rupert any more than it will for us.'

'But won't the judge and the jury see through it all?'

'Ned, give us the benefit of some intelligence. We are well connected with legal – persons. We are not short of the money required for their fees. We intend to see that you are acquitted.'

'I still don't see how it's to be done.'

'It is of no advantage to you to know the details. You have some very good friends, believe me, and you don't need to worry. One thing you can rest your mind on – Miss Redbridge's part in your escapade won't be made public, for Rupert is gentleman enough to leave her presence unmentioned. We are all agreed that you left the coach alone at Fairoaks.'

Railton, when he was being serious, had such an air of authority that Ned was inclined to accept his reassurances. Knowing that his days in Newgate were now numbered, to be finished either by his acquittal or by his death, he spent most of his days indulging himself – on Railton's cash – in gambling with his fellow-prisoners, the turnkeys leaving the cell doors unlocked for most of the day. He also drank a good deal, to take his mind off what lay ahead, afraid to think about it. His lawyer came to visit, a heavy, dry man, not anxious to say a great deal, but explicit in exactly what Ned was to say – apparently four words only: "Not guilty, my Lord," and to everything else: "I leave it to my counsel." Ned, considering him, felt very much a pawn in some complicated game, a trout on a line who would swim free or get hit on the head by a rock. Enough to send him back to the gin bottle. But two days before the trial Railton came to him, bringing him clean clothes, dark and discreet, for his court appearance, and his usual words of reassurance. But as he left, and the turnkey stood by, waiting, he hesitated in the doorway, and said, 'I should warn you, Ned – a great deal has been left unsaid between us. You will be very surprised at the way things have turned out, and when you meet Ironminster again –' he paused, perhaps wondering whether he should say any more –

'well, you will get a shock.'

'How do you mean? Does he look very ill?'

'No, it's not that. We are used to his looking ill. But this –
this business –' he gestured uncertainly, and shrugged – 'It has
changed a whole lot of things. Nothing will be the same again.
You will see what I mean in a few days' time. Just be prepared,
when you leave here, for a shock.'

Ned thought, as long as it wasn't the shock of being hanged,
he could stomach anything.

13

'GENTLEMEN of the jury, by the indictment which you have just heard read by the Officer of the Court, you are already acquainted with the nature of the crime with which the prisoner at the bar stands accused. But it is a duty that devolves upon me, as counsel for the prosecution, to state to you in a more minute and particular manner the precise nature of that charge . . .'

Ned, looking extremely smart and upstanding in Railton's clothes, expensive black coat and starched linen setting off the prison pallor of his face and the flaming copper of his bare head, made a striking criminal (as Railton had intended), his appearance, youth and subdued manner subtly contradicting his reputation as murderer. He felt subdued; more by the knowledge that if the verdict went against him, it being a Monday, he would by the same time next week be dead. He could not share Railton's confidence, still less as the counsel for the prosecution prepared to unfold his story.

He sat down, as he was bid, having proclaimed his plea of Not Guilty. Two bored jailers sat with him, one of them twirling a stem of withered sage out of the pile of pungent herbs on the bench before them. These were apparently to nullify the smell of the prisoner; the judge's bench was similarly strewn, a few dishes of early primroses glowing hopefully amongst them. It was probably true, Ned decided, that in spite of his fresh garments he smelt; he certainly itched unmercifully, and he understood that lawyers in court were very nervous of contracting jail-fever, for which reason no doubt the smell of snuff was equally strong. These trivial interests were easier to dwell on than the far more affecting sight of Ironminster sitting with Railton and Field in the body of the court. He looked dreadful, and coughed constantly. He had met Ned's eye on entering court, but made only a sad smile. Ned, for his part, had felt a deep spasm of emotion on seeing him again. He did not know whether it was for love or pity, or both, and had turned his mind away from the subject to recover his composure. Pity he must reserve for himself. It did not do in this arena of high emotion to digress from the essentials – time later to uncover the old relationships and loyalties. He seemed to have been away from the world for a century. The court-house, although stuffy and overcrowded, was a gracious relief with its plastered ceilings and long windows, from the stone gloom of the prison beyond. One was encouraged to believe in civilization and justice: the only rub being that, if justice was to triumph, he was in fact guilty of the deed the prosecution was now so elaborately describing. Ned sat without moving, trying not to let his thoughts wander, hands tightly clasped beneath Railton's fine lace ruffles.

'The deceased, Mr James Saville, was a gentleman of the highest repute, a cousin to Lord Ironminster, the prisoner's employer . . .'

The prosecution counsel, Mr Nathaniel Clarke, long-winded and self-important, described the true facts leading up to the arrival of the two coaches at The Bull, putting a surprisingly different light on the result of the wager: 'Lord Ironminster's victory being mainly due to the very skilful driving of his drag by the prisoner at the bar, which skill was much admired by Mr James and Mr Rupert Saville, so much so, in fact, that – despite their disappointment in losing the wager to Lord Ironminster – they there and then decided to see if they could secure the services of Rowlands for themselves.'

So Railton's information was true. This is where the lies started – although the next admission was true enough: 'You will understand that there was considerable rivalry, not to say animosity, between Lord Ironminster and the deceased and his brother, which will not be denied by any of the parties, and this decision to approach Rowlands was therefore not impeded by any considerations of loyalty.'

No, indeed, thought Ned. Only by considerations to see him beaten to death by a pair of hired thugs. But Mr Clarke was more circumspect than to reveal this desire.

'In order to talk to Rowlands Mr James Saville left the dining-room of The Bull alone and gave a message to a stable-boy, Bob Barnard, to ask Rowlands to meet him outside the back gate of the stable-yard, where they could talk in private.

186

This was very convenient for Rowlands, who was tending his horses in the yard. You will hear a statement from Mr Barnard to the effect that this message was indeed given to Rowlands who was in the harness-room at the time talking to Mr Herbert, the head groom at The Bull. Mr Herbert will also testify to this message being passed to Rowlands. Rowlands, on receiving the message, got up and went out of the yard.'

'As to what passed between the two men we can only conjecture from the result. Rowlands came back into the stable-yard less than five minutes after he left it and sent word into the inn that he wanted to speak to his employer. We have a witness to this effect. As Lord Ironminster was feeling indisposed, his companion Lord Railton went out to speak with Rowlands, as a result of which conversation the horses were put to immediately and the party left at once, making for home. This in spite of the fact, remember, gentlemen, that the horses had less than an hour before completed the journey from Threadgolds at an extremely fast pace and were obviously in a very fatigued state. I will put it to you that this precipitous departure was instigated by Rowlands in order to leave as quickly as possible the scene of his crime.'

Perfectly true, Ned thought. Horribly, accurately true. He glanced at Railton, who sat impassively, very serious, a different man from the prankster they were all accustomed to. Ned thought he looked strained and tired, and wondered again whether the apparent confidence was merely an act. But if he let his mind wander in that direction, he could easily panic . . . He tried to concentrate on the moment, the complacent features of his own counsel, Mr Reader, who had shown no anxiety. Or was that professional imperturbability? Lawyers did not cry over their hanged clients, but shrugged their shoulders and passed the bill to the next of kin.

'No sooner had the party left,' continued Mr Clarke, 'than a passer-by reported the finding of Mr Saville's body in the back lane. He was killed, you will hear, by a violent blow to the back of his head, which fractured his skull.'

'On learning what had happened, the deceased's brother, Mr Rupert Saville, very sensibly got fresh horses for his drag and set off in pursuit. Five miles from home, at a ford on Threadgold's lane, Lord Ironminster's coach stopped and the accused got down and ran away into the woods, leaving Lord Railton to handle the reins. Shortly afterwards Mr Saville overtook the Ironminster coach, ascertained that Rowlands was missing, and sent out a search-party with bloodhounds to follow Rowlands' trail from the ford. This resulted in the capture of Rowlands some few hours later and his subsequent arrest for the murder of Mr James Saville. These circumstances, gentlemen, can all be indubitably proved by the evidence that will be produced to substantiate them, and I feel convinced that you will have no hesitation in finding the prisoner guilty of the crime imputed to him. I would now ask leave to call my witnesses.'

God Almighty, Ned thought, could anyone have the faintest shadow of doubt that he was guilty after that narrative? Dammit, he *was* guilty! Where was this clever fellow who was going to prove otherwise? His heavy features not at all disturbed, Mr Reader was talking to Railton, stroking his chin thoughtfully. He had a sheaf of papers in his hand. He was not allowed to address the jury directly as the prosecution had just done, as Ned well knew; his side of the story had to be revealed by witnesses. In this case they would have to be perjurors, liars before God. Ned felt himself sweating. The jury, respectable-looking men soberly dressed for the occasion, muttered amongst themselves and nodded their heads. They had all stared long and hard at Ned, and no doubt seen the light of panic in his eye. Ned stared at his hands, willing himself to keep calm.

'I would like to call my first witness, my Lord, Mr Rupert Saville, brother to the deceased.'

'Call Rupert Saville.'

Saville crossed the court and climbed the steps into the witness-box. He did not look to left or right, but directly at his counsel, very upright, impeccably dressed, grave and authoritative. He did not look at all the sort of man whose word one would doubt. He took the oath. 'God see you rot in hell,' Ned thought, watching him.

Rupert gave his story without hesitation, asserting that James had gone out to meet Ned with the intention of offering him a post as coachman at Mole End. Ned half-expected a thunderbolt to hit him as Rupert uttered this iniquity, but the equanimity of the court remained unchanged. The judge actually yawned at this point, and Mr Reader was picking his nose, gazing at his sheaf of papers. It occurred to Ned that getting a man hanged was quite an every-day occurrence to these people. The judge pronounced sentence and went home to play with his children and eat a good dinner. Had he ever looked inside the walls of Newgate beyond the court-room door? Ned, getting angry and fidgety, wriggled against the bench to relieve his itching. God blast Saville! A week or two in the Common Felons would improve his soul.

'I would admit here, gentlemen, that our intention to secure the services of the prisoner was undeterred by any feelings of loyalty towards our cousin, Lord Ironminster, who has treated us with equal indifference in the past. But I submit that my brother's approach to Rowlands was entirely friendly, admiring, in fact and made in perfect sincerity and good faith.'

'This was the last occasion on which you saw your brother alive, when he left you in the dining-room in The Bull, to go and speak to Rowlands?'

'Yes.'

The rest of his story was true enough, the story of his pursuit of the Ironminster coach back towards Threadgolds and his ordering out the bloodhound party when he found that Ned had left the coach at the ford. Much importance was put by his counsel on the fact that the Ironminster coach had left much sooner than might have been expected, a mere five minutes before the body had been discovered in the alley.

'And how can one describe the journey back to Threadgolds as other than a flight to safety, which, when it was obviously failing due to the fatigue of the horses, was abandoned by the prisoner, with the condonation – no, indeed, one might say at the *instigation* – of his employer and companions? A desperate move, one would suggest, at the very moment of being taken, which did in fact defer his capture by several hours. But, thanks to the aciduous searching and pursuit of Mr Saville's party with bloodhounds, the prisoner was eventually run down and taken into custody.'

Mr Clarke sat down and Mr Reader, once more glum and expressionless, lumbered into action to cross-examine Rupert Saville. Ned detected that Rupert looked nervous at this point.

'Am I right in understanding that this journey to London, to attempt to do the distance in under one and a quarter hours to win a wager, was proceeded upon without any public notice, in order that Lord Ironminster would not know about it?'

'I did not want Ironminster to know about it, no.'

'He was very anxious to win this wager himself?'

'I believe so.'

'So, in effect, Lord Ironminster made the journey as soon as he knew you were going to make it, which must have meant that he gave his orders somewhat precipitously to Mr Rowlands, that Mr Rowlands had to drop whatever arrangements he might have made to do otherwise and set out without any warning for London? This at a time when he might well have expected to be off duty, and enjoying his evening after his own fashion?'

'That could well have been so. I believe Lord Ironminster had spies watching my stable to see when I left.'

'He will not deny it. He was aware that you were trying to make the journey before he felt ready to do it and naturally did not want to be beaten. But the point I am making, gentlemen of the jury, is that Mr Rowlands, that night, was not expecting to be called out. Thank you, Mr Saville.'

Ned felt baffled by Reader's insistence on this point, with its implication that he enjoyed his evenings in some unspecified licentious fashion. In fact, after supper in the servants' hall, he made a last round of the stables to see all was well, locked up and went to bed. Not much enjoyment there.

At this point the court adjourned for lunch, and Ned was locked up alone in a cell outside the court until the afternoon session. He had hoped he might have a visit from Railton, if not Ironminster himself, but all he got was one of the jailers bringing him a cup of ale and a piece of dry bread. He sat alone, puzzled, anxious and miserable, trying to believe that in a couple of days he would be acquitted and freed, to resume his life at Threadgolds. But it did not seem possible, with the jury all fed on the tale of his ignominious flight through the Fairoaks woods.

After lunch they were given even more details.

'You would say that the prisoner tried very hard to evade capture? That there was no suggestion of his merely taking a walk, a short-cut through the woods towards home?'

'Oh, no, sir, he led us a pretty dance, and ran very fast and fought hard at the finish to try and prevent us overpowering him.'

The bloodhound keeper was enjoying his hour of glory. 'We had to knock him down with ash-poles, sir, to stop him fighting.'

'Six against one, the swines,' Ned thought, scowling at the floor. If it wasn't his life at stake, he would have been bored rigid. The court had grown stuffy and hot and he wanted to scratch all the time, save Railton had told him to sit like a gentleman to give the best impression possible. If he wasn't going to swing, it was high time someone started to give him an alibi.

The constable to whom he had been taken after his capture was sworn in and gave evidence. Mr Reader asked him, 'Was there any evidence on his clothes or person of his having killed a man by violence? The deceased was in a very bloody state when found, remember.'

The constable was uncertain. 'It's hard to say, sir. There was a good deal of blood on the lower half of his body, but I would say it came from the lacerations made by the dogs when he was caught. In any case, the blood from his lacerations would have covered any earlier blood if there had been any.'

'Perhaps you could give us the time of the prisoner's being apprehended? I understand you have the details?'

'He was captured at near enough seven o'clock in the morning, sir.'

'But I understand from Mr Saville's evidence –' Mr Reader consulted his notes, lifting his spectacles to do so – 'That he left the coach and took to the woods at midnight, as near as anyone can tell. Mr Saville went home and called out a party of men from his estate to go out with the dogs, which did not set out until three o'clock, I am told. Have you any idea as to what the prisoner was doing between midnight and, say, six o'clock, when the dogs got on to his trail?'

'Hiding and resting up, I daresay, sir.'

'Hmm,' said Mr Reader, with what Ned considered unnecessary emphasis. He sounded as if he doubted the constable's suggestion. Nobody, according to plan, had yet suggested that Ironminster had also left the coach and taken to the woods, let alone Miss Redbridge. Ned, having concentrated hard for several hours, was beginning to feel very tired and slightly faint, unused to a hot atmosphere after the rigours of his unheated cell; Ironminster, he noticed, was sniffing at a salts bottle and leaning wearily over the table in front of him. The reek of herbs and vinegar-sprinkled vegetation, not to mention snuff and sweat and hints of the prison-stench creeping through closed doors, all conspired to make a very thick atmosphere. The judge was glancing at his watch.

'How many more witnesses have we got for the prosecution, Mr Clarke?' he asked.

'Three, my Lord.'

'I suggest we adjourn now and hear them tomorrow.'

'Very well, my Lord.'

Ned got to his feet as the court rose and the judge and jury filed out. He hoped Lord Ironminster would come and speak to him, but the jailers took him out immediately, back to his cell, where they chained him to his bed. When he complained, they laughed and said, 'Make the most of it, lad. It's roses here compared to the condemned cells, which is where you'll be tomorrow.'

Ned rather thought so too, the way things were going, and lay back on the pillows and watched the last of the sun-tipped light filtering through his poky window, fading into dusk. He felt cold and pulled the blankets over him, feeling wretchedly disappointed after Railton's optimism. The story the court had heard so far pointed massively to his guilt. The stolid Mr Reader did not impress as the sort of man to produce great surprises, a complete turn-round of opinion; Ned felt utterly condemned by what he had heard in court, and so no doubt the jury thought too. The small barred window darkened and he lay and watched the stars come out, drained now of the fear he had felt earlier when the threat of dying had been farther away. His life was of little account; no one depended upon him, save Ironminster who would be dead soon in any case, and hanging was no worse a death than most, more merciful indeed than Ironminster's was likely to be. The panic had given way to resignation, which was strangely restful after all the fretting he had done the last few weeks. The stars suggested a philosophy, putting him in his tiny place, having outlived millions of lives as puny as his and likely to outlive several millions more. If he was condemned he would send word to his father to make a proper leave-taking; Railton would arrange it. He would not like to push his pride so far that he would not do that.

By the time the stars had faded and the sky was lightening again, he felt cramped, frozen, hungry – but far more cheerful. The dark watches of the night, he decided, were conducive to thoughts of death. The morning made one far more keen to stay alive. The turnkey brought him some food, and he prevailed upon him to fetch a barber to make him look respectable, which cost him half a guinea, some twenty times the amount it would have cost outside. He then paid twopence for a cup of gin to make him feel more optimistic, and a crown to get unlocked from the ringbolt in the wall, which allowed him to put on a clean shirt and neckcloth. The jailers, coming to escort him to the court-room, mocked him for his smart appearance and hoped his noble friends had spent as much trouble on his defence – 'For you're going to need it before the day is out, my boy.'

Ned did not reply, straightening up as they opened the doors and led him into the dock. The court was crowded. Ned, aware of the curious eyes on him, kept his own cast down, and sent up a bleak prayer for deliverance. He now felt very nervous, shivers creeping up his spine, and would have given another of his guineas for some more gin, enough to stupify the brain.

The judge took his place and the proceedings commenced after a short preamble concerning the events of the day before. Mr Clarke sought permission to call more witnesses for the prosecution which, being granted, brought the stable-boy, Bob Barnard, into the witness box, to testify to his giving the message to Ned that James Saville wished to see him in the back lane.

Mr Reader got to his feet and Ned looked up hopefully.

'When you gave the prisoner this message what was he doing?'

'He was having a drink with Mr Herbert, sir.'

'Did he get up and go towards the gate into the back lane?'

'I suppose he did, sir.'

'You didn't see him?'

'No, sir. I gave the message and went back to my work immediately.'

'Leaving the prisoner still talking with Mr Herbert?'

'Yes, sir.'

'Thank you.' Mr Reader sat down again.

Anyone would know that for a lie, Ned thought – a stable-boy going back to his work immediately, but no one remarked on the unlikeliness of the statement.

Mr Clarke called Mr Herbert, and Ned was more hopeful, Ben Herbert being a cheerful acquaintance of some years standing.

'Yes, I was with Mr Rowlands when the boy brought the message.'

At this point Mr Reader stood up, with slightly more agility than he had displayed before.

'Did the prisoner leave you after the message was delivered?'

'Not immediately. He didn't seem interested. He said words to the effect that he was going to put the horses to again, ready to leave, as he didn't want to waste any time.'

'Did he say he was going home the same night?'

'I understood so, sir. He said their Lordships didn't intend to stay long in The Bull, only for refreshment. He was very anxious to get home again, I got the impression.'

'In your opinion, had the horses rested sufficiently for the return journey?'

'Yes, sir. They were the fittest horses I've ever set eyes on, sir, which credit must go to Mr Rowlands for the way he kept 'em.'

'You didn't see him leave the yard?'

'No, sir. When he left me he went back into the stable.'

'He ignored the message?'

'He said, sir, that he didn't want to speak with Mr Saville.'

'Thank you, Mr Herbert.'

Ned went on looking at the floor, remembering that Railton had told him not to show any surprise at anything he might hear. But now, for the first time, the lies were to his advantage. He felt a great rush of warmth towards old Herbert, the silly old devil, as he watched his bandy-legged progress out of court. Mr Clarke, conferring with Rupert Saville, looked annoyed.

The judge said, 'Am I to understand that nobody actually saw the prisoner go out of the yard to meet Mr Saville?'

'It seems not, my Lord,' Mr Reader replied, stony-faced. 'Unless Mr Clarke has another witness.'

,'Have you any more witnesses, Mr Clarke?'

Clarke muttered something to Saville again, then stood up and said, 'No, my Lord.'

'In that case, the evidence for the prosecution is closed.'

The judge spoke to his clerk, and there was a general shuffling and muttering, until order was called. Ned, prompted by his jailers, got to his feet.

The judge, peering down the court towards him, said, 'Prisoner, now is the time for you to make your defence. The court and jury will now hearken with patience and attention to anything you have to say.'

'I leave it to my counsel, my Lord,' Ned said.

'Very well. Mr Reader?'

'I should like to call Lord Ironminster as first witness for the defence, my Lord.'

Ned watched Ironminster cross the floor of the court and climb slowly into the witness-box. Although Ironminster was acting to help him, Ned felt instinctively that it should be the other way round: Ironminster looked as frail as Ned had ever seen him. Ned stood there, feeling darkly that if, in this life, justice were truly to prevail, not only would he be acquitted, but Ironminster too would be delivered from his wretched fate, which at this moment looked likely to overtake him sooner than Ned's own, should the outcome be unfavourable. A clerk put a glass of water on the shelf before him.

Reader said to him, 'Lord Ironminster, when you made this journey to London, was it made on the spur of the moment, without prior warning to the prisoner that he was likely to go out that night?'

'Yes. I ordered the coach to be got ready in the evening, when it seemed likely that my cousin was about to leave.'

'Did you intend to come back home the same night?'

'Yes, I did. After the horses had rested.'

'Did Rowlands know this?'

'Yes. I told him I expected to be back about midnight.'

'When you were in The Bull, after about an hour is it true that Rowlands sent a message in to you to say that he wanted to depart?'

'Yes, that is true. Lord Railton went out to him and said we would be coming shortly.'

Mr Clarke stood up and the judge nodded to him. Clarke said to Ironminster, 'Are we to believe that your coachman sent what amounted to an order to you, to say that he wanted to depart? This merely an idle desire of his own? May I not suggest that this message was a very urgent one, saying that he wanted to depart as hastily as possible, because he had just committed a murder?'

'You can suggest that if you like. But you must remember that we had agreed to stay only an hour at The Bull, and that hour was up, and my coachman had orders to call us when he thought the horses were rested enough to start back. Which is what he did.'

Clarke sat down, frowning.

Reader said to Ironminster, 'I understand that you have a very high opinion of the prisoner?'

'Yes, I have. He is the best whip I have ever ridden with, and a very conscientious horse-keeper.'

'You would be distressed if he were to leave your service?'

'Yes.'

'Were you aware that he had a liaison, a relationship, with a female servant in your household?'

Ned wasn't sure if he had heard this last question correctly and, as if to make it clear to him, Mr Reader repeated it in a louder voice. A muttering ran round the court and everyone looked much more interested. Ned tried not to look too interested too, but could feel the blood pulsing up to his ears in amazement.

Ironminster answered, 'Yes.'

'This girl, Mathilda Smith, is a maid-servant in your household?'

'Yes.'

'You say you were aware of this – er – friendship?'

'Yes, I was. I have seen them embracing.'

One of the jailers nudged Ned and whispered something, but Ned could scarcely believe what he was hearing from Ironminster, let alone from his companion.

'You did nothing to discourage it?'

'No. They are well-matched. I saw no reason to discourage it, if it made them happy.'

'I am suggesting that the accused had other reasons for being home by midnight, personal reasons that might have prompted him to send the message in to The Bull to suggest a departure?'

'Quite possibly.'

'Thank you, Lord Ironminster.'

'Do you want to cross-examine Lord Ironminster, Mr Clarke?' asked the judge.

'No, my Lord.'

'Have you any other witnesses to call, Mr Reader?'

'I would like to call Mathilda Smith, my Lord.'

'Very well. Call Mathilda Smith.'

Ned had the utmost difficulty in constraining himself – what was it Railton had said about shocks! God, but he had under-estimated the man! And what in God's name was Matty going to say in his defence? He stood rigid, trying to look impassive, and saw Matty ushered in from a doorway at the side. She walked across to the witness-box, dressed in very simple dark clothes, her red hair loose in its wild childish curls over her shoulders and, quite plainly to the whole court, pregnant. Ned, after the simple shock of setting eyes on her again, took in her condition and was in dire peril of fainting clean away. He clutched at the bench in front of him and took wild, calming breaths, feeling quite desperate. The jailers on either side were muttering some very coarse remarks, and the whole court was plainly much more interested by the turn of events, shuffling and exclaiming to such an extent that the clerk had to call for order. Ned, recovering his composure with great difficulty, saw that Rupert Saville was looking outraged, and seemed to be remonstrating angrily with his counsel, but Railton, Ironminster and Reader looked impassive.

Reader faced Matty and said, 'You are Mathilda Smith, a maid-servant at Threadgolds, and acquainted with the prisoner?'

'Yes, sir.'

'In what way are you acquainted?'

'Very closely, sir. He is the father of the child I am bearing.'

Matty's voice was soft but perfectly audible, and she spoke with neither shame nor pride, but matter-of-factly, keeping her eyes on her questioner. Whether it was a great ordeal for her or not Ned could not guess; whether she was doing it from love or loyalty or merely for payment he could not devise; her lies were monstrous, and left him breathless.

'Will you tell us what you were doing on the night of Mr Saville's murder, the night the prisoner drove to London to win the wager?'

'I had arranged to meet him at midnight, sir, in the gamekeeper's cottage at Fairoaks. I went there and waited for him.'

'And he came?'

'Yes, sir, at about the time he had promised.'

'Did he tell you that he had left the coach at the ford and come through the woods?'

'Yes, sir. He said they – their Lordships – had allowed him. They were in a very good mood, having won the wager, and Lord Railton wanted to take the reins, and he said he took advantage of their good spirits to ask permission to get down. He was afraid otherwise I would have got tired of waiting and left.'

'And he stayed there with you for several hours?'

'Until we heard the hounds, sir, and I was frightened. He got up and said he would go and see what was happening. We didn't want to be discovered together in the cottage.'

'But their Lordships had given their consent to the prisoner meeting you.'

'Yes, but that was different. I didn't want it to come to her Ladyship's notice, or to be common knowledge, in case I got dismissed. Their Lordships, with respect, sir, treat many things as a joke which her Ladyship would not, and nor would the housekeeper to whom I am answerable.'

This spirited reply brought a titter of amusement from the body of the court and even the judge smiled.

'The prisoner did not suppose the hounds were hunting him?'

'No, sir, not that he revealed to me. He was just anxious to give me protection.'

'Thank you.'

Matty got down and great curiosity and excitement followed her departure. Ned contained his feelings to the best of his ability, but was obliged to hide his face in his hands, elbows on knees, for the sum total of her evidence was too great a shock to take impassively. Not only her appearance, but her condition, not to mention the enormous validity her lies had given to his plea of not guilty – altogether too rich a confection for his mind to take in without the consternation and excitement showing in his face. And her motive – had she been prevailed upon to do it by Ironminster and Railton? Had they paid her? Had they pleaded with her? Or had she done it entirely for love? Not once had she looked in his direction, nor had she shown any untoward emotion. She had loved him once, he knew well enough – but she had obviously loved Tom Garnett equally as well (no, *more*), and, for all he knew, was now betrothed to him, if not already married. Lady Ironminster surely would not keep her unmarried in that condition for longer than was necessary? Lady Ironminster normally dismissed pregnant serving-girls, as well he remembered, for that was how Matty had come by the job in the first place.

By the time all this confusion had settled in his head, the court, after some conferring amongst the lawyers, had agreed to adjourn for lunch, and Ned was removed to his cell. He no longer had the composure to think intelligently: Matty had put his sense to flight. Perhaps she had saved his life. When he went back into court, the judge was ready to make his summing-up for jury, and the ordeal was drawing to its close.

The judge, looking towards the jury, said, 'If, on considering all the circumstances of the case, you should be of the opinion that no reasonable doubt exists, that the prisoner is the person who committed the crime, in justice to the public the conviction of the prisoner must follow. But if that should not be the case, if you have good reason to doubt his guilt, that would be a ground of acquittal.'

He then proceeded to gather together all the facts, which long story Ned tried to listen to as if he were one of the jury, but he was so nervous by this stage that he could not concentrate. He felt very hot and thirsty, and he itched unbearably, and his mind kept wandering off into amazing fantasies, mostly concerned with Matty. He noticed that Ironminster sat very still, gazing into space, looking intensely miserable, but Railton looked rather pleased and fidgeted a good deal, glancing at his watch at intervals. Rupert Saville was dour, arms folded across his chest.

'And so I would direct you, members of the jury, that by the evidence alone are you to be guided in your decision. It is better that a murderer with all the weight of his crime upon his head should escape punishment than that an innocent man should suffer death. Please go and consider your verdict.'

Ned thought that what he had heard of the summing-up had been vastly in his favour, but – such was his state of mind – decided that he had heard only what he had wanted to hear. The following hour was painful in the extreme. The court adjourned; the jailers stayed with him outside. Ned, seeing the afterooon light falling in dusty golden streaks through the high windows, thought of going into the condemned cells and wanted to be sick. He was close enough now to the outside world to want to embrace it with such love and passion as he didn't know was in him; to be convicted now would be harder than the actual drop. Yet if he was convicted he must stand there impassively and listen to the dreadful words: with so little time left to make an impression in the world let it never be said that he did not make a good and brave impression on being convicted. 'The prisoner showed no emotion' – he had seen it written in the newspapers, and admired. He would do the same. He clenched his hands to stop his fingers fidgeting and walked up and down a few paces, shutting his mind to the crude remarks the jailers were passing about Matty.

'How long do you think they'll be?'

'Well, if it's not to be tonight, they'll soon be telling us. But I reckon they'll want to get home to their suppers the same as the rest of us.'

They laughed at his impatience, but were not unsympathetic. 'The judge – he were on your side, I reckon.'

Dusk was veiling the windows and the first friendly star was showing when the court was convened again. Ned was marched back in to an expectant silence. He stood alone, the jailers stepping back. The foreman of the jury looked at the judge.

'Do you find the prisoner guilty or not guilty?'

'Not guilty, my Lord.'

It was over. Ned, according to his resolution, showed no emotion, and was dismissed to freedom.

14

'Look, Ned, old fellow, I'm afraid the shocks aren't over yet.'

Railton looked both grave and nervous, taking his arm and drawing him to one side.

'I know you want to speak to Ironminster, but Ironminster isn't in a fit state to talk to anyone at the moment. You are to come home with me. It's his wish. Tomorrow – that's another story . . . tomorrow you are to drive him to his wedding.'

'Who?'

'Lord Ironminster.'

'His *wedding*?'

'Yes. St George's, Hanover Square, at noon. He is marrying Amelia Amherst.'

Ned was speechless. Railton took the opportunity of guiding him towards a carriage and pair that was waiting and gesturing him inside. Ned got in, noticing nothing. He looked at Railton, appalled.

'Remember, it's four months since we last met outside the walls of Newgate, Ned. In Ironminster's life, that's a long time. After his last illness, he decided to do what everyone wished. No one, including himself, is of the opinion that he will have very long to suffer the state and he will enjoy annoying Rupert. The only stipulation was that the event would not take place before you were free to drive the wedding coach.'

Wedding coach . . .! But a wedding was a happy, laughing event . . . the Ironminster wedding coach should have Sarah Redbridge inside it, not the dumpy, perspiring, ever-talking Amelia. It was a disaster equal to – to his own hanging, had it happened.

'But why? He was ill before –'

'It's not entirely unexpected, Ned. The pressure has always been great, you know that. Perhaps he just hasn't got the strength to resist any more.'

'Why didn't you tell me before?'

'He didn't want you to know.'

'I don't understand it –'

'Why not? A great many marriages are for convenience, you know. I daresay I shall put convenience first myself when the time comes.'

'But *he* –' Ned stopped, unable to put it into words. He felt bitterly let down, as if in some way Ironminster had failed him. Ironminster with his extraordinary spirit, cocking a snook at convention, at his health, at his responsibilities, always game for a lark – to stoop to *convenience*. Convenience wasn't in his nature. It would have been far more convenient to live quietly, to sell his coach and horses, to lead an invalid life, to save his strength, but the Ironminster Ned thought he knew so well wasn't that sort of man at all. Perhaps his last illness had changed him.

'You were right about the shocks,' he said.

He felt rough, exhausted. He could not have believed, a few hours earlier, that anything would have had the power to make him feel unhappy once he had got clear of Newgate, but now he was unhappy.

'Come, Ned!' Railton was perhaps surprised at his reaction. 'It should be a night for celebrating. No regrets –'

Had Railton seen Ironminster with Sarah, Ned wondered, as he had seen them together? Even the last night, in the cottage, asleep in each other's arms . . . remembering that, Ned thought that Ironminster's capitulation amounted to treachery. The night in the cottage reminded him forcibly of something else.

'It was Matty's evidence that got me acquitted.'

'Yes, I think so.'

'Who thought of that story?'

'Sam.'

Sam! Ned laughed then. Of course! Sam saw to all the trickery in the Ironminster ménage, even to employing the coachman. He wanted badly to talk to Sam. There were all sorts of things he wanted to know, not least about Matty, but one wouldn't ask Lord Railton such things. Railton looked tired too. He said he was to be August's best man in the morning and Ned knew that that job would not be easy. His own might not be easy either.

'How are our horses going? Are they fit?'

'Fit enough, Ned, although nobody's driven them as a team since the night they won the wager. Pegram's scared of 'em. They're up here now though, in Conduit Street, and after the reception you'll have to take them home with the bride and bridegroom. We'll go over to Conduit Street together in the morning, in plenty of time.'

Railton took Ned into his house in St Alban's Street, and took him up to his own rooms and charged his valet to look after him, provide him with everything he needed.

'I must go back to August, Ned. He'll need me tonight. You can have your dinner served up here, and Charles will prepare you a bath, and a bed, and anything else you need. I'll bring your livery back with me, ready for the morning.'

Ned would have preferred the servants' quarters, but found it impossible to say so. The luxury of Railton's apartments was overpowering after the austerity he had become accustomed to. He moved away from the large fire and stood at the window looking down into the street, feeling very strange, the enormous relief at his acquittal overlaid by disquietude for Ironminster. For all Railton's urbane acceptance of what was happening, with his talk of convenience, Ned felt that the alliance was a monstrous let-down; he wondered if perhaps he had overrated Ironminster. Why did he feel so disappointed? It didn't matter a wit to him, after all. It made no difference to his own position in the household. He watched the lights of a carriage passing, and the same stars he had watched through his barred window the night before. What did it matter? He was too tired to come to any conclusions, a large supper and the hot fire sending him into a doze before a maid had cleared the plates away. The valet fetched him a wooden tub of water and helped him get rid of most of the vermin that plagued him, after which he rolled into bed and slept dreamlessly and without stirring until daylight, when he was awakened by Railton in a dressing-gown, his hair in curling-papers, throwing back the covers and saying cheerfully, 'You aren't in prison now, Ned – you can't stay in bed all day. There's work to be done.'

To get Lord Ironminster married, Ned remembered, after some moments working out where he was. The sun streamed in through the windows; a manservant was setting down a silver tea-service, steaming gently, and fine bone cups and saucers. Just like Newgate, Ned thought, surprised to find that he wasn't chained to the bed. He laughed, the pure joy of knowing that he wasn't going to die as radiant a thought as the sunlight itself. Nothing else mattered at that moment.

'Is it late?'

'No. Just gone nine.' This was extremely late by Ned's reckoning and he sat up quickly. 'No hurry,' Railton said. 'We can be round at Conduit Street by eleven nicely. Everything is in hand over there.'

It was a perfect spring morning, the pigeons crooning softly in the gutters and the sky very clear and pale and delicate. Ned thought of Threadgolds and going home, and felt marvellously happy, in spite of everything. He drank tea with Railton, constrained with him now that life was taking up its normal order again, anxious to get back to his own place.

Afterwards, when Railton left him, a man came to shave him, and he got dressed in the livery that was laid out in the dressing-room: his full livery for the occasion, with white silk stockings and satin knee-breeches, and the heavy, ornate coat with gold frogging. Suitably sobered by its grandeur, he pulled on the powdered wig with its curls over the ears and ringlets tied with black velvet, and realized by the familiar prickling of his scalp that the wig's close warmth was going to play the devil with his flea-bites. The smile faded. There would be no free hand for scratching once he was on the box-seat; the prospect was daunting. At this point Railton came in, extremely elegant in a coat of cinnamon-brown velvet with a gold waistcoat and pale cream satin breeches and stockings.

'What do you think? A trifle gaudy, perhaps, but someone has to make a show. August swears he is wearing black, even to the cravat, but I am relying on Sam to dissuade him. You and I are a match, at least, Ned. Let us take a glass of brandy before we depart and drink to your freedom. Better a jaunt like this than a ticket to see you hang, eh? I was beginning to wonder at one point . . .'

They drove to Conduit Street in a carriage and Ned was put down at the gate of the mews. He felt very nervous suddenly, presenting himself to the old faces after such a long absence, especially in these unfamiliar clothes, but he need not have worried. The welcome was genuinely moving, from old Pegram's unashamed nose-blowing to the youngest lad's solemn avowal of loyalty: 'We was all going to come and see you, sir, if you'd hanged.'

'I'm sorry if I disappointed you!'

'Oh, no, sir. It's just that it's not very often it's someone you know.'

Ned laughed. 'Let's see my horses then. Bring them out. If Brimstone decides to play up we might keep the bride waiting.'

His horses, he decided critically, were not the horses he had last seen, obviously having been let down in condition, no doubt to make them more manageable, but they were nice enough, and the sight of them made him feel as sentimental as old Pegram for a moment, so that he went up to Starling and laid his cheek against the horse's own and spoke to him with a caressing voice. The horse fluttered his nostrils at him, recognizing him, blowing a cloud of powder out of his wig. Ned laughed, and looked at his watch.

'Are the footmen ready?'

'I'll tell them, sir.'

Ned checked the harness minutely and the pole and pole-chains and the couplings, the horses' feet, the inside of the coach and the wheels, decided he was satisfied and told the footmen to get up. He put on his white gloves and Pegram brushed the shoulders of his coat and handed him his whip. Ned picked up the reins, adjusting them in his hand. Up on the box, holding the horses' mouths again, all the familiar smells and sounds and feelings reminding him with sickening clarity of all he had so nearly lost, he hastily eased the reins, not wanting to think about it, and concentrated on leaving the mews without taking away the gatepost, a doubtful accomplishment at the best of times. But he had not lost his touch. He arrived at the front door of the Ironminster house thirty seconds before the required time and pulled up with the door of the coach exactly opposite the door of the house. The footmen got down. Ned waited, his eyes strictly ahead like a good servant, heard the front door open and the voices on the step, Railton laughing, Lady Ironminster forgetting something. Another minute and the footman nodded to him, climbed up and they were off down the street.

'St George's with this lot, then Park Lane to collect the bride and her old man,' the footman said, with a lack of dignity that was incongruous with his formidable bearing.

It was all accomplished without incident, Miss Amherst stepping down with her father on to the red carpet before the church steps exactly as the clock showed midday. A fair-sized crowd had gathered, murmuring and exclaiming. Out of the open doors Ned heard the organ playing and then, Amelia having got her bridesmaids into order and her dress to her liking, a wedding march started up and the small procession went into the church. Ned eased his reins to move to a quieter place to wait, but was stopped by an usher coming out of the church and calling up to him, 'You're to get down, Mr Rowlands – a word with you.' Ned got down, the footmen taking the horses, and the usher said to him, 'You are to attend the service, Lord Ironminster's instructions. Come with me,' and Ned found himself entering the hushed church to the final strains of the wedding march and being shown into an empty place in the last pew near the door, the only seat still vacant as far as he could see, for the church was crowded. He got a glimpse of Railton and Ironminster moving out to join the Amhersts at the altar and the vicar waiting to receive them; he squeezed into his pew, trod on some one's foot, apologized and heard a voice beside him say, 'God's truth, the man himself!' Glancing sideways he saw Sam regarding him, grinning.

'Sam!'

Sam put out a hand and shook Ned's vigorously.

'Dearly beloved, we are gathered together here in the sight of God to join together this man and this woman in holy matrimony. . . .'

'How are you, Ned?' Sam whispered.

'Fine.'

'Where've you been? Last night? I was waiting –'

'At Railton's. He said to leave Ironminster alone until this –'

'Yes, I can understand. What a time we've had!'

'It was you, Railton said, who got Matty to say –'

'Who else?'

'What a schemer you are!'

'Yes. It was clever, eh? They said she was very good.'

'She got me off.'

'They all got you off, Ned. Did he tell you the whole story? Railton, I mean?'

'We haven't spoken much. He was with Ironminster all last night.'

'Don't you know –'

'Will you kindly stop talking!' an acid lady in front of them hissed over her shoulder.

'. . . if any man can show any just cause why they may not lawfully be joined together let him now speak or else hereafter for ever hold his peace.'

The priestly voice floated down the aisle, echoing under the gallery, fading into the street where the onlookers were peering through the open doors. Ned sat back in the pew, taking it all in, the rows and rows of elegant men and women, brightly dressed like caged birds, peering, pecking at the entertainment, the sun shining on the white plaster pillars and glittering gold ornament.

'Wilt thou have this woman to thy wedded wife, to live together after God's ordinance in the holy estate of matrimony? Wilt thou love her, comfort her, honour and keep her, in sickness and in health . . .'

The wrong woman, Ned was thinking, his eyes on the group before the darkness of the altar, where candles were flickering and pillars of black and gold like great sticks of peppermint flanked a smoky brown painting of indecipherable beings.

'I will,' Ironminster said, very plainly.

Railton was digging in his pocket for the ring. Ned saw a white pigeon fly past against the blue sky, and thought of Threadgolds and the trees all bursting into leaf. Sam blew his nose.

Ironminster said, again quite clearly, 'With this ring I thee wed, with my body I thee worship and with all my worldly goods I thee endow. In the name of the Father and of the Son and of the Holy Ghost, Amen.'

He knelt down. The vicar said, 'Let us pray.'

Ned got down on his knees and put his face in his hands. Beside him Sam did the same.

'Oh eternal God, creator and preserver of all mankind, giver of all spiritual grace, the author of everlasting life, send they blessing upon these thy servants . . .'

Ned, endeavouring to scratch his head while everyone's eyes were discreetly closed, caught Sam's eye and was moved to breathe, 'Why, Sam? Why is he doing it?'

Sam looked away, Ned thought with devotion – mistakenly, for his eyes then returned to Ned's, uncertain, slightly suspicious.

'Didn't Railton say?'

'Say what?'

'Tell you everything?'

'What do you mean?'

It was difficult to talk in the hushed atmosphere of prayer, and Sam made a grimace and waited until the organ launched the choir into a psalm, very clear and pure in the high sunlit arches of the church. Ned waited, lifting his head, suddenly very afraid of what Sam was going to say. He looked at him. Sam went on praying, his eyes shut.

'Sam!' Ned hissed.

Sam's eyes darted open, angry at his insistence. 'You should have guessed, for heaven's sake, if nobody's told you!'

'Told me what?'

'It was a deal, for your acquittal.'

'What do you mean?'

Sam would not reply. The choir sang, 'Glory be to the Father and to the Son and to the Holy Ghost. As it was in the beginning, is now and ever shall be, world without end.'

'Amen,' said Sam. He looked sideways again. 'With Justice Amherst, of course. He arranged the acquittal, if Ironminster married his daughter.'

'Lord have mercy upon us.'

'Christ have mercy upon us,' Sam intoned. 'You were guilty after all. It wasn't easy getting you off, even with Amherst's influence.'

'Oh Lord, hear our prayer.'

'And let our cry come unto thee. Ironminster was the loser, whatever the verdict.'

'Oh, God!' Ned buried his face in his hands.

Sam was grinning. 'Pray on! You're too late to change anything now, lad.'

Sam's revelation was, to Ned, the greatest shock of them all, tearing him with disgust. He stayed, face hidden, listening to the soaring, mocking organ-music celebrating this ridiculous union, awed beyond words by what Ironminster had done for him. His acquittal last night had been Ironminster's life sentence. And to think that he – Ned – had felt disappointed, let down, by the apparent surrender to convention, to convenience, to the scheming elders. It was almost a relief, in a sense, to know that Ironminster was still the same man; Ned had not wanted his loyalties shaken.

'Don't take it too much to heart,' Sam whispered to him. 'You know a good coachman means far more to him than an ugly wife.'

Sam's jibe could well have been true.

Ned lifted his head, the shock absorbed, as all the others had been, by his bewildered system. The married couple were taking communion; the sun was shining; Ned was moved unbearably by his own freedom and its cost to Ironminster. He tried to make his mind a blank, protecting himself, but the organ music got into his susceptibilities and was his undoing. Sam passed him a handkerchief.

'It's me as should be worrying,' he remarked. 'Having her on our hands. It's no rub to you.'

Ned, being in the right place for it, would have liked to pray to some avail, but all he could bring himself to say, thinking about it, was, 'Oh, God!' Perhaps God would know what he meant. On the whole it was meant as thanks, but thanks for a whole lot more than he would ever have made into words.

To his great relief, the organ then broke into a noisy fanfare to announce the completion of the ceremony, and the whole congregation started craning and peering and shuffling as the bride and bridegroom embarked on their long ceremonial exit down the aisle. Ned picked up his hat and made to slip out ahead of them, but an usher motioned to him to stay. Ned glued his eyes to the floor, praying to remain unnoticed, but at the approaching silky rustle of the bride's dress he could not resist lifting his head. August was beside him. Ned saw the sun's sheen on his black silk coat, reminding him irresistibly of Starling, the soft, pale embroidery of gold and silver on his waistcoat, raised his head and saw the face, white and drained, thin enough to look carved out of ivory, or modelled out of plaster, like one of the church decorations. August, having smiled at nobody, smiled at Ned, and winked. Ned understood the wink, although a few minutes ago he wouldn't have done.

Behind him, Sam laughed. 'He was always a damned good loser, I'll say that for him.'

At four o'clock Ned took the coach to the front door of the Amherst house to collect the bride and bridegroom, Sam and Amelia's maid who – he quickly noticed – was as unattractive as her mistress. A good deal of luggage was handed up and secured by footmen. Sam and the maid got up, and Ironminster and Amelia presently appeared and were escorted into the coach by a very merry crowd of their friends. Ned caught a glimpse of Lady Ironminster standing at the top of the steps with the judge, looking as complacent as he had ever seen her; he sent some sour wishes in her direction, no less in the judge's, unhappy to see them so pleased at August's fate. While he was still scowling, Railton climbed up on the step and said, 'Well, Ned, you'll be pleased to get home, I daresay. Things could have turned out much worse.'

'They're all right for *me*, my Lord.'

Railton gave him a very odd look and said, 'You think so? I don't think you know everything, even now.' And laughed. Ned supposed he was a bit drunk. He turned to Sam, settled on the back seat, and said, 'Sam, have you told him what's in store for –'

'I think you should get down now, my Lord. Lord Ironminster is ready to go.' Sam, a practised diplomat, cut him off very smoothly.

Railton laughed and jumped down.

'Good luck, Ned!'

'Thank you, my Lord. Thank you for all you did.'

It was very strange to be alone on the box-seat. They had two footmen up behind, and Sam and the maid. Ned would have liked Sam beside him to tell him all the news but Sam was busy flirting with the maid. Ned hadn't seen him since he had left the church, having got stranded with the Amherst servants celebrating the departure of Miss Amelia, and particularly with a little parlour-maid much too forward for her own good whom he had kissed in the cupboard under the stairs. He had left his wig propped up on a broom handle and had to go back for it. A pity *she* hadn't been Miss Amelia's companion.

His horses, smelling home, went smartly up Piccadilly towards the city, casting long evening shadows before them. Too near to Newgate for his liking, Ned hurried them on, sparing a thought for the poor devils still inside, not daring to think on his own luck. The traffic was very thick with evening and the progress up Ludgate Hill painfully obstructed, but Ned was unusually patient, enjoying the bustle, lifting his eyes to the dome of St Paul's glowing all over its western side with the setting sun like a great full-blown rose against the dusking sky. The starlings twittered and soared and Ned could smell the damp soft air blowing off the marshes below with its promise of summer coming. He longed to be back in the Threadgolds lanes, coaxing his horses through the gaps, hurrying, watching the first lights smoking in the window-panes, pulling up for a Royal Mail making up into Cheapside for St Martin's-le-Grand . . . the journey, so familiar, was this time like a great adventure, every detail sharpened by his deprived senses into fantastic importance. The horses chafed and fretted their way through the city, all stops and starts, down Leadenhall Street and into Aldgate, past The Bull – which drew a jibe from Sam behind him, but which Ned chose to ignore. He would avoid the dreadful memories provoked by The Bull in the future, if he could. At last, the road clear before them, and the horses began to settle into their old rhythm. Ned watched them affectionately, critically, feeling like a master back with his ship at sea after a long time ashore, seeing all the work to be done to get them back into shape. The coach-lamps were already lit and there was nothing to stop for, the smells of the country taking over from the smoky city, the lovely raw dampness of an April evening hanging in the hedges on either side. They passed through Bow and Stratford and out on to the road for Romford, and Ned was just thinking of springing them for fifty yards on a good patch of road they were coming to when he heard a signal from inside and Sam called to him, 'His Lordship wants you to pull up!'

Ned pulled up, and before the footman could get down, Ironminster got out of the coach, shut the door behind him, and climbed up beside Ned. Settling himself, he gave a great sigh as if of relief and said to Ned, 'Drive on.'

Ned got going again, somewhat surprised, while Ironminster shrugged up the large collar of his box-coat and did up the buttons, and pulled the apron over his legs.

'I've told her,' he said, 'that I always ride outside. And I always shall, I can't change that.'

'No, my Lord.'

Ned felt very constrained, nervous of speaking to Ironminster. Too much lay between them to put into casual conversation. It did not seem appropriate to make any sort of a speech of thanks for what Ironminster had done, for it was beyond a polite speech – or, at least, any that Ned could put tongue to.

As if he guessed what was in Ned's mind, August said, quite directly, 'You mustn't feel you owe me anything for what has happened, Ned. It is pure self-interest, if you like. I couldn't bear to lose you. I can stand being married to Amelia that much better. One chooses the least of two evils.'

Ned, not accepting the implied ease of Ironminster's position, said, 'I think you have made a very great sacrifice, my Lord. I shall never be able to thank you enough.'

August laughed and said, 'You aren't being very polite to my wife, Ned. You'll have to learn better than that.'

'No, my Lord. I shall feel grateful to the Amherst family all my life.'

'Ned, dammit, stop being so solemn. We've had enough church business today. Being serious doesn't become you. I came up here for a bit of light relief from the admonitions of my bride about our future life together, which I am led to believe will be very short, otherwise the prospect would daunt me. Tell me, Ned, did you really think you were going to hang?'

'I wasn't very optimistic, no. Lord Railton assured me it would be all right, but the prosecution's story was damning.'

'Yes, true. But old Amherst was so thorough – so keen to get his daughter off his hands – that he went to enormous trouble for us. Even the prosecution counsel was in his pay, you know, not to mention the judge being his brother-in-law. He was confident enough to fix the wedding-date, in fact, although he knew I wouldn't go through with it if you were convicted.'

'I didn't know about that. Lord Railton never told me.'

'No, we decided it would be better if you didn't know until it was all over. You had enough to worry about. And I didn't want to speak to you until after the wedding. It would have been much too painful for both of us. But once everything is *fait accompli* – well, there's not much to regret. Certainly not James.'

'I didn't mean to kill him.'

'No. Although in fact you did, in truth you were perfectly innocent, which is why I felt justified in going to such dishonest means to get you acquitted. A case of two wrongs making a right. Perjury is never to be taken on lightly; hence the enormous advantage of knowing a man like Justice Amherst. Without him, I doubt we could have managed it, for all the evidence was against you.'

'It was Matty's story that saved me, I think.'

Ironminster was silent for a moment. Then he said, 'Yes. Did Sam tell you?'

'That it was his idea? Lord Railton told me.'

'Did he tell you anything else?'

'I don't understand –?'

August did not reply. Ned felt slightly uneasy, remembering hints of things left unsaid, as Railton had so truly confessed. Were there still more? It was surely impossible? He could think of nothing that could shock him any more after the upheavals of the last few days.

The conversation was interrupted by coming to the turnpike and finding the right money. Sam got down to see to it and Amelia put her head out of the window and called up to Ironminster, 'August, you will catch your death up there in the cold! Why don't you come inside sensibly?'

August groaned quietly, and Ned had a vision of Sarah Redbridge riding up on the box between them – dear Sarah, who belonged in all justice to August. It was Sarah's existence which made his fate so unkind; without her, marrying Amelia for convenience could have been passed off lightly enough. Glancing at August, Ned knew that his thoughts at that moment were running along the same lines, and to confirm it August said, 'What price a thoughtful wife, eh, Ned? If I could have had Sarah, believe me, I'd have let you hang!' The quiet exclamation carried such conviction that August immediately

qualified it, 'Oh, confound it, Ned – I don't mean it! But you
talked of sacrifice just now, and there is none, because there
was no question of my having Sarah. So rest assured. I've
never pretended to you, you know that.'

Ned started his wheelers and eased Starling and Nightingale,
who were smelling home and anxious to go. The consequence
of what August had just said hung between them, and August
followed it up: 'Imagine it, Ned, if it had been different! If I
had had to forsake marriage with Sarah to get you acquitted –
that would have been sacrifice indeed! Thank God there are
some things we haven't had to face. We've nothing to be sorry
for, everything considered.' He then laughed, and said, 'At
least, you still don't know –'

Ned had an instinct of doom impending, and waited.

August glanced at him, amused, slightly doubtful.

'You will have to know before we reach home, and there's
not much time. I hope you won't be angry, Ned. About
Matty –'

Ned groped for enlightenment. 'You mean about her being
with child? It must be Tom Garnett's.'

'Yes, that's true.'

'Is she to marry him?'

Ned, having assumed this, had not grieved much over the
fact, not anxious for marriage himself.

'No, Ned. This is the thing you will have to know. She gave
that evidence for you in the belief that if you were acquitted
you would give a name to the child. Marry her, I mean.'

Ned felt his mouth open, the words freeze. His hand on the
reins dropped into his lap.

August said, 'She was terribly nervous about telling such
lies in court and we had the devil of a job with her you know.
Ask Sam. It was his idea to persuade her by saying you would
marry her. He told her you loved her dearly but were too shy
to declare it. Ned, for heaven's sake – you'll have us in the
ditch!' August, holding on at the lurching of the coach, turned
round and called out to Sam, 'Sam, isn't it true? Come here
and take your blame like a man. Didn't you tell Matty –?'

Sam clambered over the roof towards the box.

'Gawd's truth, my Lord, don't put it all on me! We didn't
promise her –'

'No, we just told her to wait till Ned came home . . . but it's no good pretending that she's not full of expectations. Confound it, Ned, you're *alive*, aren't you? We were pretty desperate – you just try and think up some story to explain all that happened – come up with a better one if you can! And it all depended on Matty. Without her, believe me, you'd be in the condemned cell now.'

'Most men would think it a pretty good exchange, the gallows for a girl like Matty,' Sam said, indignant.

'But *she* wants it? With Garnett's child inside her?'

August, to Ned's fury, actually laughed. 'Yes. Amazing as it might seem, Ned, she loves you passionately.'

Ned felt more panic-stricken than he had ever felt in Newgate. This shock, of them all, had as good as knocked him off the box. The horses were still all over the road, and he started to gather them together, the Threadgolds turning coming up. He checked Starling and Nightingale, but they knew the way and were steadying of their own accord.

'I can't – I –'

'Well, nobody can compel you,' August said. 'I'm just telling you the situation. She's certainly got to marry somebody very soon.' He paused for a few moments and then added, 'You get used to the idea quite quickly when it's forced upon you. I'm speaking from experience, of course.'

Ned took a hold of the horses as they came to the long slope down to the Fairoaks ford. The smell of the woods reminded him of waiting for August and Sarah. He remembered them in the gamekeeper's cottage when he had left them. God in heaven, his fate wasn't very arduous compared with theirs! He tried to think of the story as Matty had told it, that she had met him in the cottage and lain in his arms all night. It wasn't at all repulsive to him, given a few minutes of thought. The horses' hooves were quietened by the thick peaty bed of the lane, only the bars and chains rattling and jangling, the horses going beautifully. A branch of yellow catkins flicked them in passing with golden pollen and there were nightingales singing over toward Threadgolds, very spring-like. There could well be a cuckoo by daylight. The violet sky was filled with enormous water-laden clouds drifting slowly like pregnant angels. Ned was suddenly enormously impressed by all the loving care that had gone into saving his life, and all the strange patterns the task had created in its wake, mostly unintended, but accepted with an apparently careless and cheerful resignation in the same way that a wager might be won or lost. Ironminster had lost his, but he – Ned – might well have won, if he were as honourable as his friend.

'It's so – unexpected – I don't mean I won't . . . it's just that I hadn't thought of marriage.'

'You will think of it?'

'Yes. I will.'

'You owe it to her, Ned. A debt of honour.'

'Yes, my Lord.'

Somewhere in the deepest recesses of his mind the long-cherished shadow of a dream of himself and Sarah Redbridge married dropped into oblivion for ever and ever, Amen. It had had no substance beyond wild wishing, had never, truly, been acknowledged. Only by its death was it now reminding him that it had existed.

The horses were moving very freely. This was their home ground, these their woods and hedges and soft home air. Ironminster would not see another summer. Make the best of this.

He glanced at August and picked up the whip.

'Yes, spring them, Ned! Through the ford – it's very full – she'll float, I daresay, a yard or two –'

'Her Ladyship?'

The water would cover the floor of the coach. Ned could see the crest of the lane ahead where it started its long galloping dip down to the Fairoaks corner and could picture the dark swirling of the water in spring flood, the horses breasting it and their tails floating out sideways on the current.

'Oh, damn her Ladyship!' August said, and laughed.

Ned put the horses into a gallop and behind him heard the footmen and Sam blaspheming and complaining. He looked at August again and saw his face alight, the old Ironminster unchanged. The lovely slope unrolled before them and the loaded coach started to travel, scarcely held by the wheelers but not quite out of control, on the hairline between mere excitement and pure recklessness, a working compromise – long perfected – between its two mentors. This accord, to be consummated by a safe but hair-raising completion of their journey home, was to Ned the perfect ending to a very difficult day. He settled himself firmly in his seat, took a strong hold on his leaders, and used his whip again. Ironminster pulled out his time-piece and looked at it quickly.

'Twenty minutes to the North gates, Ned?'

'Eighteen, my Lord.'

'I'll hold you to it!'

Ned grinned. The horses started to gallop.